D1534788

Blanco

Blanco

ALLEN WIER

Louisiana State University Press
Baton Rouge and London   1978

Design: Dwight Agner
Typeface: VIP Goudy Oldstyle
Composition: The Composing Room of Michigan, Inc.
Printing and binding: Kingsport Press, Inc.

Portions of this novel, in slightly different form, have appeared in *Intro 6*,
Black Warrior Review, and *Window.*

The author gratefully acknowledges permission to reprint portions of "Don't
Let the Stars Get in Your Eyes" by Cactus Pryor, Slim Willet, and Barbara
Trammel, from Irwin A. Deutscher, Four-Star Music Company, Nashville,
Tennessee.

LIBRARY OF CONGRESS CATALOGING IN PUBLICATION DATA

Wier, Allen, 1946–
  Blanco.

  I. Title.
PZ4.W6477Bl [PS3573.I355]   813'.5'4   78-9660
ISBN 0-8071-0473-6

for the memory of my daddy, Ralph,
and for my mother, George Ann

How should you walk in that space and know
Nothing of the madness of space...

WALLACE STEVENS

Blanco   (Blank'ō) town in S. central Texas, located on the Blanco River; pop. 775; alt. 1350.

Blanco   (Blänco) *Spanish:* white; fair (complexion); blank; yellow (cowardly); white (person); coward; white star, white spot (on horse); target; aim, goal; interval; hole, empty; blank space.

Blanco

1

JORDAN WEST'S Sinclair station was closed, the glassed-in office dark except for the dim glow of the coke machine and a fluorescent clock, blue on the back wall. The Bowling Alley Cafe on the other side of the square would be closed by midnight. No café, no filling station, nothing stayed open all night in Blanco. The Lone Star picture show was closed weeknights, Fridays too during football season. There was no newspaper, no hospital, no jail. Blanco County was the only county in Texas without an oil well. The courthouse, built in 1886, was empty, an election in 1890 having moved the Blanco County Seat some fourteen miles north to Johnson City.

One downtown streetlight made the shadow of a highway sign on the sidewalk. A flashing yellow light strung across the highway, and ignored by truckers who barreled-ass through town all night long, turned a plate glass reflection of the empty courthouse building off and on. A windmill, looking

1

like an oil derrick above the short trees, was locked still. There was no water running over the new Blanco River Dam. But a westerly breeze and dips in the highway where flood gauge posts measured spring flash floods, suggested motion.

In a frame house across the highway and a little ways toward Johnson City, the man who had closed up Jordan West's Sinclair sat, letting his late supper digest over the ten o'clock news and trying to ignore his momma, Eunice, with whom he lived, who was, as usual, talking.

"Edna used to give a permanent *and* a haircut for six-fifty, now the haircut's two and a half extra, so I said just *cancel* mine, and I got Dot to do it for seven-fifty *with* the haircut," Eunice reached back to pull at her hair, stared at Turk. "But it's not any good, won't last through the wedding. I just don't know why Dot can't give a good permanent, it's just pin curls, just little pin curls." She spread her fingers slowly, holding her hand out before her as if she could read something written there. "But I don't care, it's short. It's short, and it's cool, and I don't have to worry with it."

Turk was watching the news on a San Antonio station. Years ago he had learned to stop listening to Momma's talk. He leaned forward in his chair, reached, and changed the channel.

"Lola Mae was telling me how her boy was going to marry," Momma began again, leaving her big rocker gently rocking as she went into the kitchen after Turk's coffee. "Said she was going to ask me to the wedding and I said I can't come I won't have a way, and she said, well you're going to be asked anyway. Get your boy Turk to bring you, she said, and I told her it was like pulling teeth to get you to take me anywhere." Walking carefully, so as not to spill Turk's coffee, Eunice stopped in front of the television and

2

for emphasis raised the cup she held in both hands, "Well, Turk, you know that's the Lord's truth, you never take me places I need to go. Anyway I wouldn't go cause she was only trying to get back at me for not inviting her to June's."

Turk took the cup, leaned around her to see the television, a news film of a three-car pile-up that had left a San Antonio woman dead and hospitalized her four children.

"'What do you want me to give him,' I asked her, and she said, 'oh, anything, give him anything. Give him some silverware, give him some of them dishes you eat off of,' and I said 'that's fine, I'll give him some of those, I can get them down at the Red & White, you get ten dollars in coupons for every two hundred and fifty dollars you spend on groceries.' 'Well, give him those,' she said, 'he'll love to get them.'"

Turk stared at the white, covered-up bodies on the highway on the television, the white highway stripe splitting the TV screen. He could read the numbers on the license plate of the wrecked car.

Eunice looked over her head at the All-Tex Feed calendar thumbtacked to the wall: Fencing, Well Supplies, Stock Trailers, Veterinary Supplies, Guns, Ammunition. On the calendar, a cartoon: two cowboys buying one box of shells, two cases of whiskey, six cases of beer, the cartoon clerk saying: "Well, I reckon that's all the important supplies you boys need for your hunting trip."

She stared at the vertical column of Turk's big penciled PD's over the dates of each Saturday. The calendar was where he did his bookkeeping. He had paid her his room and board through the end of the month. She was wondering if he could've made a mistake, maybe he hadn't really paid her for this last week, maybe he wrote two PD's last time.

He blew on his coffee between gulps, the steam fogging his glasses as he watched a rest home burn in Baltimore. Arson was suspected in the fire in which six old women lost their

3

lives. Authorities estimated damages would run into the hundreds of thousands of dollars.

She gave up on the calendar. He'd never forgotten to pay her before, and, if she was honest with herself, she remembered tucking the money into the back of Armon's picture. Things sure would be easier if Armon hadn't died so soon. Now, after so many years, she still missed him. Thinking of her dead husband, who had been tall, nearly two feet taller than she was, she looked up at the high ceiling. As if, she thought, I might see him floating around up there like an angel. What she saw instead were cobwebs.

"I'd rather have cobwebs than a broke leg," she said, "so I just don't climb." She looked to see how Turk reacted to that. He closed his eyes. No sympathy for the aged, she thought. He made her mad, just sitting there, sipping his coffee with his eyes shut. She thought he farted. She didn't hear him, but she thought she smelled him. She wished she would hear him, then she'd *really* have something to say.

He sighed, opened his eyes, stretched, bent over and un-laced each of his shoes, kicked them off. Then he worked his socks off, holding the toe of first one sock, then the other, against the floor with one foot while he pulled the other foot out. He reached on top of the television for his nail clipper, the kind with a key chain, bought off a cardboard display for a quarter, and began clipping his toenails.

"Don't you get your nasty toenails all over my house."

He cupped his hand under his foot, reached the empty coffee cup with the gold stalk of wheat on the inside and dropped a thick nail in the cup. There were eighteen or twenty cups just like it in the cabinets. She had gotten them in huge boxes of laundry detergent and then left the opened boxes in the pantry and in the bathroom closet where he turned them over getting towels out and finally he had to throw most of the stuff away, the whole house had begun to

4

smell like a washateria. She bought things, then forgot she had them. Once he'd found eight plastic dispensers of dental floss, two in the kitchen drawers, three in the medicine cabinet in the bathroom, one sitting out on her dresser beside her cold cream, one in his closet, and one completely unrolled under her bed.

"Listen to me when I'm talking to you," she was up again. She snapped the television off, seemed about to launch into something else, then, surprisingly, said nothing. He watched the gray dot disappear in the center of the green TV screen. She sat down slowly, ran her hand down her shin. Feeling for lumps, he thought. She glared at him over the edge of the table top.

Snick. A toenail hit the television screen.

"Now Turk, what'd I tell you? Stop it right now. I mean it, it's hard enough to keep a nice house with all the dust of west Texas blowing in, with rain makin mud for you to track all over my floor, and if it isn't mud you're tracking it's those old black streaks on the linoleum off your nasty shoes. I have to keep this old house as decent as I can for June's wedding. There'll be nosey people traipsing all over just looking for dirt. Thank goodness Cage doesn't have any people to bring down."

Turk clipped another toenail, thinking of Cage as he squeezed the clipper. Cage with his big-shot, yankee ways. What a prick he was.

"You don't even care about your own sister's wedding. Lord, I am tired of putting up with it. I'm getting too old. You know I'm not supposed to get worried. You know what the doctor told me. I don't like it. I don't like it. But I try to do what he tells me. And you could be just a little help it seems like."

He didn't even look up.

"I take care of you. Cook you three good meals every day.

5

Keep this house for you. I'm an old woman, you won't see me much longer. I'm ailing, you know. What are you going to do after I'm dead and gone? What will you do then?"

"I'll take my meals at the Bowling Alley where it's quieter, for one thing."

She pursed her lips, looked around the room. Then she narrowed her eyes and said, "Sleeping with a divorced woman. That's what kind of man you are."

"I'm not sleeping with anyone."

She stopped rocking and gave him a triumphant look, then rocked harder.

"You know I'm not sleeping with anyone."

"You'll have a field day after I'm gone. I just can't see why you let Sally play you for such a fool. I swear, Turk, you're stupid as a betsy bug."

"You're jealous. You hate to be here alone for half an hour. You can't stand for me to have a good time. You know you aren't about to die and you're just worried that I might marry Sally and then you'd be alone. And you don't have to worry about me marrying anyone. I'm not."

"Marry. Marry. That's right, you won't ever get married. Not you. That's what kind of man you are, just wild. Just too wild and irresponsible to have a family. Everyone else has a family. Robert Allen, bad as he is, has a family. June's finally getting married, and look what a catch she got. Worth the wait, I'd say. But you. I never will have a grandchild unless it's from June and Cage and then it won't carry the Marrs name."

Turk pictured an ugly little baby with Cage's queer little moustache on its ugly little red face. The Austin newspaper lay folded on the edge of the table. Momma had been swatting flies with it and there was a tiny bloodstain on a front page photo of a train derailment.

"Sally wouldn't marry you if you were the last man in Texas. She wouldn't marry you if it harelipped the governor.

6

Why should she, she's got you for during and in-between husbands."

"Momma she's widowed and divorced, not married, and I never saw her while she was married."

"Besides, who'd want an old bachelor who works part time at a filling station and cutting grass at the graveyard? Not me. Not anybody with any brains. Why I'd sooner run through hell in drawers drenched in gasoline."

"You don't even know what you're talking about."

"I guess I do. I guess I know what that Sally is up to. I know she never calls here you don't go traipsing off to Austin to see her. Clear to Austin to see her, and you can't take me over to Lola Mae's for her son's wedding. I know Sally's been through three husbands already, all younger, richer, and better looking than you are. I know. She's closed in on you like an iron on a starched pocket." She had each arm flat on the wooden arms of the rocker, bent straight at the elbows, gripping the flat ends of the rocker arms. She rocked steadily, up and back, staring perfectly straight ahead, her eyes moving only up and back with the rocker.

He got up, took his shoes into his bedroom, sat on the edge of the bed putting his socks and shoes back on. Seeing her swallowed up by the big old rocker she looked tiny, her gray hair hard and bright looking beneath the dining room lights. She was getting old. She really might die soon, though she sure seemed strong as hell. He felt a little guilty, but he had to get away from all this talk, just rattling on and on. He had to have a little space around him. "I'm gone. If anyone calls, I'll be down at the Bowling Alley."

"I'm not your answering service."

"If anyone calls, I'll be down at the Bowling Alley."

"What if the highway department calls?"

"This time of night? Besides I told Jordan I'd run the Sinclair this weekend."

"You ought to let Jordan West run his own business. He

7

doesn't pay you decent. The highway department might get to be a regular job. Why do you let everyone run over you?"

"I'm working at the Sinclair this weekend. You tell anyone that calls, I'm at the Bowling Alley for a while." He was already at the kitchen door, going out.

"Turk, don't you walk out on me while I'm talking to you. I'm still your mother and don't you forget it."

The screened door clapped shut behind him.

"Do you hear me? Do you hear me, Turk? What time are you coming home?" She was up, picking up his cup and saucer, the spoon, the sugar bowl. His toenail clippings stuck up like sprouts in the gray layer of sugar and coffee left on the bottom of his cup. "Turk," she was still yelling, the sound of his car pulling onto the highway drowning her out, "you didn't even finish doing your toenails. I swear, if you aren't enough to make a preacher cuss."

2 THE ORANGE propane truck Robert Allen drove was parked outside the Bowling Alley Cafe, and as soon as Turk opened the door he heard Robert Allen yelling at him.

"Turk, she's gonna pour coffee in my shirt pocket."

"Well, he didn't have no cup, so I told him I'd fill his pocket full and he could drink it with a straw." Sudie was laughing, and the hot coffee was sloshing dangerously in the round glass pot she held out like a basketball.

"It'd be the only thing in my pocket," Robert Allen went on, "I sure don't have no money there."

"Reckon I better buy the coffee then," Turk said, giving Sudie change out of his coin purse, which he snapped shut, folded in half, and slipped back into his shirt pocket. Then he stuck a big safety pin through the pocket and through the purse inside the pocket and back out through the pocket and clamped the safety pin. His shirts all had two holes in the left front pocket where he carried his money. Taking off his thick bifocals, he slowly rubbed each lens with a paper napkin, "Goddamn, it's getting so I can't see anything anymore."

9

Robert Allen was spooning crushed ice from his water glass into his coffee.

"Can't hear worth shit, either," Turk said, putting his glasses back on.

Robert Allen was blowing loudly into the heavy white mug, watching the chunks of ice disappear in the coffee. Turk squinted out the window, through the reflection of the booth they were sitting in, through his own face, to the Real Fine Food sign, the orange neon arrow aimed right back at him. A white pickup pulled in, pink-orange beneath the neon. Up against the window its lights went off. Two men in khaki shirts, khaki pants got out and tapped the glass, grinning at Robert Allen and Turk as they passed by the window.

Inside, they whistled at Sudie. "Sudie," one said, "you hadn't gone and got yourself a boyfriend since we were in here last, have you?"

Sudie just laughed and said, "Boyd Madden I told you I'm saving myself, waiting for you to grow up."

Boyd Madden straddled a stool at the counter where Sudie already had set two steaming mugs of coffee down. His friend walked straight to the jukebox. Passing close by Turk and Robert Allen he punched them each on the shoulder and asked Sudie, "Say, Sudie, these two jokers gone partners with you? They're here ever time I stop." He stood at the juke box doing a sort of bowlegged dance while he punched out three songs. Passing back by Turk and Robert Allen he picked Robert Allen's hat off the hatrack and dropped it on Turk's head. Turk just pulled the too-big hat down over his eyes and took a pull on his coffee.

Behind the café were four bowling lanes full of teenagers bowling and old men sitting around little tables playing dominoes. The rumbling of bowling balls sounded like far off thunder. Just as a ball hit the pins the jukebox came on, Lefty Frizzell singing "Long Black Veil."

Robert Allen asked Boyd and Jumper, the only name anybody had ever heard the other man use, why didn't they join them, but Boyd said not this time, they had to gulp and run.

Turk was on his second cup of coffee before Robert Allen had taken his first sip.

"So, little June's gonna marry the man from Ohio." It was just a way of getting started talking. "You ever been to Ohio, Turk?"

"Yeah, I been. There and New York and Chicago and California. Even went to Guam in the army."

Of course Robert Allen knew Turk had been in Guam, but he asked him anyway, "What was Guam like?"

"Bout like anyplace. That was a long time ago. Guamos was just like Mexicans—didn't seem much different to me." Turk's memories of Guam were not too good, they had become mixed with television images of tropical places he thought of vaguely as foreign islands. People with dark skin, dark oily hair, the hospital where he had jaundice. He remembered drinking in a lot of bars that looked alike and going with dark-haired girls to small rooms, each with a bed and a dresser and just room enough to walk sideways between the bed and the wall. A snapshot of some grinning Guamos, an old couple and five or six kids, stuck on the mirror over the dresser, some flowers made of colored toilet paper, a rosary hung over the corner of the mirror. He remembered paying a girl eight dollars to sleep with him, remembered she refused to pull off her black turtleneck blouse because she didn't want to mess up her hairdo. She rolled the turtleneck up over her shoulders and left it around her neck like an innertube. Afterward he scalded himself, leaning over the basin, pouring hot water on himself from a pan, afraid of V.D.

"How come you never got married, Turk?"

He looked straight at Robert Allen, trying to figure out whether Robert Allen was kidding. He wasn't smiling. To keep from getting into it, Turk answered with a question, "How come you did?"

11

"Oh," Robert Allen was smiling to beat the band now, "I guess you might say it just come naturally, Florene and Curtis being the natural results."

Turk slurped his coffee.

"I always figgered you and ole Sally'd finally get hitched," Robert Allen's grin showed his big yellow teeth.

"Screw you." Everyone kidded Turk about Sally, as if Momma's riding him all the time about her wasn't enough. Sally was a schoolteacher in Austin who used to be the ribbon clerk in Dyars' Store, before they quit selling ribbon. Old Man Brown Smith Speer used to say Turk'd wore a spot in the floor where he'd stood talking to Sally all the time. Then Sally married a man from Longview and moved away. Two years later she was back in Blanco, divorced. She didn't stay long before she went to Austin and got a job teaching first grade. Turk drove over nearly every weekend to see her until she got married again. That time lasted nine months and Turk took to visiting her again. Folks began to laugh at Turk. Before, they had wondered what a cute thing like Sally saw in him, then they began to wonder why he kept fooling with a girl like Sally. Her third husband got killed in a car wreck and left her ten thousand dollars insurance money. Turk knew folks joked about him and Sally, but he liked seeing her and maybe, he admitted to himself, maybe he even liked keeping everyone wondering what was really going on between them. Sally never had lied to him, she always told him when she was seeing other men and somehow he just never thought he wanted to get married and have to have a regular job. Momma was still mad at him for inviting her to June's wedding, but he knew Sally wouldn't come on a bet.

Robert Allen was pouring salt on the table, trying to balance the shaker in the cone of salt. While he worked with the salt he sang,

I got sand in my coffee,
and sand in my tea,
and when I die they gonna bury me,
in them shiftin, driftin sands—of Tex-as.

Watching him Turk realized he had coffee with Robert
Allen at this same café, same booth usually, two or three
times every day. At night, like tonight, in the morning, like
tomorrow morning, and in the afternoons, whenever Jordan
West's boys would drop by the Sinclair after school and
watch things awhile for Turk. Jordan had the franchise on
the Sinclair, but he took most days off to go deer or quail or
dove hunting or fishing or because he had some extra beer in
him he felt he needed to sleep off. Jordan drank one case of
Lone Star beer nearly every day. He was one of those men
who always seem to have plenty of money to do whatever
they want to do. Turk couldn't understand it. Jordan grew up
in Blanco just like him, finished high school and joined the
army. Then one day he showed up in a nice car and not long
after that he had the franchise on the station. Then he drove
up one day in a panel truck from a dry cleaners in San Antonio. Told Turk he was running a little cleaners on the side.
Later he got married and built a new brick house across from
Blanco High. Now he had the propane gas company in
Blanco and in Johnson City—Robert Allen worked for
him—and he had just put in a washateria in Blanco. His wife
had two boys from her first marriage, and both of them
worked for Jordan when they weren't in school or going
hunting or fishing with him. Men like Jordan were hard to
figure. Cage was like that too, Turk thought, but not as easy
going as Jordan. Where Cage seemed like a real wheeler
dealer, at least partly bullshit, Jordan was a solid old boy.
Turk wished June was getting married to Jordan instead.
    And then there were men like Robert Allen and himself

13

who worked for other men all their lives and spent their free time drinking coffee together and kidding around.

"What are *you* looking so serious about?"

Turk rubbed his chin like he was thinking hard, "Well," he said, "if you really want to know, I was wondering how a man could grow to be as ugly to look at as you are, Robert Allen."

"Shit, I'll go take a leak on that bullshit." Robert Allen slid out the end of the booth and headed back to the men's room. He didn't look anything like Turk. He had a long, pointed nose, while Turk's was more the shape and color of a big strawberry. Robert Allen was tall and skinny, had blue eyes, and almost no beard at all. Turk wasn't fat, but he was muscular, at least he used to be, and his arms were like cedar limbs, dark red, knotty, twisted with veins. He had dark hair with a bald spot on each side of his forehead, leaving what some people called a widow's peak. He always looked like he needed a shave, even though he shaved every morning and usually again in the evening. Like most men in Blanco, Robert Allen wore cowboy boots with long pointed toes, but Turk always had on his black work shoes with big round steel toes and thick gray work socks that Momma bought him by the dozen. She also bought his dark green work shirts and trousers by the dozen, so she didn't have to run the washer so often.

Before he got married Robert Allen had lived in an old office over a deserted cotton gin on the Austin highway. He had a bed in the office and could look out a small window at traffic on the highway. Now, he and Dot and Florene and Curtis had a house trailer in behind the gin with an iron deer and a pedestal with a blue reflecting ball on it, in their front yard. There was a black mailbox and a yellow plastic newspaper tube by the highway. Dot was so big pregnant she had trouble getting in and out of the trailer. Florene and Curtis teased her, and sang, *fatty, fatty, two by four, can't get through*

14

the kitchen door. Dot had been to beauty school before she and Robert Allen got married, and she had a diploma and a license so she opened up a beauty shop in the gin office where Robert Allen had lived. It wasn't fancy, but it was cheaper than Edna Stoppelman who had the La Petite Beauty Salon in Johnson City. Dot was teaching Florene how to set waves and give shampoos. Robert Allen spent a lot of time fixing up around the place, painted blue shutters around the windows on front of the trailer, put in a goldfish pond and a rock garden, but the goldfish died and the pond kept drying up, so he filled it in and got the iron deer instead. He took Turk with him in the propane truck when Turk wasn't working, and they always came back drunk and Dot would laugh and say that was just like a couple of men, and she'd put the rubber sheet on the bed because Robert Allen always wet it when he was sleeping drunk. All this made Momma mad as a cat, and she wouldn't tell where Turk was if Robert Allen came looking for him.

The orange arrow outside the café blinked off just as Robert Allen came out of the men's room, and Sudie flipped the sign over, putting the Come In We're Open side to the inside.

Robert Allen told Turk about a book on taxidermy he had sent off for. He had been talking for weeks about learning taxidermy in his spare time and putting him a taxidermist's shop in next to Dot's beauty shop. Turk said that sounded pretty good.

"I figure the hardest part is the eyes," Robert Allen said.

"What do you mean?"

"You know, the eyes and the tongue never really look alive. But I've got a secret plan for putting little plastic balls of water, I'll dye the water with some of Dot's food coloring, put the balls in the eye sockets so they'll reflect light and jiggle a little when someone slams a door or bangs on the wall."

15

"What about the tongues?"

"I hadn't solved that yet, maybe just more red paint."

When Sudie finished washing up and finally chased them out, they decided to run out to the Hilltop and have a beer and a barbecue sandwich to rest their stomachs from all the coffee.

3 BY THE time Turk and Robert Allen got out
to the Hilltop all the lights were out. The red Chevrolet
pickup was still parked out front, so they knew that Oscar
Pettit, who owned the Hilltop, was still around. Turk pulled
his car up beside Robert Allen's big orange truck and put it
out of gear, the motor still running. Robert Allen was already
out, urging Turk to hurry.

"Come on, slowpoke, Pettit'll still give us a beer and some
barbecue."

"He's all shut down, no reason to bother with it."

"Reason enough is I need me a cold one. Come *on.*"

"You always need you a cold one. I'm going home to bed
and leave Oscar in peace."

"All right, you don't want to bother Pettit, let's go in to
San Antone, get drunk, stay out all night. Come on, we
haven't done that in a long while."

Turk was tempted. It was a nice warm night, but not too
warm, nice night breezes and real starry out. But it was past
midnight, be at least one by the time they got there, everything would be closed. Dot was likely home waiting up for
Robert Allen, Momma was for sure home still awake, lying

17

in bed listening for his car to ease into the side yard, watching for his headlights against her dresser mirror. If he went tonight he'd feel like warmed-over hell tomorrow.

"Count me out tonight, Robert Allen. It wouldn't be any fun. It's all in your head wanting a beer so bad. Go on home, we'll hit San Antone this weekend, get started before it's too late to have a real time."

Robert Allen shrugged, gave him the finger, turned and walked toward his truck. Just before he disappeared around the front of his truck he bent over, sticking his butt up, aimed at Turk, and farted loudly, "That's what I think of you, Turkey."

Turk laughed to show he knew it was a joke, tooted his horn lightly, slipped the car into reverse. Someone came to the door of the Hilltop and stuck his head out and Robert Allen waved and hollered, "Good night, Pettit," as he pulled the propane truck out in front of Turk.

Turk drove slowly, watching Robert Allen's taillights get closer together until they became one red light and disappeared over a hill. By the time he topped the same hill, Robert Allen was out of sight. Turk passed the auction pens, the packing house and meat locker. Across the highway, the cemetery, where every two weeks he mowed the grass, driving the tractor up and down the hill, pulling the mower over the uneven ground, bumping along in the sun. Then walking behind the smaller power mower that propelled itself over so many graves with stones that said his name, MARRS, a short word in plain letters, a word he heard in the mower blades, in the sound of the grass rushing out the opening in the side of the mower. A small word cut in the big, slick faces of gray and brown stones, hard to read on stones near trees where leaves hid letters in their dark shadows.

His daddy, Armon, was out there. Armon *Luther* Marrs, but they charged by the letter, so all he had on his marker was

18

ARMON MARRS, and his dates. If you paid for the death date they cut the birth date for free. Soon enough he'd put Momma in next to Armon, then he would really be alone. June down in San Antonio with Cage, Sally probably with some new husband, Dot and Robert Allen already working on a third baby. Sally'd probably get her someone like Cage. Someone with a moustache. And money in the bank. He knew why he'd never asked Sally to marry him, he knew she never would. He was not the kind of man a woman like Sally would be interested in. Sally and June seemed a lot alike in some ways. He really knew Sally a lot better than he knew June, but he saw them both as women who knew what they wanted and aimed to have it. Sally by forgetting what people said about her and June by taking her own time about everything. When June finished school and went to San Antonio everyone said she'd be finding her a husband right away, but she didn't. Most people had just about given up on June, nearly forgot about her, she came to Blanco so seldom. There were enough years separating Turk and June that it was almost like two different families. When they were kids she was just a little sister he ignored and he was in the army when she was older, and then, by the time he came back home, she was old enough to take off on her own for San Antonio. It seemed weird, her marrying a man so much older than her. Cage seemed sort of mamby pamby to Turk, a little fat, not much to look at if you asked him. But June had always been weird, always been quiet, kept to herself. She made good grades in school but never had many friends. Somehow she never seemed a part of the family or of the town. She didn't fit in with other Blanco girls. Turk couldn't imagine June and Dot, for instance, spending much time together. They always acted friendly enough, helped each other out from time to time, Dot asking June over to the beauty shop whenever June was in town, but somehow it always seemed like June

19

was Dot's older aunt or something, someone Dot looked up to. Of course, Dot was actually years older than June. But then Dot didn't have any what you'd call real good friends. Dot was a good gal though. She didn't care how much money a man made. Sometimes Turk thought he should have married Dot. He could have. What a hell-raiser Dot had been.

On a picnic at the river, them just out of high school, him and Robert Allen and Jerry Jenkins and Billy Joe Cobb, Dot lying out on the rocks bragging she'd never had it with any boy that could really satisfy her. Jerry and Billy Joe started in telling lies about Robert Allen, bragging on him. Everyone drinking whiskey. All the boys were fixing to go into the army, there was talk of a war, maybe a big war. Before long Dot and Robert Allen were making bets against each other. Then they had their clothes off and were wrestling around, giggling, kicking little sticks and rocks down the incline.

Turk watched their shadows, huge and misshapen, against the bluff, the smell of cedar burning, the smoke of their bonfire rising out of Robert Allen's back, a skinny fire devil, as he moved on top of Dot. The shadow of the fire beneath Robert Allen's shadow moving over the flames. Lowering himself, it looked like, into the fire, a ritual, some secret ceremony seen in a movie at the Lone Star, a dance, torture, push-ups in a fire. Dot, the whole time, propped on one elbow, flipping flat stones into the river, trying to skip stones into the fire's reflection on the water. The only sounds, the stones plopping and the popping of the fire.

Dot must have liked it better than she let on; they got married a week later, just before Robert Allen joined the Army Air Corps.

Now they had twins, a trailer house, Dot's beauty shop, and another kid and a book on taxidermy on the way.

Turked stopped the car on the low-water bridge and looked out at the river. It was a dark, moonless night, clear and sharp. He could see so many stars, plenty of stars. He would have to bring Sally out here soon, they hadn't been to the river for a long time. Since the state had made a state park out of the few picnic tables and grills nobody but a few tourists ever came. They made it illegal to drink in the park and it cost a dollar to get in now. It didn't seem fair to have to pay to go picnic on the river where you'd picnicked and played and fished for free all your life. But at night he figured no one would bother him and Sally.

Turk's daddy had liked the river. He used to bring them in the spring when the deep pools filled up and they'd fish for catfish. Big, ugly catfish, blue catfish, yellow catfish, mudcats. Fishing with Armon on the river was one of the few things Turk could remember doing with June. She would sit for hours holding her pole and staring down into the water, never talked, never wiggled around. Armon couldn't swim, but he liked the river, liked coming down the dirt road in a dust cloud, liked running trot lines by the light of a lantern.

Armon told them stories. Again and again he told them about old Juno Speer, how he got drunk all the time and his wife locked him out of his own house. How he got so drunk one Christmas night he waded the river, ice forming along the edges, and went home wet and roaring and his wife locked him out and he was too crazy drunk to dry off and he went and slept in his wet clothes in the smoke house, slept under hanging hams in the smell of pork and caught pneumonia and died the next day before sundown.

Armon told stories about how it used to be. Told Turk about the long line of men before them, *a long, hard line of men led you west into Texas,* he told Turk. Eunice's three bachelor uncles rode through Texas from Mississippi on their way to California riches. Passing through Texas they stopped near Blanco and bought acres of cheap hill country. Then they wrote back to Mississippi and told the family to come ahead. Eunice was eight and rode in an open wagon looking for Indians all the way. The next time she saw her uncles was

21

after Turk was born. She was walking from the house to the store and met three men with long beards going the other way. When she got back home the men had shaved and washed and changed their clothes and were sitting on the front porch waiting for supper. Twenty years had passed like a day and they were back from California, rich, nobody knew from what, and wanting supper. Armon said Turk was bawling in his crib after supper and one of the three old men went in and picked him up and carried him out on the porch where he was sleeping on a cot, and Turk shut up and slept the whole night with that old man on the porch.

Turk was sure it must have happened, but he couldn't remember a bit of it, hard as he tried.

His daddy told him and June stories about what they had done when they were young. Things they themselves had done, but Turk couldn't remember at all. He tried to believe he had done all the things his daddy said he had done, but it didn't seem possible. He tried to think back as far as he could, and it always made his head swim. Like looking up at all the stars or trying to count the flowers in the wallpaper in Sally's living room or trying to guess when he'd driven a certain distance and not looking down at the odometer until he was sure he had gone far enough—it made him angry, and, sometimes, a little scared. In school he had read about things that everyone said had really happened in history, but he couldn't figure out why he should believe it. It had been the same way in Sunday School. Sometimes they showed him pictures, but how did he know they were true? When he tried to remember what things had been like in the past, so long ago, he was never sure if he was remembering the pictures in his mind or if he was making up pictures to fit the stories everyone told him. He couldn't remember his daddy's face. He had the picture on Momma's dresser to go by, *How old was Armon when that was taken, Eunice? Why that was right after Turk was born, I remember because it rained all day and the*

22

*photographer tracked all over my floors and kept worrying us about
the light for the picture taking, but you can see how good it come
out,* but that was the way Armon used to look. What did he
look like now? Right now when Turk tried to picture him.
Was his hair turned white? Did he still have a white handkerchief sticking out of his breastpocket? Half moons on each
fingernail? A knot on his second finger from bearing down so
hard on his pencil? Where were all the ways that made a man
stored up? Was all that lost, just because time kept moving?
There seemed to be no such thing as sudden death, we all
pass away a little more every day, drifting like sand down a
dry hillside, giving up our lives like loose grass, slowly wearing down, losing our shape, carried away by rains and steady
wind.

The river moved quietly, steadily, slowly under the
bridge. No noise, no headlights in Turk's rearview mirror.
His car idled as quietly as whispers, as evenly as his own
breathing.

He couldn't remember what Sally had looked like when he
saw her for the first time. Years ago, he knew, her skin had
been smooth and tight, now it was getting wrinkled. Her hair
used to be softer and her voice used to move up and down.
She had lived different lives since then, three different men
in three different houses with her. Did that make her three
different women? Three different mouths had chewed meat
across the table from her, had kissed her mouth, her same
mouth, in three different beds.

In an old photograph, Turk had seen himself standing
barefoot on the fender of a Model-T Ford holding his daddy's
shoulder for support, himself only half as tall as a man. Now
he stood heavy on thin white legs, blue veins down his shins
under thin patches of curly hair, his belt holding up his belly,
his nipples little leather pouches, folds under them. Now he
was hard of hearing and could barely see without his heavy
glasses. Where had those dark, sharp eyes staring out at him

23

from the boy's face in the photograph disappeared to? Sitting tonight in his car on the bridge over the same dark Blanco River that Old Juno Speer had swum across on a Christmas night years before Turk was born, right now in 1959 he felt the same as he had that day in 1920 when he'd jumped up on the fender of the Ford and grinned at the camera. In that photograph the sun made a white spot on the windshield of the square black automobile. The metal fender must have been hot against his bare feet, but he could no longer feel the heat of warm metal under his feet. Tonight his feet, bigger, whiter, were heavy in his work shoes, and tired. Tonight, inside another Ford automobile, he could not see his hands on the steering wheel in the darkness, could not see how his veins bulged out, how his skin was now wrinkled over his hands like they had been under water too long.

4

FIFTY MILES south of Blanco the hills were lower, smoother, the horizon wider. From June's apartment window she could see neither the oak-shaded and lovely San Antonio River and the old Spanish missions of downtown, nor the new shopping centers and the subdivisions that surrounded the city with their identical rows of rooftops visible from the new expressway which linked them together. Her view was of the thick green grass, watered daily by the apartment manager Mr. Tony, the one tall streetlight, and the one tall palm tree, both of which rose side by side out of a strip of grass between the sidewalk and the street.

She and Cage turned from the window and faced the mirror on her closet door, watching each other watch. Looking at Cage's reflection, June saw a flickering moustache in an old movie. From the front row of the Lone Star when she was a girl, up close, salt and pepper faces filling the screen, a moustache like Cage's popping and sizzling above her, the film gray and drizzly like the sky that topped the view from her window this morning.

He was late, he had to hurry. His fingers on her shoulders

25

were warm and damp, she thought of dough, the smell of yeast, rolls rising white and full, she imagined his fingerprints on her skin. When he kissed her goodbye the moustache was damp against her upper lip. She felt a cold spot where her tongue touched his gold tooth.

She held the slat of the venetian blind down with her finger, watched him walk to his car. When he got in, the car leaned with the weight of him. June imagined the sound of springs giving, fabric tightening, the slow creak of the heavy car door as he pulled it shut behind him. Heat waves rose from the street like the waves on June's TV screen, and the big car seemed to sink bumper deep in the pavement as Cage drove slowly off, June's luggage in his trunk, going up to Temple where he had a deal cooking with a car salesman. Her clothes—blouses folded softly, nylons neatly rolled, underwear tucked into the secret elastic pockets of her suitcase, silk against satin, the smell of her—locked in. He would meet her at Momma's in the new car. He would have to switch her luggage. He would carry her smells, blouses with the faint stains of her sweat under their arms, across the showroom bright with new cars, and his hands would sweat when he stood outside in the drizzle putting the new suitcases with her gold initials into the new trunk.

When she thought of the new car he would buy she remembered the dream she had had last night. In the dream she saw herself sleeping in her bed, her bedroom just as it was this morning, only in the dream Cage was not sleeping with her. She was alone and the door opened and five men in dark overcoats, dark trousers and jackets visible beneath the coats, came quietly into her room. The last man to come in was Cage, who stared at her but did not seem to recognize her. The other four faces were blank. Just four fleshy ovals without eyes or noses or mouths. The first man gestured for June to get up, his arm moving slowly, a dark circle where his mouth should have been, moving, pulsing regularly, a dark

26

circle that swelled, then shrank and disappeared entirely in the empty face, the sound of an amplified heartbeat from a TV show about heart surgery thumped each time the dark mouth hole swelled out. June got up and the men led her outside into a predawn fog, the landscape indistinct grays and blacks. They stood under an old-fashioned streetlight, it looked like the streetlight in a plastic silhouette someone had given June of a London carriage and horse. A long black limousine pulled silently up to them, it had no driver. The men led June to the driver's side, and the doors all opened. She slid in behind the steering wheel, the seat cold and spongy. She imagined that she was sitting on Jello, when she put her hand down against the seat it sank into a thick layer of blue and gray mold. The five men got into the limousine, and the doors shut, soundlessly, all four doorlocks went down simultaneously, like nails going in without being hammered. The steering wheel turned slightly and the heavy automobile moved into the fog, driving itself. June watched the accelerator pedal moving down slowly and felt the car tilt, then she realized they were moving up a long ramp. The climb seemed to take hours, higher and higher they went. No one spoke. Finally, the limousine leveled off and entered some kind of expressway. There were no other vehicles going in their direction, but traffic going the other way was heavy, pair after pair of yellow headlights passed, slowly disappearing into the heavy fog behind them. The ride did not seem to take as long as going up the ramp had taken. Soon the brake pedal went down slowly and the wheel turned to the right. They curved down onto another ramp and stopped, the doors opened, the five men got out. The man with Cage's face opened the trunk while the other four men led June onto a bright green island of grass. The fog seemed to be lifting and June could see that they were on a hillside formed by the exit ramp that led to another expressway which intersected the one they had been riding on, the new expressway passing

27

beneath the one they had left. The figure with Cage's face had gotten something from the trunk and come toward her. Everything seemed to take a long time, but June was not scared. When he reached her, the man with Cage's face took her hand and ran it along a very soft length of rope and a very soft, smooth leather collar he had taken out of the trunk. He seemed to be showing her how soft and old the rope and collar were, it was as if he thought she was blind and had to feel things to see them. Then, still expressionless, he slipped the collar over her head and fastened it snugly around her neck. Then two of the other men walked to the center of the island of grass and one held a wooden stake which the other drove silently into the ground with a huge wooden mallet, the stake and mallet June thought were from a circus or revival tent. Then all five dark-suited men returned to the limousine which continued down the ramp, passed beneath the first expressway, then appeared on the other side, climbing yet another ramp back onto the same expressway and returning in the direction from which they had come. The dream ended with June leaning her head down to take a mouthful of the green grass as the fog disappeared and cars passed her without notice.

She had not told Cage about the dream, it had not disturbed her. She did not worry about what it meant. She thought it didn't mean anything and, somehow, there had been something pleasant about it, something that was nice about dreaming it, nice even now when she remembered it.

She let her robe slip down around her ankles, stepped out of the ring it made over her feet, felt in her drawer for nylons, garter belt. She twisted the run in one stocking out of sight on the inside of her knee, clipped the dark bands around her thighs. Like hanging clothes on the round clothesline behind her apartment.

She put on her favorite yellow dress, the dress that made her feel confident, like she looked good. She hated going to see a doctor and was especially nervous about going to a clinic run by the public health department. "It's nothing," Cage had said, "just a quick check to make the license legal." The free clinic had been his idea, since it was required by law and they paid for the clinic with their taxes and she wasn't sick or anything. "When you're sick, or having a baby," he'd said, "then we'll want a private doctor. The best. But why worry with the time and expense of doctors' offices and getting an appointment for today?" Since she didn't have her own doctor in San Antonio, she had been to Momma's Dr. O'Connor once, but she didn't like him and didn't like the idea of him talking about her to Momma, didn't even like to think of him looking at Momma naked, touching and poking her, and then looking at her and touching her the same way, and since Cage was probably right that she couldn't get an appointment fast enough, she agreed to go to the health department clinic. As she left the apartment she stopped for a last look in the mirror, licked her thumb and rubbed the flakey skin between her eyebrows. She smiled at herself in the mirror, winked, said, "So long, spinster," and hurried to her bus stop, wishing she had her own car.

5

THE CLINIC was in the basement of an old, two-story brick house. An air conditioner stuck through one window, an ivy plant sitting on top of the air conditioner, the glass above it covered with tin foil. Through the other window a cat's eye view of the sidewalk and street: legs, feet, tires. The waiting room was crowded with women reading big magazines.

June turned the paper cup to see the red horns and grinning eyes printed on it, No Devilment Here, she read. Like in a honky-tonk, for drinking beer. But the cup was warm with her urine. She held it away from her, out over the arm of her chair. It was so yellow it surprised her. Finally a nurse took the cup and told June she'd be called soon.

The waiting room walls were each a different pale color, green, pink, blue, yellow. In one wall was the door to the hall and steps up out of the basement. In the opposite wall, the door that led to smaller rooms, rooms with padded tables, scissors and knives, dark brown bottles. Rooms with microscopes and strange smells where right now someone was pouring her urine into a test tube, looking at her urine.

In a glass window with a round hole in the bottom a nurse sat between a typewriter and a telephone. June imagined the nurse pushing a button that would shoot a little red ticket out of a metal slot in her booth, like the woman at the movie show, the little red ticket sticking out like a tongue at June, someone behind that door that led to the inside rooms who would take her ticket, tear it in half, tell her to keep the stub for the doctor. Beneath the ticket window a poster showed a fat, red apple, grinning, shaking hands with a tall green, grinning celery stalk, soft celery leaf hair, wide cartoon eyes: Eat Us For A Healthy Baby.

Most of the women in the waiting room were Mexican. There was a sign on the wall in Spanish that June couldn't read. It made her nervous not being able to read the Mexican words so she stared at the pipes that ran along the ceiling. The pipes were the same pastel colors as the walls, green, pink, blue, yellow, the same as Cage's shirts. Paper cups and colored walls and colored pipes like in some honky-tonk. A long tube in the fluorescent light was flickering overhead, bouncing light off the colored pipes like an old Wurlitzer bubbling, throwing colored shadows, Ray Price wailing out of the speaker, when June was younger, listening and dancing, "Don't Let the Stars Get in Your Eyes."

Two small boys came running into the clinic followed by a fat, pale woman with red pimples on her forehead. The woman came down the steps sideways. She carried a baby in a flat, plastic carrier with a handle over the baby's stomach. She looked back over her shoulder at the clock as she slammed the door by swinging her big hip into it, her heavy shoulder strap purse swinging, a bright turquoise scarf wrapped around her head. The other women in the waiting room looked up from behind their magazines to smile at the little boys who were running, then walking, giggling, then

31

squatting, then running again between the rows of chairs.

"You boys stop," the fat woman said without much concern or enthusiasm, "Stop that, now."

The boys squatted, giggled. The waiting women smiled at them, at the fat woman, turned pages in the shiny magazines, *Life, Look, Ladies' Home Journal.* The fat woman leaned over slowly and picked up a magazine from the floor, and, without having to straighten to standing again, reached out and held onto a chair, paused a minute while she breathed loudly, then pulled the chair toward herself while she sort of skated toward it. When she was close enough she dropped heavily into the chair and swung the baby down beside her like a six pack of beer. Dark, bluish skin, it lay perfectly still, looked dead.

June tried to hear Ray Price again, tried to picture the bubbling lights of the jukebox.

A thin, young woman with long black hair came out of the door from the smaller, inside rooms. The nurse in the window was typing, she called the young woman, "Did Doctor say you were going to have your tubes tied, Mrs. Hernandez?"

The young woman looked embarrassed, shook her head. She looked around the waiting room, seemed to look right at June. The fat woman's two boys stopped giggling and stared at the young woman.

"What did Doctor tell you, then?"

The woman half smiled, moved toward the nurse who continued to talk loudly from behind the glass.

"Are you planning on having any more children, Mrs. Hernandez?"

The fat woman lowered her *Ladies' Home Journal.*

"Well, Mrs. Hernandez, you're twenty-five. If you don't get yourself fixed that's another twenty or thirty years using the diaphragm. And you can't ever let yourself forget it. Is that what your husband wants?"

32

June tried not to hear the loud nurse. She stared at the floor, the two boys were sitting there tearing pages out of a magazine. She watched four female legs move by in the basement window. Two of the women opposite her were smoking. One held her ashes in her hand, the other let them fall, on the slick pages of the magazine, on the concrete floor. The fat woman let her magazine close on her lap, folded her curd arms across her huge breasts, and closed her eyes.

The streetlight through her window, almost like moonlight, the sheets white as sugar. Cage put his hands on her, could cover a breast with one hand, pushing her nipple in with his thumb. She lay sunk in the bed, feeling his weight on her. She wanted a pillow over her face, to lie in the muffling of pillow and his weight on her, the radio on softly, listening there to the music. He quit touching her breasts when he pushed inside her, nudging her legs apart with his thighs, locking his arms around her. His watch cold and smooth in the small of her back, his breathing warm in her ear. Trying to hear his watch, she felt it ticking against her spine. She could not hear Cage's body moving, she was listening to the music, Kitty Wells, "Your Wild Life's Gonna Get You Down." What did it look like inside her? Catfish lie in deep pools in the river, where the water is dark and cold. June never made noise, never scared the fish in the pools in the river. If she could not hear the fish moving in the water, how could they ever hear her from deep down in the pools in the river? Tip of the pole and light on the line and colored cork on the water. She wondered what it looked like inside the pool of dark water. She wanted to watch the fish swallow the hook in the cold water. When Cage pushed inside her, dark colors. A dark room like she had never seen before. Dark, wood, heavy, chocolate. Round-seated chairs with heart-shaped backs lined the walls. Straight, dark-legged, with puffy seats and padded, heart-shaped, pin-cushion backs, puffy and pink like macaroon cookies. Chocolate smell,

33

smell of pink marshmallow stuffing. A great glittering light fixture hanging down into the room, from deep in her insides, a huge layered wedding cake of glass. Dim diamond lights in the dark room, light that sparkled softly like the sound of wind chimes on Momma's porch. And men came inside the room in dark suits, men like the men who came for her in her dream and rode away with her in the limousine. But these men wore long coats with tails, white gloves, black top hats, each carrying a cane like the blind man June used to see on the bus she rode to work. But these were glass canes and made no sound on the dark thick carpet as the men came inside her room. When Cage squeezed her arms and came out of her, the room disappeared. She, beneath him, his chest against her breasts, herself flattened against herself, beneath him, hoping he would not move, hoping to see the room again. And when he came out she was numb where he had been, so numb she thought part of her had disappeared with him when he came out of her. And when he came out she lay still, wondering if there were other rooms inside her.

The young woman, Mrs. Hernandez, had left. The nurse in the window was typing again. The fat woman was breathing heavily, eyes closed, almost snoring. Her dark-skinned baby was on the floor, motionless, buckled into the plastic carrier. The other women looked the same, legs crossed, faces hidden behind magazines.

June idly turned pages in a *Saturday Evening Post,* a new automobile raced across two pages, its shiny hood reflecting the still-flickering fluorescent light. A car Cage would buy, heavy with chrome, long, silvery. So much horsepower, so big, such soft seats.

A new nurse entered the waiting room from inside the clinic, called June, led her to another room. June wondered why she had been called ahead of the women who had been waiting before her. Maybe because, like Cage said, it's only a quick check for the wedding license. The nurse asked June if

34

she was Mexican American. No. The nurse making marks in a manila folder. Age: thirty-two. Address: June didn't know—she would be moving, she didn't know the new address. Cage would pick it out, she didn't know yet. The nurse wrote: none. The nurse told June she would have to phone in for her lab results later. Husband's name: June told her, but said she wasn't married yet. The nurse looked up, her lips pursed, eyes narrowed as if she was about to tell June she didn't know the answers well enough and would have to go stand in the corner, but she said nothing. In the folder she wrote: pre-marital. Her future husband's occupation: real estate. His approximate earnings: June didn't know. The nurse looked up again, shook her head slowly, made some mark in the upper right hand corner of the folder and told June to wait. June tried to read what the nurse had written, but the stiff, white sleeve of the nurse's arm moved across the edge of the folder. Then the nurse took the folder, stepped into an office across the hall and dropped it on a desk, leaving June alone in the small room with an empty table and several metal folding chairs.

Across the hall another nurse came out of another room next to the office where the first nurse had dropped June's folder. Through the partially open door June saw a doctor kneeling, two bare feet sticking out over his head. He was twisting a metal lamp, aiming light up between the feet. The nurse stepped back into the room, the feet jerked, the metal stirrups squeaked. June's hands were shaking, a trickle of sweat ran down her spine. She held her elbows in close against her ribs, wondering if she smelled bad. If she didn't stop sweating she'd ruin her yellow dress. There was no mirror in the room. She touched her hair nervously.

Cage held her nice when they danced. She put her head on his shoulder, smelling him, watching his pants cuff and the heel of his shoe when he made a backwards step. The music was slow, twangy, sad.

When the nurse came back June got up and silently followed her down the hall to another room. Here were an examining table, a lavatory, a tall metal cabinet with glass doors revealing rows of brown bottles and colorless syringes and one shelf covered with a white towel on which was laid a row of metal instruments. This shelf reminded June of a table setting, a white placemat with knives and forks spread out, strange little butter knives, sharp steak knives, heavy dinner forks, short salad forks, long, strange-looking pickle forks. She imagined this silent nurse tucking a big bib into the collar of her nurse's uniform and spreading June out to slice her up and eat her, dabbing at her lips with the big balls of cotton stacked in a jar on the little table next to the metal cabinet. The nurse ignored June, pulled the white paper off the examining table and put down a new sheet. Then she told June to take off all her clothes and lie on the table. June imagined the nurse licking her lips.

The table was warm, even the metal stirrups were warm, felt damp. June wondered whose feet had just sweated in these same stirrups. A doctor came in reading her folder, said hello without looking up, and began to move the lamp into position for the examination.

The instrument touched her, cold, metal. Scissors to cut her open, a bellows to pump her apart. Her legs shook. The kneeling doctor stopped and told her to keep her legs still. She tried, but his hand in her hurt, her legs jerked. He pushed harder, *my hand hurts, too,* he said.

June closed her eyes, tried to imagine what it looked like inside her, tried to see the men in the room again. All she could see were the green, pink, blue, yellow pipes in the waiting room. The cold pipes ran up into her body like into a factory, a refinery, a power plant. The doctor was moving the bellows, filling her with gasses, blue and yellow gasses hissing up inside her, but she couldn't see. The doctor, a stranger, could see up into her, but she could not see her own room.

36

She opened her eyes and the doctor was holding a long stick that looked like a paint stirrer. He put the stick into her, she saw the stick disappear like a sword down a sword swallower's throat at a sideshow, saw it come back out again. She pictured the doctor inside her, walking around, inspecting the pipes, looking at valves, gauges. The doctor finished, slipped the stick into a waxed paper envelope, told June to be sure and phone in for the lab results.

Left alone to dress, June ran her fingers over her stomach, slowly felt between her legs. She wondered if the doctor had left the metal instrument inside her. She thought she still felt the metal against her insides. He had taken something out of her with his stick and put it into his envelope and had left her the metal instrument in return. A packrat, leaving something worthless for something of hers he had taken. She wished her fingers had lights on them so they could shine up into her, wished they had eyes on them so they could see. She felt herself, trying to see. Her hand shook, was slippery with sweat. Her throat was dry. She hurt.

Walking to the bus stop from the clinic was painful, she was still sore. She stood, waiting for her bus, wishing she could lie down in the grass. Soon she could quit riding buses, Cage would buy her a car of her own. He would have a car and she would have a car. Cage's car, June's car, side by side in a huge garage in back of a huge house Cage would buy her. She would tell Cage about the car in *The Saturday Evening Post*, the color of Silver Mink.

The bus was hot, the window wouldn't budge. June looked for the blind man she saw every morning on the bus she rode to work, but he wasn't here, this was not his bus. She read the posters over the windows, but many of them were in Spanish like the posters in the clinic. The strange words made her feel like she was in another country, far from anyone or anything she knew. The man driving the bus looked

37

like a foreigner, he had thick dark hair. She could see his undershirt through his sweaty bus driver's uniform. The shirt clung to his shoulders and chest, the pants were tight around his thighs. There was no one else on the bus. Maybe this was not her bus. Maybe she had gotten on a bus that had taken her away to some other country. She was alone on this bus, maybe they were kidnapping her. She wondered what the bus driver was thinking. Did he want to stop and talk to her? Tell her about the kidnapping, say he was sorry, they made him do it. Hold her hand, dark hairs covering the back of his hands, make love to her on the empty seat across the back of the bus, their skin sticking to the red plastic. She watched his hand, quick, easy, shifting gears, his foot moving up and down on the clutch. Cage would get her free, he would pay any ransom.

She wondered if Momma and Turk liked Cage. She thought no one really liked Cage but her, and she could not remember just exactly what Cage looked like. She had seen him just a few hours ago but she had trouble seeing all of his face at once. He was not like the other men she had known. He was from up north. One day he had come by the warehouse to take her boss to an Optimist Club luncheon and Cage and June had been introduced. She remembered how he had reached out to shake her hand, just like she was a man, only gentler. And she had known from the way he looked at her that he would call her.

She wondered if she would miss her job at Texas Cut Flower. She liked the men and the hammering as they filled the long cardboard boxes with layers of fern and gladiola, nailing wooden braces inside the boxes. She liked drinking coffee from the heavy mug with her initials fingerpainted on the bottom with red nailpolish, liked sitting on the packing tables smelling green waxed paper and cold flowers from the walk-in refrigerator.

The bus hissed and stopped, a fat woman got on carrying a

wicker basket and a paper bundle tied with twine. The driver nodded to the fat woman and didn't look as much like a foreigner as he had before. The fat woman grabbed a silver pole and pulled herself into a seat. June remembered the fat woman at the clinic pulling herself into a chair. What was inside fat people that took up so much room? What did the kneeling doctor at the clinic shining his light up into the fat woman see? Was there a big, empty room inside her? Cage was fat. June didn't want to be fat, ever. She was still sore from the examination and imagined being sore all over from fat inside her pushing out against her skin all the time. She would get Cage to lose weight after they were married.

The fat woman yanked the cord, pulled herself up. The bus lurched to a stop, the woman skating to the door. June almost got up and followed her off the bus. Through the window June watched the woman cross the street and disappear between two houses.

Where was she? The city didn't look familiar. This was not her neighborhood. She tried to remember what her neighborhood looked like. She was afraid she might miss her stop. She would keep looking out the window until she saw the tall palm tree and that would be across from her apartment. She would never sleep there again. That was past. She was moving. Cage would buy her a house. Her own house. What kind of house did she want?

The rain had almost stopped. The sky was cloudy, close, muggy. June was again the only passenger on the bus. She was moving. She looked at the houses she was passing and wondered what kind of house she wanted Cage to buy her. The bus moved fast, passing people, passing cars, passing houses, not stopping for anything.

6

Saturday noon

Dear June,

Got your short letter and Cage's nice check. I guess if you weren't marrying Cage I'd just have to go on the welfare with all the mexicans. Tho with the high cost of living welfare is not much good. The cost of being buryed is so bad too I can't see any way out.

Turk is down at the graveyard mowing grass. Jordan has one of his boys at the Sinclair until Turk gets through. I hope he doesn't go off to Austin tonite to see you know who. I hate to think of being left here all alone on a Saturday nite with all the Mexicans in Blanco out on a drunk. It is so hot but I still keep my windows and doors locked tight. Besides how I'd worry about him on that Austin hiway. A bad wreck up at the Henly cut off last Thurs. killed an old man crossing the hiway and a Nigger woman in the car. I hope you can read this, I have artharitis in my thumb making it hard to write.

Naomi is down with her back again. Turk wouldn't take me to see her this weekend so I called her but they wouldn't let me talk to her so she wrote me a letter Friday and I got it yesterday. Naomi said Olivia and her daughter-in-law came up and brought Olivia's granddaughter. She is 6 weeks old and the marriage was just last Feb. I had an idea that was her trouble, Olivia's, worrying about that. Thinking it might be one of Naomi's stories I called up Lucille Waters and she said yes, Olivia does have a new grand-daughter. Naomi told me right after the wedding that Lucretia, the little daughter-in-law, was square, she was so fat but I never caught on. She, Olivia, is telling it that Lucretia has been married way over a year. And all of those old ladies at the wedding know better of course—Olivia is just well on the way of loosing her mind. She called me as much as 4 times a day last week and told some of the awfullest things I had to put down the phone half the time. She said, you tell Manny to come see me, he is an old Mexican that hangs out at Pearl and Eddies, is in jail half the time and drunk. No one knows if he is stuck on Pearl or Eddie is stuck on Manny's wife who is only 19 and allready has three kids. Well I wouldn't ever speak to Manny and Olivia can have him. Manny has a wild boy by some other woman before he got married and Naomi says one nite they were all fighting and drunk Manny was betting $100 his boy could whip another mexican. Everyone says Olivia paid that boys fine. Olivia says she and Manny are just good friends. I think I could beat that nasty Mexican for friends. Olivia is just on the way of loosing her mind.

So you see what kind of place Blanco is getting to be and Turk would go off to Austin and leave me here alone all night. Guess he will be home for supper before long. The way he acts to me and I keep fixing his meals and he barely gives me rent money. That's just a mother's love I guess. All he has to do is ride that old mower around and get $12.

What time before the wedding will you get here? I hope it is at least two days. I'm glad you can quit that job at that nasty flower place. You won't need that now that you've got Cage and it wasn't a nice job for a girl. At least the church is air conditioned. This weather is about to get me down. Its just too hot to get up in the morning. Sure wish I could afford air conditioning. Naomi has one of those little General Electrics in her window in her bedroom and she says it works just real good.

41

When its dry the dust blows in and when it rains the air is so sticky it warps my bones so I walk crooked. ha. But it is true.

Well, I have to finish Turk his supper. Hope I don't slip and fall down bending over that old cook stove. Call me and tell me what day you will be here.

Love,
Momma

June folded Momma's letter and stuck it in her purse next to the appointment card and the ten dollar bill. The letter was the last she would get at this address. The appointment was to see the doctor at the clinic the day after she got back from the honeymoon. On back of the appointment card was the number to call for the lab results, day after tomorrow. Cage had given her the ten dollars to catch a taxi down to the Greyhound station and to buy a ticket to Blanco.

Going there to marry him. June wasn't sure when she had decided she would marry Cage, but it was before he had decided to ask her, she was sure of that. She had never thought much about getting married before. Only one other man, Ed Jacks, ever asked her. Ed had a job at the Texas Farm Bureau, and he talked about his job and about going back to college but was so stuck in the mud he always took her to the same Mexican food place and then always wanted to come back to June's apartment, to play cards, he told her. Ed was a card nut. He knew all kinds of card games and made up new games for them to play. The only kind of cards June liked were card tricks, the kind Armon used to bring home to try out on her and Turk when they were kids. Ed would patiently explain the rules of a game and deal them each a hand, and June would always ignore the rules and save up diamonds and clubs because she liked them best. Then Ed invented a game called Bury Your Heart with a Spade, the object of which was to discard all your hearts and spades while you collected sequences of diamonds and clubs. June decided she didn't even

42

like diamonds and clubs anymore and told Ed to learn how to make cards disappear. That hurt Ed's feelings but not so much that he quit calling her and asking her to go eat Mexican food with him.

Going through her apartment for the last time, June turned the faucets in the kitchen and bathroom off as hard as she could twist. Then she let the venetian blinds down in her bedroom, the clunk of the wooden blind against the window echoing in the empty room, the afternoon sun through the blinds zebra-striping her shins. All she smelled was dust. It was hard to believe she had lived in these small rooms for over ten years. She had only lived in three different places in her life, in the house in Blanco, in a boardinghouse when she first moved to San Antonio and was looking for a job, and here, in this apartment where she and Ed Jacks had spent many Saturday evenings, too many Saturday evenings, sitting on the used couch she'd gotten from one of the cheap furniture and appliance stores squeezed in next to army surplus stores and pawn shops on a run-down street near downtown. Standing in her bedroom, looking around, she felt no attachment, no sadness in leaving.

She opened an empty closet, air from the closet door swinging the bare coathangers against one another, making a soft metal noise. Cage said coathangers reproduced faster and quieter than rabbits. Leave a coathanger alone in an empty closet and the next time you open up that closet hangers will come jumping out like Easter bunnies. June smiled, remembering all Cage's talk about coathangers and the cleaners his mother had worked for in Ohio. Before she left, June took all the empty coathangers and stuffed them down into the garbage can outside the back door. Pushing and bending them down into the garbage left a network of crisscrossing red marks on the palms of her hands, like the lines on a roadmap.

The only time Ed Jacks had ever taken June to his

43

house—he lived at home with his parents and his younger brother—had been the night he'd asked her to marry him. It was a hot night and they sat around a new maple table in the dining room. Ed's mother asked June if she had ever heard of the Singer Sewing School. Ed's father sat at the table in front of a full cup of coffee that he kept lifting to his lips without ever drinking any. Ed was trying to hold her hand under the table, and June was listening to the water run through the straw in the water cooler in the living room window. June excused herself to go to the bathroom. She locked the bathroom door behind her and looked around. An olive green towel lay wadded up against the bottom edge of the tub, as if someone had put it there to soak up water. There was no bar of soap in the dish on the edge of the tub, none above the lavatory. She opened the medicine cabinet to see what kind of toothpaste Ed used, to see if he had an electric razor, to learn what she could. And, there in the bathroom in Ed Jacks's parents' house, she decided not to marry Ed Jacks. There was no toothpaste, no electric razor. There was nothing in the medicine cabinet but medicine. Dark brown bottles, green bottles, clear plastic bottles, dented silver tubes, metal pill boxes, the same blue and white checkered label, WHITE CROSS PROFESSIONAL PHARMACIES, the labels all lined up with the white cross emblems in rows, like a military cemetery. June remembered the blue neon sign, WHITE CROSS, she had seen a few blocks from the house, when Ed drove her over. Except for a laxative with no name on it and some nosedrops for his little brother, all the medicine was for Edward Jacks. He had nosedrops, eyedrops, eardrops, vitamins, nerve pills, pain pills, sunburn lotion, ointment for rash, salve for fever blisters, big red capsules for allergy, tiny white pills for toothache, two bottles of cherry and one of lemon cough syrup, a tall bottle labeled *rub sore area three times daily,* and several other bottles of pills and liquids labeled only with dosage instructions. June shut the cabinet door, it

44

clicked closed with finality, and washed her hands, practicing a couple of smiles in the mirror.

In the dining room Ed's father still had not drunk any of his coffee. June smiled at him and he smiled back. She was relieved when Ed said they should be running along. After they were outside, Ed told her he was going to show her where he worked.

She had expected the Farm Bureau to be in an old wooden building with one or two rolltop desks littered with papers, like the doctor's office, when she was younger, in Blanco. She pictured Ed at work looking like the Philip Morris boy, someone who carried a tray of coffee and sandwiches to his boss every day at noon, then spent the rest of the day sweeping up with a push broom. Instead, there was a new, brick building, a stainless steel elevator that took them to a floor of large rooms filled with rows of pale green metal desks, each desk with a pale green typewriter and a pale green adding machine. Ed's desk was set off by a shoulder-high glass partition, his name, Edward Jacks, on the glass. He had been promoted, he told June, he was now a supervisor. He took a clean sheet of Farm Bureau stationery, typed a line across the top, unlocked the copying machine with a shiny key, and fed the sheet into the machine. The copy that came out was slippery, smelled like an empty mayonaise jar, and was still warm when he handed it to June: WILL YOU MARRY ME? She took the pen off his desk, wrote, NO, and gave him back the copy and one of the smiles she had practiced in his medicine cabinet mirror. That night when Ed walked her to her door she let him kiss her goodnight, for his pride. He hadn't called her since.

She slammed her apartment door, had to slam it again, harder, heard the lock catch, and headed down to Mr. Tony's to leave the key. The apartment manager was from someplace up north, Chicago or Detroit. Mr. Tony was what everyone called him. He told June once that he sometimes

45

missed the snow and the sausages but that he liked the sun and the barbecue better. Mr. Tony talked funny but he was always nice to June. She had told him she was getting married and moving out, he would be expecting her with the key. He met her on his front step with a clown's exaggerated sad face.

"You know," he said, "I hate to see you go away. You my favorite best tenant. And now I won't see you again evermore."

Mr. Tony stood smiling at June in shiny pleated suit pants, dark and heavy, brown wingtip shoes, and a white pearl button shirt, wrinkled looking as wadded up cellophane. His black hair receded back off his high forehead and curled down over his shirt collar. June felt like asking herself in and visiting with him. She had never been inside his apartment. Probably it looked just like hers, the same rooms, the same windows. She didn't even know for sure if he lived alone, though she had never seen anyone else around his place. She was suddenly sad that she had never gotten to know him, this short man with his shiny, baggy pants who stood, smiling, waiting for the key. She just stood there looking at a spot beneath his ear where his hair and the stubble of his beard didn't grow. A soft-looking island of skin where no hair grew.

"Well," he said, smiling even wider.

She held out the key, and when he stepped forward to take it she hugged Mr. Tony briefly, just long enough to kiss him on the little island of baby skin. He smelled like floor wax.

For a second he seemed embarrassed, then he laughed, "Well," he laughed, "Thank you so much again." Then he was gone, and June was walking down the sidewalk still smelling the floor wax.

Her daddy, Armon, used to come home from working at the feed store in Blanco and pick her up and rub his rough chin into her neck until she would beg him to stop, and he

46

always smelled like floor wax. He used to send word home, *send June down here to see her daddy.*

Years ago. Before he died. *Send June down here.*

The store empty, she walked up and down the aisles, smelling burlap, leather, feed. Where was he? Stacking boxes of shotgun shells? Unpacking cases of whiskey? Putting prices on stiff, new denim shirts? Up and down the rows, shelves of boxes, barrels of nails too tall to see over. *Daddy, where are you?* Another trick on her? He was always pulling tricks. Joking, he said.

Behind the counter, his cigar still smoking in the heavy, glass ashtray. Something, some noise, some motion in back, in the back of the feed and ranch supply store where the shelves were not neat, where colored labels with the names of far away places on them were packed away in dark wooden crates. June hated the back of the store. It was dusty, smelled strong of animals, damp cardboard, rust, rotting grain. No windows in back, only the bare bulb hanging, swinging on a long cord run from the wall socket, tacked up the wall, run out to the middle of the room, hanging from the beams overhead. Electric wiring running across the raw lumber between the heavy studs of the unfinished walls.

Daddy, Daddy.

Huge wooden spools taller than June. New rope, chain. The light softly swinging, casting shadows. Then a gentle creaking, wood giving, the sound of weight, a tightening.

Oh. No. Daddy, no. His huge shadow swinging like the light bulb. Hanged himself. *Oh Daddy.* Running into a great coil of rope, the little hairs sticking out, the rough, tickling texture of rope sticking her hands. *No, no.*

Laughing. A joke. Come back here June, it was only a joke, a great joke. See, Daddy is right here. Ole Armon ain't gone and hung himself for real. See the rope looped around his ole chest, here, see, around here under his arms, hidden beneath his coat, up his back, up behind his neck, behind

47

his collar where the false noose was knotted. A smooth round rock held under each arm, pushed into his armpits, stopped his pulse. He didn't need to be that careful, she didn't touch him.

He was always that careful, he took every precaution. A careful joker, a very practical joker, he thought of everything. What a card. *He's a real card, a real character.* June had heard men in the store call him that. *Armon,* she had heard them laugh, *you ole son-of-a-gun, you.*

She had always been his favorite. That's what everyone said. June, his favorite, his pet. How could she have been? She hadn't gotten to know him yet. They had never really talked. *You're your daddy's favorite, that's for sure,* Momma would say. June was the youngest and she was pretty. June Estelle Marrs, her daddy's pet.

He hadn't lived long enough. She had never gotten to talk to him. She would have asked him if she really was his favorite, and why. But now that was all gone. He would have wanted her to have a big, fancy wedding. Think of the jokes, all his practical jokes. All the old shoes and tin cans in town tied to their car; HELP painted on Cage's shoe bottoms and some need to kneel worked into the service, a word to the preacher just before the service would do the trick; the air let out of their tires; all the old-timey tricks he would have known to pull.

June looked up and saw a stoplight and realized she had walked all the way to Broadway, a main street loud with traffic. The rain had stopped but the sky was still gray and threatening. She could probably catch a taxi here, at least she could find a phone booth and call a taxi. She had never ridden in a taxi. When she had told Cage that he'd laughed and given her the ten dollars and said he hated to marry a gal before she lost her taxi cab virginity. When he laughed like that June thought he sounded like the way she remembered her daddy's laugh.

48

Now, years gone by, Armon was dead and she was going back to Blanco to get married, and he would not be there to laugh and pull jokes and give the bride away. She had told Momma she didn't want any substitutes, no family friend or handsome relative, she would just give herself away.

She took out the ten dollar bill. She hated to waste money on a taxi when she had already walked half-way downtown. There were plenty of cars going by, it seemed like she could just get a ride with someone. She hadn't ever ridden in a taxi, but she hadn't ever hitchhiked either.

She held out her thumb.

She was amost relieved when the first few cars just kept on passing by. She tried not to meet the glances of the people in the cars and was about to go call for the taxi when an old Plymouth, white, rusting out along the bottom, pulled over, one brakelight bright white where the red plastic had been smashed.

There were three women, all in white dresses, crowded into the front seat. June got in the back and slid across behind the driver, who was singing, yelling:

Wa-ter-mel-ons, come and see-ee,
Ev'er-one sold on a gare-un-tee-ee,
Red ripe wa-ter-mel-ons, sweet and ju-cee-ee,
Fit for you and fit for Lu-cee-ee.

The driver pulled out into traffic again without pausing in her song and without asking June where she was going. After another verse of the watermelon song the woman in the middle offered June a drink from a silver flask.

"No, thank you. I'm just going downtown," June said. "My car broke down and I'm late for a meeting downtown at the bank. My husband is meeting me—he's head of the bank."

The driver smiled over shoulder and nodded, "We headed right through there, no problem at all." She slapped the

49

steering wheel with her left hand and the car jerked to the right as the other two women clapped their hands together. Then the driver slapped the wheel back to the left with her right hand, and the others clapped their hands together again. The woman on the right held the flask up again and offered June some. No? She nodded, grinned at June, passed the whiskey over to the driver.

"We're celebrating," the driver yelled. "Lucy here is getting hitched," she clapped the top of the curly blonde head in the middle, Lucy, June figured, beating out the tune to another round of *Wa-ter-mel-ons.* Lucy turned around and winked, "Tonight," she said.

"That's nice," June said, "That's really nice." She thought she should ask them to stop, ask them to let her out right here. She should have called the taxi. But she could see the buildings of downtown not far ahead.

"Whoo-ee, I'm so drunk," the driver laughed, "I couldn't find my ass with both my hands." Then she gave the wheel another slap for emphasis. "We run a bakery, lady, best bakery in Texas. Spent all morning fixing up Lucy's wedding cake. Taking the afternoon off. You didn't have that meeting you could come on along with us."

Lucy was bobbing up and down to some song in her head. The woman on the right, whose hair was blue-black and piled up on her head as the headliner in the old Plymouth, reached back over the seat and grabbed June's hand, "I'm Peg. You already met Lucy, and that floozie drinking at the wheel is Carmen." Her hand, so white with flour it looked to June like a white, Sunday glove, squeezed June so hard it hurt. She let go to jerk the white hand over Lucy's bouncing blonde head and point through the windshield, "Lookee, lookee."

Carmen swerved, pulled up at the curb. Another hitchhiker, a boy, a teenager carrying a big sleeping bag rolled up in front of him, hugging it to his chest.

"We're giving everone a ride today," Carmen screamed, "Our car is a whole fucking parade."

Peg was drinking from the flask. She tipped it and her head back together, her hair flattening against the teenager's sleeping bag which stuck up between him and the back of the front seat. Then she reached beneath the seat for a full bottle of whiskey and tried to pour into the little mouth of the flask. She laughed every time she spilled the whiskey. The car smelled like whiskey and bakery flour and gardenia perfume.

June was sweating, wiped her hands on the seat. The boy was staring at her. He offered her a cigarette. She said no. Peg offered him some of the whiskey and he took a long drink, the tendons in his neck bulging and tightening after he swallowed. Peg started another song:

Oh, nuts, hot nuts, get 'um from the peanut man,
Yeah, nuts, hot nuts, get 'um any way you can,

Lucy, giggling, joined Peg in a verse:

See that girl dressed in pink,
She's the one makes my finger stink.

June thought maybe she should be nice to the boy. He could protect her if these women tried to rob her or hurt her. She could still feel Peg's hand on her arm where she had squeezed her. There was a deep tan line under Peg's neck where her makeup ended. It made her look like she had on a mask. Her eyebrows were thick and black, long false eyelashes, blue-green shadows over her eyes. Maybe she is a man wearing a mask and a dress. Maybe they all are. June tried to see if any of them had on a wig. She glanced at the boy to see if he was listening to their song. He was watching her. She smiled at him. His lips parted slightly.

"Thanks anyway for the cigarette," June said.

"No sweat," he said, smiling, letting smoke come slowly out of his nostrils.

51

"I got a verse," yelled Carmen,

See that man all dressed in red,
He'll wanta fuck me after he's dead.

Lucy shook with laughter as Carmen and Peg belted out the chorus again. The boy reached over and patted June's hand on the seat between them. His fingernails were black. June was afraid one of the women would see his hand on hers. They caught every red light. His hand was hot on her skin, the same skin Peg had squeezed, the same skin the doctor had touched this morning, and Cage even earlier. June thought about how many people, many of them strangers, might touch her in a single day. The boy's hand lay there on her skin, limp and hot. She thought of the doctor's clean white hand inside the clear rubber gloves slipping up inside her. This boy's hand was dirty, his fingernails uneven, one nail was black, the finger purple where it had been smashed. She imagined this purple finger up inside her, the dead fingernail coming off and floating up into her, the purple finger bleeding, the black fingernail turned to ashes, breaking up, taken into her bloodstream. The doctor would have her back for tests and find the ashes in her blood. *You have death in your blood,* he would say. The purple finger would bleed out of her, dripping for days. *You are discharging blood.* The doctor would put the blood from this dirty purple finger on his slide, *you are discharging blood daily, your blood is type A, you are discharging blood and it is type O, what is wrong with you?* She would feel the purple finger floating around, feel it touching all the places inside her. The doctor would want to look, to find out where the blood was coming from. The nurse would spread her on the table, put her feet in the metal stirrups. June would hold her legs together to keep the purple finger from falling onto the floor. The doctor would grab her knees, his white rubber fingers sinking deep in her skin, leaving red prints on her thighs, his rubber gloves squeaking. *I have to*

52

find out where the blood is coming from, this cannot be your blood, where did you get this blood, the doctor shouting, people banging on the examining room door, the nurse yelling at June, the people yelling through the door, *what's wrong with you?*

Carmen stopped short at a yellow light. The car behind was honking at them. Now the light was red and Carmen was shouting out the window at the driver who was honking. June pulled the back door open and jumped out, "Thank you," she said, "I see my husband at the corner," and hurried across the street as the light was turning green. It was starting to drizzle again.

She kept walking. Through brass and glass revolving doors into a department store. She passed through the perfume department where smells hung sweet and heavy in bright scarves pulled through the clamped hands of a row of legless mannequin torsos. Without stopping she went out another revolving door to another street and looked down the block for the bus station. She saw a row of buses and started running down the street. Out of breath a block down the street she realized she was hurrying to a parking lot of charter buses at a hotel.

By the time she asked a policeman how to get to the Greyhound station and walked the four blocks, the bus that would take her to Blanco was about to leave. She got on just in time, the motor already running, and before she was tilted back in her seat the bus was dipping out of the depot into traffic.

7

ON THE bus June realized she hadn't eaten all day. She'd be at Momma's in about an hour. It was always good to be hungry at Momma's. After the first few minutes of exchanging news and looking around there was little to do but eat and listen to Momma tell and retell her stories. For some reason Momma took great pleasure in watching people stuff themselves with her cooking. She cooked for Armon for thirty years, June thought, habits like that are hard to break. Chicken-fried steak and milk gravy, brown beans, macaroni and cheese, fresh okra, yellow squash, and homemade biscuits—Momma's best supper. Of course Armon had to have two or three kinds of meat, and he wouldn't sit to table without homemade biscuits and gravy in front of him. Thirty years, three meals a day, the same table, the same room. After he died June always used his coffee mug, sat at his place. She could remember the day they brought him home like it was yesterday.

Years ago. A hot, dry day. June was twelve. Four men carried him like a heavy sack of feed home from the store. A man at each corner, like they were fixing to swing him into the river and he would hit, splash, shout, come swimming and running after them.

During droughts the Blanco River dried up and its bed turned the same yellowish brown as the old photograph of Armon that Momma kept stuck in the mirror corner above her hairbrush on the dresser. The white cracks that split the caked river bottom also split Armon's picture. The same picture that had stared at June from Momma's mirror ever since June could remember, the picture that would still be there today when June got to Blanco, that same face of Armon's had watched June the day he died.

Her daddy, Armon Luther Marrs. From a town in Missouri called Joplin, a name Armon said sounded like the noise horses' hooves made on brick streets. June had never seen brick streets, and the picture she had in her mind when Armon told her that was like the beautiful picture of fairyland in a book Armon had brought her back from Kansas City the time he had gone up there to see his daddy buried.

Where you want him, Eunice?

June's twelfth birthday, four men carried her daddy home. The first of June, the rent due on the house, rented from Armon's boss who knocked four dollars off the monthly rent for every Saturday Momma worked with Armon at the feed store.

In the sickroom. Put him in the sickroom.

June did not want to go into the sickroom with the men. The sickroom was Turk's room, empty because he was away in the army. When Turk was home and June got sick they traded rooms. If it was Momma or Daddy sick, Turk had to sleep on the sofa-bed. June hated sleeping in Turk's bed worse than anything else about being sick, but his room was between the kitchen and the bathroom and that's where Momma made you stay.

Four men eased Armon onto Turk's bed.

Looking for elbow room, Armon had come to Texas. He

55

ended up in a narrow space behind the counter of Juno D. Speer & Co., General Merchandise, where he hoped to make it rich. But Juno died, leaving the store to his only son, who left Armon out of work. Armon's sales experience and friendly face got him a job across the square at All-Tex Feed, where he not only sold feed and ranch supplies, but also guns, ammunition, western wear, and whiskey. A safe bet for a job in Blanco, the demand sure to outlast the supply.

June felt guilty seeing her daddy passed out, his face red, his tongue coming out of his mouth. She looked away, looked back, had to look, even though she hated to see him like this. Dr. Meyers had seen the men carrying Armon and was at the house right behind them. In the kitchen June made coffee for the men. Momma and Dr. Meyers were in the crowded sickroom with her daddy. She pictured them squeezed in between the old iron bed and the wall. She heard them, talking softly through the closed door, ran water hard in the kitchen sink so she would not hear what they were saying.

She had heard before, through closed doors. Night after night, through thin doors and wallpapered walls she had lain in bed hearing the rhythms of night-talking. Momma getting up, slap of her bare feet and screak of the faucet, the soft splatter of water in the sink when Momma soaked a towel for his head. A rat rattling over their heads in the empty attic. Listening, hearing her own heartbeat and hearing her own soft breath, hearing her daddy bounce his head against his pillow, bed springs squeaking, her daddy's head hurting.

His face sunk in the pillow, lost in the white pillowcase, not roasted the color of a cedar limb like other Blanco faces. He stayed inside, worked in the store. Others, tanned and sweating others, loaded cattle onto trucks, nailed boards, dug postholes, talked low, looked away when Armon wet the tip of his pencil against his tongue and added up their bills at the store.

56

Other men sat quietly, drinking the coffee June poured, waiting, while Armon was dying in there in Turk's room. They avoided her eyes, stood in corners, leaned against the kitchen counter, stared out the window over the sink, never looked at June, never looked at the closed door of the sickroom where Armon's head hurt deep into the soft pillow.

June opened the refrigerator door, moved bowls from the bottom shelf to the middle shelf, shut the door. Cold air, damp against her face, drawn out of the refrigerator into the hot kitchen, sucked into the hot sickroom where the murmuring had stopped.

Damn Turk for being in Guam.

There was nothing to do. He had passed out before, but not for this long. Something not right inside his head. Dr. Meyers had taken some fluid out, sent it off to be studied somewhere, the report not back yet. Dr. Meyers had said the first time that New Orleans wouldn't do Armon any good, no more than they could do for him at home, said it would cost like the blue blazes.

In the sickroom with Momma, June stepped sideways along the bed, held her arms tight against her sides. Dr. Meyers stood by Armon's head. Brother Spurgin came in too, eyelids lowered. Her daddy was porcelain. Stiff legs beneath the sheet drawn tight over his feet to his chin, where it was tucked like a big napkin. No shape showed beneath the sheet. Ready for burial. Pick him straight up, his stiff body horizontal, the sheet hanging down on all sides like an oversized tablecloth. Wrap the sheet around him like the shuck around a tamale, fold it and pin it, drop him in his grave. He will shatter when he hits.

A body on stage, a magician of levitation, the Houdini movie. He floats off the bed, eyes opened, staring at the glass doorknob. That's how he's doing it, hypnotizing himself. Dr. Meyers grins, moves a broom around the body. No wires. Brother Spurgin snaps his fingers three times, shouts, *Praise*

57

the Lord. The men in the kitchen crowd into the sickroom clapping, whistling. Brother Spurgin looks at June, eyes bulging, *Can you say Amen?* The men lean closer to the suspended body, they whisper, *Amen, Amen.* Her daddy laughs, bows. He stands on air, takes a step forward, takes a step backward. He takes the sheet and gives it a hard shake, and doves and rabbits shake out of it. He holds the sheet out like a bullfighter holding out a cape, shows both sides. He pulls back his stiff white cuffs, ties a knot in the sheet, pops it with a jerk of his wrist, and the sheet disappears.

Momma is watching her.

Dr. Meyers says, *He can hear you, child.*

Hello Daddy. How are you, Daddy? She wants to know how it feels to be inside that head, heavy with pain. Wants to know how the world looks from in there. Is the room blurred like breath on a frosty windowpane, do voices sound far away, slowed down? That's what she really means when she softly says, *How are you?*

Dr. Meyers puts his fingers on the icy forehead, *Armon, if you can hear me, grind your teeth together.*

There is a small movement at his temples.

He can hear us, all right.

Brother Spurgin holds a soft, limp-looking Bible in both his hands, flexing it back and forth like a gambler loosening up a new deck of cards. Against the black cover of the Bible his hands look very white. The edges of the pages are gold and when he bends the book in and out the pages ripple and the gold edges catch the light, shine, snap like teeth.

Yep, he can hear us for sure, says Dr. Meyers.

All afternoon it was like that. Standing, sitting, watching, no one knowing anything to say. People came in and people went out, they brought hams and cakes. June kept busy keeping the coffee pot full and hot.

Armon did not die until the next day. Still sleepy, June opened the door to Turk's little room. Momma was at the foot of the bed, old Mr. Berryhill, who always idled around the feed store and called Armon his best friend, was at the head of the bed saying Armon looked better this morning, looked a heap better.

Armon was still staring at the doorknob. His lips moved, separated with a noise like a spoonful of sugar sliding into a cup of coffee. When he spoke June almost missed it, a hoarse whisper, and tiny strands of saliva floated on his breath, off his lips, spider silk, snail trails, boiled okra juice.

What time is it, Eunice?

His pocket watch tickless on Turk's dresser. Momma stepped out of the bedroom, got the time off a railroad watch one of the men held up, stepped back in.

Eight-fifteen, Armon. How you feeling?

His voice louder, *Eunice, you're telling me a story.*

Why, Armon, you know good and well I wouldn't tell you a story.

He stared at the doorknob. His head nodded, letting the sheet slip from under his chin. The sheet rose a little on the air, then sank, settling softly on his chest, which sank too, then stopped, still. Dr. Meyers, watching through the partly opened door, came in and checked his pulse, pulled the sheet tight over his face and tucked it under the back of his head. Momma got up and walked out without saying a word. Mr. Berryhill shook his head, told Dr. Meyers it was funny, he'd really looked better today.

Years ago. But June could remember everything. Even the button broken in half on Dr. Meyers's suit jacket. She had watched when he leaned over to pull the sheet over her daddy's face, afraid the button was going to fall off, maybe drop into her daddy's mouth. Northing more than a broken button, and she had remembered it all those years.

Through the tinted glass of the Greyhound window, June looked for the Lackey Tree where a man had been hanged, she'd heard the story all her life, for axing his wife and two kids, hiding their heads in his water well for days. She couldn't remember if Lackey was the murderer's name or the name of the rancher who owned the hanging tree. Either way, she thought, Mr. Lackey found a pretty easy way to get into history. She always looked for the tree on the way to or from Blanco, was always disappointed that it was so short. She wondered how they managed to hang a man from a tree so short. This time she missed the tree. Maybe she had already passed it, the bus was almost to Blanco. Maybe someone chopped it down. Axed the ax man's tree. Or maybe it had gotten old and just died.

The bus sped up the brown, round hills bordered by barbed wire and rough, twisted fence posts cut from rough, twisted cedar trees, then went even faster down between the hills, crossing low, flat bridges where rain filled gullies and ran over the highway. When they passed the Hill Top Bar-B-Q and the Pearl Beer sign with the moving waterfall, she dug in her purse for her compact that didn't snap shut good anymore and got powder all over everything in her purse. She made faces at herself in the small mirror which threw small dancing clouds on her hair and on the bus seat. She dusted powder across her nose, lipsticked each lip, smacked them together, bit both sides of a Kleenex, patted a corner of the Kleenex on her tongue and dabbed her eyebrows with it. Finally, she smiled different ways into the mirror, pinched each cheek several times, brushed powder off her front, and dropped the compact, lipstick, and tissue back into her purse.

The bus whooshed through a pool of water on the highway, passed the cemetery where Armon was buried and where Turk mowed the grass, then crossed the Blanco River. Rain dripped out of an old mesquite tree onto two wooden picnic tables near the river. The rock building on the right was the bowling alley and café, then came an empty building that used to be a hardware store. A black Chevy station wagon and a red pickup, parked diagonally in front of All-

Tex Feed. June had not been inside the feed store since Armon died, twenty years ago. Next door was the drugstore, Lee's, and on the corner, the bank. On around the small square were three filling stations, the post office, a Red & White grocery store, the Lone Star picture show, and a new washateria where Juno D. Speer & Co. used to be. Smack in the middle of the square was the empty old stone courthouse. For a while, after the county seat was moved to Johnson City, it had been used as a hospital, but now you had to go to San Antonio or Austin or Johnson City if you got sick. Momma had written June something about a man renting the courthouse from the county and turning it into a museum of the wild west.

At the corner by the bank, the bus turned, heading north, on to Johnson City. June could see the house farther down the highway, across from the lumberyard. Between her and the house was the green Sinclair sign. Turk might be there right now, filling someone's gas tank, wiping smeared bugs off someone's windshield. She saw Cage's new car, parked in Momma's yard. She pulled the cord and the bus slowed.

The house needed paint. It leaned forward, toward the highway. The big live oak in front, by the side a hackberry and a gum tree. In back, a lopsided shed where a fat wringer washer sat hugging itself, a fig tree that made June itch when she was younger, and the trash barrel where Momma burned garbage.

By the time June was off the bus Momma was on the porch to meet her. The oval glass in the door behind Momma framed her like an old photograph.

"Cage's in the kitchen with Turk. Robert Allen called and said they'd be by directly. Did you see ya'lls new car? He wouldn't let a soul ride in it till after you got here." Momma was rolling her eyeballs, raising her eyebrows, not waiting for replies. "And he's got a new suit on, and a *case* of whiskey in

61

the car." She stopped talking long enough to squeeze both June's cheeks and hug her. She was much shorter than June, and June could see her scalp, white beneath her gray hair. She smelled like she had always smelled, like her down comforter, like the inside of the cedar chest where June used to hide when she was little.

June walked slowly, nervous she realized. Inside, the house was dark and cool, the fan by Momma's bed turning back and forth, blowing the white curtains, blowing the white bedspread, blowing the pages of a magazine on the chair beside the bed where Momma kept a jar of Mentholatum and her flashlight.

"The house is nice and cool, Momma."

"Well, its been so hot. Then this rain. Now everthing's all sticky. I left the fan on while I was cooking, my old stove heats up the house something awful. But this is a good house for keeping cool Texas style." Texas style meant opening all the windows at night when it was cool and when the morning sun started getting hot, shutting the windows and pulling the shades to keep the cool inside. "You don't need fans at night," Momma said, "there's always good night breezes."

They stood in Momma's bedroom, the front room, while June looked around. Momma looked too, as if something might have changed since *she'd* been here last.

The same bed Momma and Daddy slept in night after night. When she was little she used to wake up and go get in bed with them. Momma and Daddy breathing together, on each side of her, steady rhythm of their breathing. She would be awake, her own quiet breath hidden beneath the soft down comforter. Sunk deep in the middle of the soft mattress, only her eyes outside the covers, she would peep out, looking for the streetlight in the narrow crack of window beneath the shade. In the winter sleet might be ticking against the window, wind rattling the house. In spring it would be crickets she heard. And, always, the big cattle trucks backfiring down the hill through town. Poptrucks, she called them.

From the kitchen June heard laughing and cooking going on. Cage was waiting for her. For a frightening second she was afraid she wouldn't recognize him. The radio was on in the dining room, Eddy Arnold was singing "Tennessee Stud," plates were clattering down onto the oilcloth-covered table, surrounded by five different straight-backed chairs and the big rocker that had started rocking by itself the morning Armon died.

Off the dining room was Turk's room, the sickroom, which had to be gone through to reach the bathroom. At night June could always hear Turk snoring and see the white dial of his alarm clock that ticked all the way to the kitchen. The bathroom door didn't close good, and Turk's room always smelled like Air Wick.

Cage waved to June from the kitchen doorway where he was talking to Turk. She winked at him to keep him from hurrying her, then heard herself saying, "Just a second, Cage." He smiled and kept talking to Turk. Turk looked at her but said nothing.

Turk's real name was Clinton, but Turk was a nickname stuck on him at school because someone said he was dumb as a turkey. So everybody said, turkeys would throw their heads back when it rained, to get a drink, and then forget to bring their heads back down, and would drown. Turk seemed to like the nickname better than Clinton, and most folks had forgotten he had another name.

There were two other rooms, both off the side of Momma's bedroom, the living room with its huge old sofa-bed that came the day Armon died, twenty years ago, and June's old bedroom, seldom used now.

"The very day," Momma always told folks, "Armon died, I got my new sofa bed. Ordered from San Antonio. They delivered it the very afternoon of the day he died. I wanted to take it back, we needed the money something terrible what with the funeral and Armon not believing in insurance, but he had signed for it and that was that. I've never been rich, I'll tell the world, not then nor now neither. You go right in my living room and sit down on that sofa, been twenty years of sitting on it. Why, there's hardly a coat of paint been put on this house since Armon passed."

It was true, things hadn't changed much. There was a television, some magazines Armon never heard of, new things in the newspapers, but the same newspapers, the *Austin American*, the *San Antonio Light*. Nothing Armon couldn't have got the hang of.

The shelf above the sideboard might not have been touched since he died: a ceramic pitcher he used to drink milk out of, a big white spool of thread, a box of Band-aids, an empty brown medicine bottle, a yellow tape measure, skeleton keys.

On the heavy old sideboard: the same mahogany silverware box, a cup towel, more spools of thread, old birthday cards, the wooden recipe box, the Emerson radio, place mats with scenes of Big Bend National Park, scissors, a tin can full of pencils, a wadded-up hairnet, a pincushion, a fingernail file, two clothespins, one ten-penny nail, a big glass ashtray, empty button cards, a jar of face cream, a tin of aspirin, rubber bands, adhesive tape, a worn family Bible with the first few pages of Genesis and the last few pages of Revelation gone.

The same gas heater beside the rocker, a box of Blue Diamond kitchen matches on top. Dust on the doilies on the chair arms.

June told Momma she wanted to look around a minute, told Cage she'd be in right away. Momma smiled her of-course-I-understand smile, the smile that said she knew June was nervous, wanted some time alone and that that was as it should be. Momma thought it was a school-girl nervousness about getting married, but it wasn't that, it was something else. June wasn't sure what it was, but it had more to do with being back here and remembering things so vividly than it did with getting married. Momma always told folks that June was a moody girl. Once you got known as a moody girl, June thought, you had a ready-made excuse for nearly anything. With Cage, June used that excuse or let him think she had strange female reasons. Sometimes she thought she might like to get pregnant just so she could let Cage worry about her and pamper her all the time. Like a lot of people, Cage believed the picture-show vision of women as illogical, exotic, indecipherable creatures who were to be humored more often than understood. Maybe, June thought, that was why some women had so many children, to have all those months of days when they could escape without being questioned. Pregnant, they were in control of all the invented mysteries of childbearing and motherhood. But even if she didn't get pregnant she knew Cage would always believe her female problems, like days she simply wasn't feeling quite right. It had been the same when she was younger, playing sick and staying home from school. Dot had told her that sometimes she wouldn't make love with Robert Allen for days, saying she was having a bad time with her period. Then, after he got real anxious, she would get him to promise he'd take Florene and Curtis somewhere without her, so she could rest. She had told June that if you used your head being married was a seller's market. June guessed Dot really did dread being with Robert Allen some days as much as June had dreaded going to school on exam days. So they both played hooky. June would not be like Dot. She was smarter, had more control over her life, more control than that. But she was glad Cage believed her so easily. And, she admitted, she liked figuring what he would enjoy believing. Everyone, it seemed, wanted to believe her, especially if she made sure she told them some things they wanted to hear. Cage was happy as long as it

65

looked like he was running the show. As long as it was that simple, June figured she knew how to get along just fine.

The front porch was damp, dark, and quiet looking. She slipped out, silently pulling the door closed behind her. The highway, empty and noiseless for a moment, was wider than it used to be, passed closer to the house. The live oak was bigger, the pecan gone. She sat on the dark wet roots of the oak tree that stuck up around its base. The roof of the house had been patched, but was still swaybacked, still tin, the color of the water in the tank out back before it dried up. Everything looked the same, yet looked different. She had been home to see Momma lots of times since she moved to San Antonio, but before, she never saw everything so clearly. Today she felt much older than she ever had before. And the town seemed to stand out, calling attention to itself, like a scene seen through a stereoscope.

There were more buildings, fewer people. Lee Davis who had run the soda fountain in his own drugstore for thrity-five years was dead now, a new prescription drug counter replacing the soda fountain. June guessed there was more call for medicine in Blanco these days than for chocolate malts. Everyone had gotten old and their kids had gotten out. The courthouse was empty but still standing. The bank had a new pink marble front, but probably hadn't changed inside, probably still had the same money in the vault as the last time June had come here. Maybe, she thought, maybe money, perhaps papers Armon had carried over from the feed store twenty years ago. Or was there some law that made them turn in old money for new every so often? She didn't know. Maybe they should make them change the people every now and then, too. Freshen up the town some.

Of course there were more cars and trucks and, naturally, more filling stations than when Armon was alive. Like the Sinclair where Turk sometimes pumped gas and changed tires. The widened highway to San Antonio was faster.

66

Times had changed and Blanco had changed too, but not much. Armon might not recognize the times, but he would know Blanco.

The brown, rugged hills the new highway passed through were still nearly impossible to farm, covered with Spanish oak, live oak, scrub cedar, mesquite, needle grass, mesquite grass, yucca, and prickly pear. Sheep and white-faced Herefords still roamed under the short, twisted trees. They had the new dam, but the river still ran dry nearly every summer.

When June finally took a deep breath and went into the kitchen, Cage stopped talking and hugged her, kissed her quickly on the neck. The moustache was what got June first every time. When he smiled it moved out wider, his small, even teeth showing, one gold tooth flashing when he talked. He had on the new suit pants, a long-sleeved yellow shirt. His new suit coat was folded neatly over the back of the kitchen rocker, which was now in the opening between the kitchen and dining room. His tie was clipped to his stomach with a silver swordfish. He leaned over when he talked, he was so big, eyes bulging, little red veins networking his nose, tiny balls of sweat in the thick black and gray moustache. He'd been telling Turk about the deal he'd made on the new car, watching June through doorways and windows, waiting for a chance to show her the new car. Now he wanted to take her for a spin. Turk took his coffee and went into the dining room, telling June, not Cage, telling her, "Listen, Sister, the highway is slick with rain."

She followed Cage to the side yard. The car was a Buick, dark green. The chrome shone, even on this rainy day, and beads of water formed on the waxy green finish, green as new money. They walked slowly around the car, their reflections changing with the lines of the car, vertical and willowy, horizontal and heavy. Cage lifted the hood like an artist un-

67

veiling his latest work, talked about horsepower and speed. June stared at the engine, dark, complicated. Cage walked around, opened the trunk, leaned over, reached in, and slapped the back of the rear seat to show June how much room there was for baggage. He had already carried their suitcases inside. His straw hat, stained purple beneath the band, sat on the spare tire like a crazy hubcap. Dark bottles of whiskey stuck up out of a cardboard honeycomb, a man in a black coat and a top hat, a yellow cane in his gloved hand on the label on the box. Cage put his big pink hand on June's stomach to move her back when he slammed the trunk shut.

Inside, the car was almost cold, smelled like new rubber, money. The engine started smoothly, the windshield wipers hummed, moved confidently back and forth like heartbeats.

They rode slowly around the square. June imagined them in a parade, some stately procession. She watched the long, green automobile in plate-glass windows where it swam like the fish clipped across Cage's tie. Cage turned on the head-lights and they gleamed like teeth in the store windows. He turned on the heater and a leaf crackled in the vent as the fan breathed in hot air.

Cage was talking happily, telling June about the deal he had made, what a good car a Buick was, how long it would last them, how quick it handled. She listened idly, feeling the soft seat under her thighs and watching a turkey buzzard gliding in smooth, easy circles above them.

They took Momma and Turk for a ride. The sky was gray and still, it was getting cooler, no car but theirs on the road. Only the sound of the windshield wipers squeaking against the almost dry windshield and Cage's keys hitting against his knee as he drove. Turk sat in back beside Momma, looking, somehow, cramped in the big, heavy car. Momma talked, said it was just rearing back to come a good storm. Said it felt like a blue norther fixing to blow in, she'd swear it was if it wasn't the middle of summer.

8

ALL AFTERNOON they stayed in the kitchen and dining room, eating and talking. Robert Allen, who usually managed to visit near suppertime, came by with Dot and their children, Florene and Curtis.

The house had always been full of visitors. Salesmen Armon would bring home from the store for supper, Momma's relatives, Turk's buddies. During the depression, people came and visited for weeks because Armon drew regular wages the whole bad time. Momma cooking all day long, feeding everyone. Robert Allen had come to live with them for a few years because his folks couldn't afford to keep him. So many people always made June feel alone. She never had to say anything, someone was always talking. Daddy worked at the store all day, Momma cooked and talked all day. People came and sat in the kitchen drinking coffee with Momma, talking.

It seemed she had spent her life listening to other people talk. Their stories were her stories, they made up her life for her. When she was alone or unhappy she would listen to the stories and imagine a different life. As she got older she made

69

up stories of her own and found out that her imagination could make her totally free. She could become anyone, do anything, be anywhere.

The stories hadn't even changed much from that old time to today. Hearing Robert Allen laugh about old Miz Turpin, so dumb she couldn't tell beans from buzzard tails, Momma raising an eyebrow asking Robert Allen just how smart *he* was, June could not be sure time had passed at all. The rooms and the sounds seemed the same now as then.

The depression, years ago, the house full of people, June playing on the kitchen floor with Momma's pots and pans, the heavy black skillets, the cast-iron meat grinder, the huge cream crock, the egg beater that cranked like the ice-cream freezer, putting small pans inside bigger ones, stacking forks on top of each other, covering pots with heavy lids, making it dark inside the pots. The soft black toes of women's shoes, the pointed toes of men's boots, the mud, the sheen of stockings, white shins between sock tops and pants cuffs. The smell of metal and dust and feet, a fine mist of steam, a stinging drop of grease, the yellow, white, yellow, white pattern of the linoleum.

You all'l have a field day after I'm dead. Momma said this every time she washed dishes and tried to find room in the crowded cabinets for all the mixed sets of plates and glasses and cups.

Eunice, you gonna outlive us all, working like you do. This might be anyone, old Miz Turpin, Mrs. Wagner, Naomi Phelps, Mr. Billy Berger, anyone sitting in the big rocker drinking coffee, talking.

Now you just promise me one thing, Momma would say, *you promise me you'll come over here and have coffee with Armon when he's home alone, keep him company after I'm passed on.* Then she'd laugh and pour another cup for anybody who might be sitting there listening.

Heard about Roe Blackwell, I guess? they'd say.

70

What'd Roe get into now? Momma would ask.

Well, they would begin, *you know he owes everybody in the country, but then who doesn't, these times are so bad.* Then would come the story about how they'd seen him with those three boys of his, fine looking boys, hard to see how they manage, pulling that wooden wagon Roe made, pulling it all about town, picking up scraps of wood, how someone saw them pull little ole pieces of roof tin out of the trash pile over to the blacksmith's, stacking everything on that wagon, that youngest boy up on top, keeping their load on. The Roe Blackwell story about how Roe and that young wife of his from Twin Sisters were digging a house out of the ground. Out beyond the cemetery. Digging with boards and pieces of tin, scraping way back into the hill, holding the walls back with those old boards he hauled on his wagon.

June had heard the Roe Blackwell stories again and again, but she never got tired of picturing his house in the ground. Roe Blackwell and those three fine boys and his young Twin Sisters wife, all deep in the side of the hill, way back inside the ground, nailing up old boards, old tin signs and roof patches, bracing the low ceiling with fence posts Roe worked loose late at night. June used to listen to the story and imagine living with Roe Blackwell and his three boys and young wife, deep in their cave, digging a new room whenever they wanted.

Got a new baby don't they? Momma might be sitting on the wooden stepladder by the stove, a little two-stepper she sat on, leaning over to peek in the oven, check on Armon's supper.

No more'n a week ago. Born right there in that hillside. And they would tell about Dr. Meyers riding out in the dust, parking his car right outside and delivering a baby in that dirt house. *Said Roe's wife asked how much she owed, Dr. told her five dollars, times so bad. Said she pulled a twenty out from her bed covers, asked for her change.*

71

I'll declare, Momma would say, shaking her head, pursing her lips, June never sure if this was approval or disapproval, but she loved the ritual of hearing the story, then watching for Momma's pursed lips. Momma's reaction became as much a part of hearing and imagining a story as that twenty Roe's wife pulled magically out of her sheets.

Now Roe Blackwell was dead and his Twin Sisters wife, no longer young, lived somewhere back east. June couldn't remember what had happened to his three fine boys. They had all left school to join the army as soon as the Second World War started and June had forgotten what they looked like. Probably like most of the boys she had gone to school with, poor boys with bowl-shaped heads, hair skinned close across the backs of their necks and above both ears, wide, open faces with noses that were always red, sunburned and peeling in summer, windblown and running in winter.

Kids who looked like Robert Allen and Dot's kids in striped tee shirts and cheap, off-brand blue jeans with double knees and bright orange stitching. June wondered who would remember just what Florene and Curtis looked like if they went away. Maybe that was why Dot kept a wall in her beauty shop full of school pictures of each of them, a picture for every year, the dates printed neatly across the bottom of every picture. June liked Florene and Curtis because they were both so easy to please. They liked everything, nothing seemed to bother them very much, nothing seemed to excite them very much. They were small replicas of Dot and Robert Allen, only a little clumsier than their parents. June had taken care of them once when Dot had been in the hospital in San Antonio. They weren't much trouble, except that they didn't know how to take care of themselves very well. June had to tie their shoes and button their buttons for them, even had to show Curtis how to flush the toilet in her apartment. June told Momma she figured they were just shy, staying with her, but Momma said they were just plain stupid.

72

Just like their daddy, Momma said. Momma always said Robert Allen wasn't in line when the Good Lord gave out brains, said he didn't have the brains God gave a brass monkey. June had taken them sightseeing, one day the Alamo, the next day the zoo. They had a picnic in Breckenridge Park and then went to the alligator house.

It was round, a circular bamboo railing overlooked a pit about six feet below, a thatched roof, cone-shaped like a straw hat June had seen in a movie about Chinese people, overhead. Standing down in the center of the damp concrete pit, a man cracked a whip over the heads of a dozen alligators lying in a ring around him, loud moving spokes, their tails to the man swinging the whip. The alligator man spoke into a microphone strung around his neck, invited anyone brave enough to come down and sit on the back of Old Joe, the oldest alligator in captivity.

Old Joe wasn't very pretty, June thought, wouldn't make a very nice handbag, but there was something appealing about him, a kind of wise look about his eyes, she decided. Florene wanted to go down the narrow concrete steps and have her photograph taken sitting on Old Joe's bumpy back. Curtis didn't much want to, but when June told Florene she'd go with her, Curtis had to give in. As they went down the steps the crowd clapped, and the alligator man said here was a gal brave as she was good looking and two mighty brave kiddos.

Old Joe lay still, half-shut eyes unblinking. Up close June decided that what she had thought looked wise was just a glazed, sleepy look. Smaller, greener alligators around Old Joe roared and rolled their heavy tails. The alligator man poked at them with a long pole, and they jerked away from Old Joe, short front legs rasping against the concrete. June stepped between Old Joe and one of the smaller alligators, put her hand out on Old Joe's back and easily sat, smiling up at the crowd. Florene and Curtis quickly straddled Old Joe, sitting in front of June. Old Joe's back swelled slowly and

73

sank as he breathed. His feet, dark, webbed, gray-brown. Around them the other alligators squirmed and roared, the whip popping behind them. Next to them, a long, blunt-ended jaw opened, thick yellow teeth stuck out of gray gums, a heavy yellow tongue rolled eaily, like a swell in a lake. Above them a woman leaned over the railing and flashed her camera at them twice. Old Joe's tail twitched a little, that was all, and June, Florene, and Curtis went around the cat-walk, back up the narrow steps, and headed to the snake house.

Today, Florene was quiet, sleepy. Curtis, in the big rocker, rocked fiercely, hold a Dr Pepper tight against his lips, sloshing Dr Pepper into his mouth when he rocked back, then into the bottom of the bottle when he rocked forward.

June sat in the dining room talking with Dot and Momma, mostly listening to Momma talk. Cage was in the kitchen with Robert Allen talking cars and weather. Turk had run over to the Sinclair so Jordan West could have supper at home. June guessed Turk was glad for an excuse to get out of the house. She would be glad to be gone, too.

From where she sat she could see Cage leaning against the counter by the kitchen sink, his elbow resting against his waist, a drink in his hand. Every few minutes his arm hinged at the elbow mechanically raising the drink to his mouth. The motion caught the gray light of the kitchen window in the weak yellow whiskey.

Cage seemed to be listening more than talking, too. June let her eyes go out of focus, saw two outlines of Cage's profile, as if Cage were stepping out of himself. There was something wise looking about Cage's eyes too, something that seemed sure and confident and June liked that about him as much as anything. He was always excited to see her. Older than she was, he always acted younger. Maybe, she thought, the thing she liked most about him, maybe even the reason she wanted to marry him, was his apparently endless energy. He was always planning something, scheming and dreaming, telling June about the future. It made some people nervous to be around him, but June liked it. It was like hearing stories in the kitchen when she was little, only most of Cage's stories hadn't happened yet and she was in most of Cage's stories.

Momma was talking about the wedding, Robert Allen was talking about something—cars, still? Something else? June wondered how long she had been sitting, daydreaming, drifting above the room almost asleep. She heard her own voice, then she was up, walking to the bathroom. She had said something to Momma and Dot about brushing her teeth, freshening up. She felt almost drunk, out of control of her body. Was she staggering? No one acted surprised. She must be doing okay, looking all right.

Cold water on her face felt good, but as soon as she stood up from the faucet she lost the effect and was drowsy again. She pressed on her eyeballs, made red spots in the medicine cabinet mirror. She wanted to lie down in the bathtub and go to sleep. She ran a comb through her hair, letting the teeth of the comb scrape against her scalp, and when her hair caught she pulled it hard, making it hurt. She could hear Momma moving about in the dining room and heard food being set out. Turk must be back, she thought, and as she went back to the dining room he passed her, nodded, going straight to the bathroom where June heard him running water and pictured his hands in the lavatory, covered with a mixture of grease and soap suds.

Supper was slow. Turk, face shining, hair wet in dark points around his face, sat at the end of the table tearing slices of soft white bread into chunks and pouring the thick milk gravy over them.

Just as Turk was forking a big slice of roast beef onto his plate, Cage started stirring sugar furiously into his iced tea, and, suddenly, tea and ice cubes poured from the big glass with the colored stripes, all over the table.

75

"Damned if he hadn't stirred the bottom out of his glass, damned if he hadn't," Turk said. "First time I've ever seen that, first time anywhere."

Cage tried to stop the flow with his napkin. Momma kept saying it didn't matter, the glass was a jam glass. June got up and ran into the kitchen for a dishrag, soaked up the tea, picked the glass and ice off the table, and brought Cage back a fresh glassful.

Cage talked a lot during the rest of the meal, telling everyone about a new piece of property he was going to develop soon. June listened—he had told her all about the new development—and liked hearing again his description of the property, the houses that would be built. June saw Turk watching Cage, listening quietly. As he talked, Cage held his iced tea, clinking the ice in his new glass.

When everyone had eaten, Momma brought in a steaming pot of strong coffee and a pecan pie she had made especially for Cage. Cage offered Turk and Robert Allen cigars, Turk shook his head and took a big slice of pie, Robert Allen said he didn't mind if he did, though he hardly ever had him a stogie. Cage pulled a small silver pocketknife out and made a cut in the end of his cigar before lighting up.

Outside the sun was coming through a temporary crack in the dark clouds. It was deep orange against the gray-green sky and threw a bright orange slice of light through the gauzy white dining room curtains onto the cluttered table and the arms and faces of the people sitting around the table. June watched the smoke from the cigars and the steam off the hot cups of coffee rise into the momentary orange glow and felt good. For a moment, hearing familiar voices around her in this familiar room, she felt like she belonged to this family. Even Turk seemed seemed friendlier this afternoon. Thirteen when she was born, Turk had always been a stranger to her. He had joined the army when she was just nine, came home seven years later, after Armon died, nearly deaf from working on airplane engines. He had always seemed like a stranger, a roomer, a silent man who slept by the bathroom. Sometimes she wondered why he stayed in Blanco, how he could stand to live with Momma, listen to her talk all the time. She wondered if he ever thought about doing something with his life, wondered if he ever made plans for the future the way Cage was always doing. Maybe, she guessed, he didn't ever think about himself. Maybe he didn't realize what a failure he was, how wasted his life was. And, she thought, maybe he liked his life. She knew he had Sally to go see from time to time, probably had other girls too. Could be he had girls all over Austin and San Antonio and did outrageous, crazy, fun things no one ever knew about. June pictured the headlines, I LED TWO DIFFERENT LIVES, a bad newspaper photo of Turk and Momma on the front porch, the old house sagging behind them, another photo of Turk in a flashy suit at a cozy table in a high-class nightclub, his arm around a beautiful young girl in a sequined dress. Watching him drink his coffee, his eyes deepset and almost black, June could imagine him, in a different setting, being liked by a woman, could imagine him doing almost anything. He set down his empty cup and tilted his chair back with his legs, opened his mouth wide to yawn, threw back his shoulders, moved his arms up and back stretching. He had to go back to the station for a little while, to be there to close up at dark so he'd have the money out of the till for change the next morning to open up with. Cage offered to drive him, said he needed to gas up the Buick. June smiled at Cage, trying to be polite, trying to get along with her family, and she realized she had lost the feeling of closeness and again felt as uncomfortable with these people as Cage must. He came around the table and leaned down and kissed her before they left, and for a moment she thought she would call out to him, tell him to get their bags and take her somewhere far away, right now. Then he and Turk disappeared through the side door and then she heard the Buick backing out of the yard and then she was alone at the table. Dot and Momma were already in the kitchen fixing to go to work on the dishes. Robert Allen had gone into the living room to take a nap.

Well, she thought, just one more night. After tonight she would never have to sleep alone again. After tonight Cage would take her away and buy her a house and her own car, and he would always make plans for the future and tell her about them and everything would be better and she would be happy.

June offered to help Momma and Dot with the dishes, but Dot told her to enjoy her last night of freedom, cause she'd have plenty of dishes of her own to wash from now on. June said she'd just have to make sure Cage got her a dishwasher. She left Dot shaking scraps off plates into the garbage can and went outside for a walk while there was still a little light. As she closed the door behind her, she heard Momma yell, *Aren't you afraid you're gonna get rained on?* and she walked a little faster to get out of earshot.

78

9 "RUN'ER UP here just a mite. More—hup, good." Turk was walking backward into the garage bay nearest the office, leaning over, taking quick looks under Cage's new Buick. There wasn't much business, and Turk had suggested they put the new car up on the rack and check her out. "Okay, come ahead," he stretched his leg out, kicked the metal runner into place, "that's got it."

Cage's neck was twisted back over his shoulder, his knuckles white, hands squeezing the steering wheel, straining to see if he had the rear wheel on the narrow metal runner. He sat a moment before opening the door, breathing deeply, and when he did start to slide out he hit the horn with his stomach. It made two quick notes, a puppy's bark that echoed in the hollow service station.

Turk chuckled at the horn, stood staring at Cage through the tinted windshield, enjoying the damp air, his sweaty shirt sticking to his back. Cage's new shoes snapped loudly against the concrete floor as he walked around the big automobile to the passenger side where Turk was waiting to run the grease rack up. Cage seemed out of place in the garage,

79

his expensive suit was stiff, made him walk awkwardly up-right and slow, careful not to rub against a dirty wall or brush against the tires stacked on the floor. Cage, larger and heavier than Turk, seemed dwarfed by the high walls and the rack of huge wrenches and the gleaming row of silver sockets, so many different tools suggesting secrets, mysteries Cage could not unravel. On the other hand, Turk, in his wrinkled work clothes and two-day beard looked confident and right at home among the strong smells of rubber, gasoline, rust.

On the highway a couple of streetlights had come on, though there was still enough dull light through the clouds to see fairly well. The station was bright with harsh lights that reflected in the wet glass office walls where the rain had blown earlier, and each big rectangular pane of glass in the garage doors bounced light back inside. Turk and Cage were alone except for Jordan West's son in the office, tilted back in a metal chair behind the cash register listening to nasal singing from a transistor radio tied with a long cord to an overhead fluorescent light. The radio was slowly turning, moving gently back and forth like a lure on a line, the song slowly pulsing, loud then low, loud then low. Golden Coun-try Hits. Through the green glass of the Sinclair station the occasional drizzle seemed to keep tune to the sad songs. Cage could see yellow squares of light down at Eunice's and he wondered what June was doing right now. Seeing the little house lit up down the darkening highway and picturing June and Eunice and Dot and Robert Allen and the two kids in-side, talking, moving about, made him feel more isolated in here, with Turk, in the station garage.

Turk threw a switch and the Buick shuddered, began to rise. A tire tool clanged against the concrete, knocked off the end of the right runner. Turk ran the car up near the ceiling, watching the cylinder, streaked with grease, slowly rise out of the floor like the black pellets he lit when he was a kid, snakes they called them, small black cylinders he

80

touched a match to and watched rise and grow into long black tubes of ash, coils of black, before a breeze blew them away down the highway.

Turk watched Cage who was beneath the car, looking up, touching, jiggling, tapping rods and pipes and joints. "Like a woman, huh Cage," he said, just to see if he could get Cage's goat, "you like to look up under their skirts to see if they're any good." Cage seemed not to have heard. Turk couldn't figure him, didn't know his ways. For that matter, he didn't even know June, his own sister, any better. But she was his sister. She didn't talk funny like Cage, and she knew how to hold her fork and, unlike Cage who had asked Turk if that was a possum dead on the highway, she knew an armadillo when she saw one.

Turk stepped beneath the car, carrying a light on a long cord, the bulb in a wire cage like a catcher's mask, a wire hook on one end which he hung over a muffler bracket. He walked slowly under the length of the car, looking up, his eyes shifting easily from bolt to bolt. In a garage, Turk was almost graceful. In the office his fingers got stuck between the keys on the cash register and when he wrote out a credit card sale his writing looked wiggly and cramped like a grade school kid's. But down under an engine he was in his element, things made sense. He didn't know why, he never studied it, but he was at home with machines. At a rear wheel he stopped, spun the tire, listened. Like a safecracker, his skill came naturally and he played it by ear. Cage reached up to wiggle the tail pipe, white hot at the end, jerked his hand back and scraped it against the bottom of the car.

"Watch out, you'll burn yourself, Cage."

Cage's eyes narrowed, but he smiled wide and nodded, stepping out from under the car.

Turk took the trouble light off the muffler, there were cut marks where he had dug his nails into the rubber handle. Cage stepped out of his line of vision and he imagined Cage

81

throwing the switch on the lift, dropping the car silently on top of him.

But Cage was only moving to look out front where an old black station wagon was pulling up. The boy in the office tilted down and eased outside, moving with the rhythm of Hank Williams, "Move it on Over," moving with the rhythm of the Juicy Fruit moving in his jaw. Two men in levis and muddy boots came over and looked up under Cage's Buick. One of the men, the older of the two, maybe the father of the other man, leaned over, supporting himself with a hand on the rear of the car, and slapped the right rear tire several times. Turk knew there would be a hand print left on the new finish where the man leaned.

"Buick, huh?" the old man said.

"Cost plenty money," the younger man said. "Didn't she cost you some money?" he said to Cage.

"Well, I got a very good trade-in," Cage began.

"I wouldn't have no Buick," the old man said to the younger man, interrupting Cage.

They both looked at Cage, stared him right in the eyes, and he smiled that wide smile of his and shrugged.

Turk stepped out from under the car, put the light on a cluttered shelf across the back wall. Jordan's boy had finished gassing the old station wagon and was back in his chair, tilted again against the shelves stacked with dust-covered boxes of air filters.

The two men didn't seem in any hurry to leave. They asked Turk about the engine.

"A six cylinder," the younger man said, "is smartest."

"V-8s just swilll gas," the older man said.

"Guzzlers," said the younger man.

The older man nodded seriously, "Cost like hell to repair, and break down all the time."

"I like a good road car," Cage said. "You can't beat a Buick for a good, smooth road car."

Turk flipped the switch to lower the Buick, pushed against the side to straighten the car so it would settle down evenly on all four corners. He caught Cage looking at the grease prints he left, smiled, pulled the red rag from his hip pocket, and wiped the side of the car, leaving a shiny halo that distorted his reflection in the dark green metal.

"You take that Ford we got," the old man leaned against Cage's car, rested his wrinkled hand on Cage's shoulder, "that there car is made for speed. She's light and she's fast and she just keeps going and going." He stared at Cage for a minute, no one spoke, then he laughed. He laughed and laughed, giving Cage a good push, let his hand slide off Cage's shoulder. Still laughing, he put his arm around the younger man's shoulder, and they led Turk out to their old station wagon where they pulled a mud-caked spare out of the back and showed Turk a nail in the nearly bald tread.

Turk said he figured he could make it right, and he started rolling the tire across the wet pavement, watching it get darker as it picked up rainwater off the pavement. Smiling, he rolled the tire into the garage where Cage was still with his car, wiping at the smear Turk had left on the side, spreading it bigger.

Turk hefted the tire up onto the red iron pedestal by the Coke machine, dropped the rim over an iron rod, and spun a big wing nut down to hold the tire in place. He worked the rubber off the rim with a tire tool, pulling down and slowly swinging around the tire, walking a short circle, doing a slow dance around the tire changer, working his arms up and down like he was pumping a handcar down a railroad track or pumping water from a well, like an Indian dancer he had seen once at the Gillespie County Rodeo moving his arms before him. The veins in Turk's arms stood out, sweat reflecting light, and he knew Cage was staring at his muscles.

He thought about Cage making love to June, pictured Cage, big, white, moving up and down on June. His sister,

83

but mainly because people told him she was. He wondered about her just as he wondered about any other woman. He could understand Cage going for her, she was not bad looking, still pretty young, several years younger than Cage. But what did she see in Cage? His new suits, the new Buick, all those houses he was going to build? Maybe June had never had anyone else ask her to marry him. She was strange, he couldn't remember her ever having any real boyfriends when she lived in Blanco. Of course he had been away in the army, she had left as soon as she got through school. He didn't know what she'd done down in San Antonio. He hadn't even ever seen where she lived in San Antonio. About all he could say for sure was that she was pretty quiet and not bad to look at. She'd always made good grades in school and spent lots of time in her room reading mushy magazines. Somehow, now that she was getting married, he was more curious about her. Seeing Cage made him want to get to know her, at least try to figure her a little better.

Finally the two men in the station wagon paid Turk for fixing the flat and left, driving off in a cloud of blue smoke. Turk got a Dr Pepper, slamming the lever of the Coke machine down hard, popped the top off with a loud twist of the bottle in the opener. Cage watched from the doorway between the office and the garage, his arms hanging at his side, his hands feeling large, weightless, as if they might float up, lifting his arms toward the ceiling. He pushed them both deep into his pants pockets, they jumped around inside the slick lining, jingling keys on one side, change on the other. Turk got a bag of peanuts from the big glass fishbowl jar with the red wooden lid, carefully putting a nickel on the ledge at the base of the cash register, and shook the peanuts down into his Dr Pepper.

Jordan West's son, who had not said a word to Cage since they arrived at the station, told Turk he was tired of waiting for his daddy to come get him and would walk home.

84

"We'll give you a lift if you want," Cage offered.

"We'll give you a lift if you want," Cage offered.
word to Cage since they arrived at the station, told Turk he was tired of waiting for his daddy to come get him and would walk home.

"We'll give you a lift if you want," Cage offered.

The boy looked at Cage, at the shiny Buick in the garage, then said to Turk, "Thanks just the same, I'll just head on home. Do me good to hoof it, gotta start getting in shape for football."

The boy left and Cage got himself a Coke and a Hershey Bar. Putting his nickel next to Turk's he said surely Turk's boss wouldn't charge him for a nickel bag of peanuts?

Turk had never thought of Jordan West as his boss, but all he said to Cage was that he was used to paying his own way.

Drinking the Dr Pepper, Turk relaxed. He watched the funny way Cage put his Coke bottle all the way into his mouth, his lips wrapped around the middle of the bottle neck, and he was tempted to poke Cage in the belly just to watch him spew Coke down his fancy shirt. The candy bar was soft and left chocolate on the tips of Cage's fingers. When he finished eating the candy he put each finger in his mouth and sucked the chocolate off, making a loud smacking sound with each finger, like ten kisses.

Riding back to Momma's, Turk didn't talk. He watched the hood of the Buick, deep green under the cloudy, evening sky, and he was glad the wedding would be over by this time tomorrow. Cage was thinking of tomorrow evening too, thinking of June beside him, the two of them close together, locked inside the dark, quiet car, going somewhere else, going sixty miles an hour.

85

10

ARMON'S name, her name, MARRS, carved in simple block letters. It was a new discovery every time she came to the cemetery, as if she was never really aware of her name except standing here at this grave, smelling the auction pens at the packinghouse across the highway, listening to the twisted little live oaks tremble in the wind that seemed to be always blowing out here on this hill. Her lips moved, MARRS, repeating the word silently. Tomorrow she would get rid of that name and go away with Cage. She would become someone else, someone new. She knelt, wet grass prickling her knees through her stockings, one shoe sinking in the mud, the stone wet. Her eyes closed, she felt the letters, braille-learning. Around her the trees dripped, rainwater slipping down through leaves and dark branches to fall onto tombstones with soft slapping sounds.

June's hands were pale, almost blue, her veins close to the surface. One small hand held the other. Poor body, she thought, dying so fast. Veins that would eventually turn a rusty purple and push darkly through her skin, skin that would spot, become loose and wrinkled, gray, dry. She held her hands against her sides, up under her armpits, covered them with her arms. She lay back on Armon's wet grave, feeling the cool wetness slowly seeping through her clothes into her body. Above her she saw the metallic glint of an airplane reflecting, for a second, the light of the sun which had already gone down, and a cloud, gray fetus, floating, cut from a larger cloud by the slice of the airplane, jet trail umbilical cord.

June had been born a month too soon, a hard birth. Momma had been swimming in the river the first day in June. The sac June was in burst, and the fluid around her ran into the muddy Blanco River. Born dry for a Texas climate.

In a box, in the ground beneath her, were the bones of her daddy. In town, in the bed where her daddy had slept every night for over thirty years, her momma's bones lay. No one lived in her momma's body now, not even her momma's young self. Just an old case, the beat up crate the goods had been delivered in. Momma, poor Momma, who always talked, always seemed busy. A woman who lived alone with a roomer who was once inside her own body. An old woman whose bones lay inside her loose skin, sleeping alone every night with a flashlight beside her bed. She had once gone swimming in the river, had nursed June with firm full breasts that now were dry gourds that hung to her stomach. Her hair was old and thin as the grass on Armon's grave, her dark eyes had grown pale. Her toenails, hard and yellow now, still grew.

June shook her hands until they felt tight and young again. Her body was still nice. It was a certain number of years old. It would be a day older when she and Cage got married. She would not feel any older inside her body. Maybe, even now, Momma felt young inside her old body. But one day June would not be able to shake the veins in her hands down under tight young skin like shaking down the red line in a thermometer. One day she would be trapped inside a used-up

87

body, but she would feel the same as she felt now. She was more than her body. Her skin shrunken into itself, she would slip out someday, air from a shriveling balloon, her body would collapse like a tent on its poles, but she would be gone, up through the trees like smoke leaving a burned-up log.

She would not ever sleep alone again.

Walking back to Momma's, she passed the school. It had been painted bright yellow last year, but it was the same building. Rain ran off the red tile roof, made it look like it was shivering.

June had few memories of her childhood. The school did not seem familiar. Even Blanco, where she had lived so many years, seemed strange. She was more at home in San Antonio in her small apartment, sitting in a dark theater with Cage, answering the phone at work or writing out orders on thick pads of yellow and pink sheets with a carbon that left her fingers blue. What was she doing back in this town, this strange place?

She would walk on back to Momma's and wait for Cage and Turk to get back. They would all drink another cup of coffee and then go to bed, June and Cage sleeping in different beds at Momma's, sleeping in different rooms for the last time. Tomorrow they would go to the Baptist church and get married. Then they could sleep in the same bed even at Momma's. Cage and June, June and Cage, getting married in the Blanco Baptist church, Cage and June who had never been in a church together. The Baptist church June had not been in since she moved from Blanco.

The same old stone church building. Across the road from the school. June had sat in her school desk and stared at that same church, sometimes daydreaming her wedding. The same sad square of lawn in front of the church, the patch where the grass had never grown well and where every Sunday following a rain June would get mud on her Sunday shoes.

Sunday mornings, years ago. Saving seats for girlfriends, feeling Momma's eyes on the back of her neck. Waiting then for girls she no longer knew, girls whose names and faces she had forgotten, Mollys and Linda Lees and Sue Ellens and Carolyns. Putting her Bible in one seat, the Sunday School lesson book in one, a hymn book and a pair of gloves in two more. Tearing strips off the pink mimeographed program, marking pages in the dark green hymn book. First song, "Holy Holy Holy."

Brother Spurgin in the same black suit and blue tie he wore every Sunday, coming in from the side door like a groom waiting for his bride to come down the aisle. The choir filing up into the choir loft, singing as they marched, open hymn books held out, mouths frozen in wide O's, two fans mounted high on the wall aimed down at them, flipping pages, rippling robes. The Christian flag, white with a red cross on a blue square on Brother Spurgin's right, by the piano which no one played. On his left the American flag, a gold eagle on the staff. Mrs. Tatum pumped the organ steadily with thick, white legs, smiling up at Brother Spurgin.

The other girls, coming in late, taking the seats June had saved, whispering while Brother Spurgin gave the opening prayer, standing, heads bowed, sneaking glances all around them. Singing with the standing congregation, "Power in the Blood." Be seated, please, for the scripture reading. Coloring in the steeple and windows printed on the front of the pink program, passing the ball point back and forth, notes about a girl who was not there. A special number by the choir, "Oh for a Thousand Tongues to Sing," followed by the love offering, men passing shining plates, plates moving down the rows like plates around the Sunday dinner table. Money passing from hand to hand like change moving across the bleachers to the vendor at a ball game. Sneezing laughter and giggles into their soft white gloves stuffed like gags against their mouths, faint red lips left softly tattooed on the palms of the gloves. *Guess who's with Fred Hinkley in back of Fred's Dad's Dodge, parked right out back.* Brother Spurgin moving, head lowered, to the pulpit. That was something, to spend Sunday morning with Fred Hinkley in the back of Mr. Hinkley's Dodge.

Sunday afternoons were slow and still. Heavy roast dinners, Sunday-dressed visitors, women talking quietly, washing dishes, sitting in the hot kitchen, men in the dining room talking, smoking, listening to the baseball game on the Emerson, children asleep in rows on the double beds, on pallets on the floor if it was too hot or there were too many for the three beds. June always felt like she had to whisper on Sunday afternoons.

Sunday nights, crickets loud during prayers. Dead stained glass, dark purple bruises. No sunlight slanting through the red robes and yellow crooks of shepherds in the windows. In strange, religious-looking letters, on the yellow scroll across the green hill where June's favorite shepherd stood: In loving Memory of Brother Marvin J. Tatum. The shepherd had heavy red lips that always smiled down at June.

Sunday nights fewer people came, they didn't dress up as much, men in shirt sleeves, women without hats, everyone looked bare. The auditorium felt empty. The high ceiling echoed footsteps on the tile floor, scattered coughs, wooden seats folding down.

June listened for echoes. She was in a great cave. She was deep in some beautiful seashell, surrounded by the sound of ocean, some giant holding her, holding the church building up to a giant ear, listening to June's breathing, giant fingers curling around the steeple, covering the windows, blacking out the colors of the stained glass. Deep in the giant's fist when the sermon ended.

Dearly Beloved, let us pray.

The giant's voice shaking the floor beneath her, tilting the church in the giant hand, shaking the building, trying to shake June out of this strange building, out the little hole of the front doors.

The invitation hymn, "Jesus is Calling." June feeling sorry for Brother Spurgin that no one was going down the aisle. *Why should you lin-ger and heed not His mer-cies?* Brother Spurgin's arms opened, moving slowly with the music like wings. *Mer-cies for you and for me.* Whispering with her friends, telling them they should rededicate their lives. No one had gone down the aisle. Brother Spurgin's arms slowly folded as he prayed. *Only one more stanza.* The choir humming softly as he spoke. *If no one comes we will close the invitation. But if just one comes we will add another stanza until no one comes.* He smiled, looking right at June, saying, *The Holy Spirit is right here inside this church with us this evening, won't you let him work his will with you tonight, won't you let Jesus come into your heart? All it takes is one step, just one step into that aisle and He'll go with you all the way. Come along, now, as we sing just one more stanza.* His arms went slowly up, outstretched. *Come on, now, do it for Jesus' sake.* June wanted to see Brother Spurgin move those arms up and down and slowly fly up through the ceiling. Everyone softly singing, *See on the port-als he's wait-ing and watch-ing.* June told them they could all go together, she'd go with them, down the aisle to put their arms around Brother Spurgin. Brother Spurgin calling loudly over the singing, *Don't wait until it's too late, He's here waiting to take you now.* June thought of the giant. *Watch-ing for you and for me.* They all promised one another. One after the other they slipped into the aisle and moved toward the front. Brother Spurgin walked up to meet them, his arms coming down to envelop each one of them. But June was still at her seat, holding the back of the pew in front of her, her feet looking very far below her, her knuckles pink.

91

She knew they'd be mad at her for not keeping her promise, but they couldn't be too mad right after rededicating their lives to be good Christians. Watching Brother Spurgin beam out at the congregation as he led them in the closing stanza, June no longer felt guilty. Maybe, she thought, the Holy Spirit didn't mind a little help in moving people. Brother Spurgin said the names of her girlfriends outloud in his closing prayer, and when June went down with the rest of the congregation to get in line to give each girl her love and support, the shepherd was smiling down at her, like always.

June and Cage in that same church to get married. Brother Spurgin had died, years ago, not long after Armon. Most of June's childhood friends had moved away as soon as they were old enough. The church had a new air-conditioning system and a new preacher named Bailey. June had never met Brother Bailey who was out of town tonight, preaching a revival over at Comfort, but who had assured Momma he would be back in plenty of time for June's wedding.

Walking back to Momma's she came up to the house from the back, coming down the side street in the dark. A blue-white sheet of light flapped across the sky outlining a dark row of thunderclouds rolling in from the north and lighting up Momma's side yard long enough for June to see the new Buick parked there and know that Cage and Turk had beat her back.

92

11

AS THE screened door clapped shut behind June, thunder rolled over the house, and the rain started again, hard, steady. June closed the wooden door and the sound of the rain was muffled. The kitchen was deserted, dishes stacked in the drainer, rows of glasses and coffee cups upside down on a cup towel spread out on the counter. The door to Momma's room was closed. June eased the door open and in the dark room could barely see Momma's shape on the bed, asleep already.

All the lights were on in the living room, it looked barer than usual. Squares of light fell through the panes of the double french doors into the dining room where Cage lowered the newspaper he was reading and gave her a big smile. Dot was working the crossword puzzle in last Sunday's paper, Florene asleep in her lap, and Curtis was still in the big rocker. He was intently watching Turk and Robert Allen who sat facing each other across the table, playing a hand of double solitaire.

"Where have you been so long, honey?" Cage folded up the newspaper.

93

"Oh, I just took a little walk."

In the silence after she spoke, June could hear only the snap of a card Turk put on the table and the heavy, slow creak of the house itself as she went and sat by Cage. It too seemed to have grown old and tired. The foundation had settled unevenly, and the floors in the different rooms slanted slightly in different directions. Like these old floors, her memories seemed askew. Vague somehow, incomplete. She couldn't account for more than snatches of her life. She could remember that night in church, could see Brother Spurgin standing with his arms raised as clearly as she saw Turk right now, sitting under the light hunched over the cards on the bright table top, could remember the hymns they sang better than anything she had read in the paper in the last week, could picture the stained-glass shepherd's face but couldn't recall the faces of the girls she had persuaded to walk the aisle. If that was what getting old was like, getting things mixed up, setting some memories in focus while you lost others entirely, then maybe the reason Momma talked so much, said the same things over and over, was just that she was trying to hang on to her memories. Trying to memorize her life, talking about things so much because it was her way of trying not to lose so much. Then what about Turk, he hardly ever talked. Was it, as he said, because he had lived with Momma so long, never able to get a word in edgewise, and had gotten out of practice? Or was he, like June, silently imagining the life he had lived? For as long as she could remember it had been more fun—sitting on the kitchen floor with Momma's pots and pans listening to stories about Roe Blackwell and his dark house dug into the hill, pretending the black roasting pot was Roe Blackwell's deep room, putting the pot over her head to breathe the cool, dark air deep in the earth—to make up a life than to stay strictly in the life she was living. She had sat in school and looked out at the church and been married again and again, always to a vague,

94

faceless figure from far away who was rich and, somehow, magical. Tomorrow she would go to that church and get married one more time, to a man who still seemed vague, a man whose face she was always surprised by, remembering usually only an abstract detail, the gold tooth shiny and wet, the moustache like a comic-book caterpillar stretched across his lip. He was from far away, and he did anything she asked him to. He told her stories about the places he had been and the places he would take her, and she knew he was magical for her. She remembered dances, sometime, while she was in high school, once or twice while she was in San Antonio, feeling the music in the floor, every time she dipped, stepped down, feeling it come up through the bottoms of her feet, the smell of sizing in her date's new shirt, sweat slowly turning cool as it slid from their tightly held palms down the underside of her forearm. There was always the motion and sounds of his legs moving into the width of fabric her dress spread between her legs, her legs naked and slender beneath layers of dress and lining and slip, his legs tight at the thigh as he leaned into her, a vibration of music and muscle and material that was like leaves and tree limbs shaking together, like teeth chattering inside loose lips, like the multiple outlines of a blurred picture. All that, and a song remembered, someone with a teardrop voice, she couldn't remember the year, a few years back, someone singing to her, her alone, telling her, *Love blooms at night, in daylight it dies,* telling her, *Don't let the stars get in your eyes.* The tiny lights in the ceiling, dimmed for the dance, dropping shadows and spots of light on their shoulders as they moved in swaying circles on the slick floor, the swirling shadows of twisted strands of crepe paper hung like colored clouds above them, *So keep your heart for me, for someday I'll return, And you know you're the only one I'll ever love.* And always the voice was the man without a face, the man who had stood on the steps of the old stone church in her imagination and waited for her to grow

95

up, *Too many miles, Too many days, Too many nights to be alone.* When Cage came along older, sure of himself, stories to tell and plans to share, it was as if she had simply been waiting for him to come back. Now, the house strangely quiet, she wondered why she hadn't asked Cage to take her away somewhere to get married. When Momma was hurrying about, talking, calling June by her name, June believed in her, believed she was her Momma. Now, with Momma asleep and out of sight, it was as if she didn't exist. His elbows on the table, arms up, hands hanging loose off his wrists, Turk looked old and frail. He was rough, wrinkled, weather-beaten, but almost timid looking. June wondered if he pretended he was younger, smarter, stronger, wondered what he dreamed when he lay in that iron bed night after night, the same bed he had slept in all his life. Like all her memories Momma and Turk seemed a part of her life only some of the time. She guessed the reason she had come back here to get married was so she could meet Cage in the stone church she had been in so many times before in her imagination. She had left Blanco for good as soon as she was old enough to make believe, rode away on magic carpets the same way Armon had become a practical joker and laughed his way out of town. That was how he got his freedom. She thought freedom explained a lot of things, Armon's tricks, Momma's talking so much she didn't have time to think, her own daydreams, and, maybe, Turk's secret imaginings. Of course, now she had Cage, and he would take her away tomorrow.

The radio June had turned off for supper came on again, playing loud German polka music, "The Beer Barrel Polka," and she looked up from the Buick Owner's Manual she had been looking through with Cage. Robert Allen was up, waking Florene, getting Dot and Curtis moving, ready to go home. June heard Curtis pumping the broken sewing machine, its squeal coming through the loud polka. Turk stood in the doorway between the dining room and living room, his head back, mouth open wide, arms out and back, stretching, yawning, the light from the living room bright behind his head turning him into a dark shape, the light seeming to come from out of his body, outlining him brightly like a dark cloud and making him look suspended in air.

Cage went to bathe and get ready for bed, Turk left with Dot and Robert Allen saying he'd run down to the Bowling Alley and see what he could get into before they closed.

Alone in the house except for Momma sleeping and the sound of Cage in the bathroom, she thought about how it would be once she and Cage were married, nights like this in her own house, the lapping sounds of water and soap while he bathed. She got a stack of old magazines from beneath the sewing machine, carried them into the living room where Cage's bed was ready to be made, Momma's sheets and quilts stacked on the sofa.

She lay on her stomach on the waxy smelling floor, turning pages slowly. She came to photographs of wild African antelope and spread the magazine flat, watching an animal in flight. Stretched out over a blur of dark grass, his tail up, his eyes shining, he stretched from one page, leaping across the fold, to the opposite page. The article was about the diminishing amount of wilderness for the antelopes and how poorly they had adapted to captivity. She stared at the animal caught by the camera in flight. In his skin she could see creases, hair, pores. Beneath the photograph she read: *Hartebeest, wild, fierce-looking, but timid beast, rarely defends himself, even when cornered.* The Hartebeest's muscles ran like thick cord over his thighs and back, his horns curved out, then back, dark pennants in the wind. Fine dark hair showed between his back legs, like pubic hair, black, barely showing, damp looking, like the thin dark grass the animal was running through, like the tiny, bare black limbs of the one silhouetted African tree in the distance.

97

The overhead lights glared down on the slick pages of the magazine, light reflecting off the dark shape of the hartebeest, and June thought of Turk, standing in the light, stretching, arms out like horns. The magazine pages smelled like a drugstore, iodine, the examining room in the clinic. June took a last look as she peeled the pages back against her thumb and let them ripple back into place. Her thumb against the paper sounded like playing cards clothespinned to the moving spokes of a kid's bicycle, and the antelope jerked by like in a movie.

12

JUNE didn't know if it was the rain or the squeak of the oven door that woke her. It was dark out, but she couldn't tell if it was that early or just the rainy weather. She lay under the quilt listening to the puff of the pilot light, the weight of someone moving in the kitchen, the murmur of the weather report on the radio. She got up, liking the feel of her bare feet on the cold floor, and pulled on jeans and a blouse. She hurried to the bathroom, through Turk's room where he lay snoring on top of his covers, one arm up over his forehead, the other sticking straight off the bed.

Aiming for a spot between two rust stains, June spat toothpaste and water. She splashed cold water on her face, not bothering to dry, letting the air on her wet face wake her.

Cage was the one up. He surprised her when she stepped into the bright kitchen. She had expected Momma to be up, not him. Cage smiled a silent good morning, poured her a cup of coffee as she kissed him, the taste of coffee from his mouth mingling with the toothpaste taste in her own. She sat on the floor by the water heater and put on her shoes, watching Cage dip crackers in his coffee, something she'd

99

remember after they were married, to keep a jar of crackers on the kitchen table. The radio was talking about the prices of beef and pork in Kansas City.

Cage seemed different, smaller, quieter. He had on thin blue socks with red diamonds on each ankle, light blue pants, a sleeveless undershirt. His chest was white around a deep, pink vee, where his dress shirts joined his body. His arms were white down to his wrists, where his sleeves had stopped, and his big hands looked like pink gloves.

June poured milk into her coffee, watching the color change. The glass-covered cake pan had some pecan pie left in it, and she cut a piece and ate it with her fingers. Cage was reading the label on a bottle of blackberry wine he had brought Momma. He wore a thick gold ring on his little finger, two small red stones on each side of a diamond that flashed as he turned the bottle in his hand. He had told June that was her Aladdin's ring, all she had to do was rub it three times and the genie in the ring would grant her wishes. He set the wine bottle down and looked at her.

"Today's the day," he said. He had a surprise for her and handed her a sealed envelope. "Wedding present," he said. Opening the envelope while he watched, she felt like a contestant in a beauty contest or an actress up for an Oscar. In the envelope was a Polaroid picture of a house, a big one-story brick house stretched across the photograph. "It's your—our new house," he said.

June did not say anything. She looked at his big, pink hands. Thought of those hands on her breasts. Thought of the ring on his pudgy little finger, cold on her bare skin.

They sat, listening to the sound of their own quiet sipping and swallowing, the refrigerator motor, the steady fall of rain.

100

13

CAGE HAD the wedding bands in his coat pocket, wrapped in a tight wad of tissue paper. The ceremony lasted only twelve minutes, June timed it.

Outside, Florene and Curtis pelted them with rice.

"Don't throw it that way," Cage yelled, "Throw it up and let it fall down on us. That way it hurts and you might put someone's eye out."

In the Buick, June smiled out at Momma with the face of someone June remembered from a movie. Someone beautiful smiling through the window of a slow-moving train, her mother or her lover standing on a gray station platform, saying goodbye.

Then she was gone with Cage, in the disappearing car.

101

14

SEEN through the rain, the lights of a giant refinery, like stars coming down for a landing, seemed to twinkle as they floated by on the left. Houston had disappeared in the darkness behind them. Cage felt the presence of the Gulf spread out in the darkness ahead. Beyond the Buick's headlights Cage could not separate land from sky, could not see where land and sky met the wide, dark Gulf. June slumped against him, warm, her lips parted in sleep. They were dry and safe in the closeness of the car, but out there where everything merged into one whole darkness was a kind of terror. Quiet, still, held somehow in check, but terror nonetheless. Cage felt as if the car might slide off the edge of the highway into an abyss. He gripped the steering wheel tightly, imagining the highway as a narrow and slippery causeway over which they were dangerously racing toward safety. When a Houston-bound bus passed, it sent water like an ocean wave breaking over the headlights, hood, windshield, blacking out Cage's vision. He held the steering wheel straight and hoped the highway did not curve. Time stopped momentarily when the water washed over the car sealing them in, Cage and June, adrift in a dark diving bell. He pressed hard on the accelerator, the car swallowed forward, the speedometer needle jerking like a compass finding direction. A speed limit sign whipped by, the road rising up to meet them, disappearing beneath the hood. He felt the car, heavy and relentless in his hands.

The green light of the dashboard on her face, June looked lovely in an eerie, almost wicked way. Her teeth luminous in the light, lime-colored and large, her open mouth a slice of darkness bitten from the air. Her loveliness was angular. Dark hair framed her face in tight curls, her cheeks high and thin, like she was always sucking something tart. Leaned against him, her breasts were pushed together swelling up from her blouse to catch the green glow of light. Cage had wanted to tell Turk how June arched her back in lovemaking. He had wanted to describe the silent force of her body, thin and urgent beneath him. He felt the heat of her hand where it rested on his thigh, touched with the tip of his finger the diamond he had given her, the diamond cool and hard. He pressed the ring until her hand twitched, raised his finger into the dim light, and saw the red imprint of the diamond slowly disappear from his skin. He wondered how he had gotten her here, inside this big quiet car, moving with silent speed through the Texas night. His wife. Cage and June, Mr. and Mrs., together from now on. She was quiet, liked country music and going to movies and stormy weather. She loved to get presents and always liked everything he gave her. Sometimes she was so quiet, seemed so distant, detached, that he wondered if she really loved him, but then they would make love and she would lift her body up against him so hard he almost hurt, and he forgot his fears.

She belonged with him now. He would take care of her from now on. He would buy new clothes for her, take her out to dinner, help her out of fur coats, pull chairs back for her again and again, hold doors open. He would buy her

flowers even when there was no occasion. They would drink
fine wine in crystal glasses every evening, and every evening
they would undress in the same room. He would buy a new
house. Cage and June's house, Cage and June's room. He
would bathe in front of her, she would bathe in front of him.
They would sit on the same toilet, wash with the same soap,
his razor would sit on the shelf in their medicine chest, in
their bathroom, with her tweezers. Asleep, vulnerable, they
would lie together, dreaming while their bodies touched,
their steady breathing taking in and letting out the same
shared air, like a secret, theirs alone. No one else really knew
her, no one knew how full she was of passion.

Inside the car, it was warm and still. Outside, the land was
speeding darkly, silently, by. He had not seen another car for
miles. Nothing existed but the short strips of pavement that
kept coming out from beneath the front of the Buick, beneath the headlights, keeping pace with them.

All around him, empty space, wide and open. Behind him
was Ohio, his past. Ohio, where there had always been
lights. Driving across flat cornfields, the lights of cars, trucks,
farmhouses. In Ohio, distant lights of small towns, cities,
endless turnpikes, airport beacons, runways, railroad cross-
ings, power lines. Lines of dim car lights, lines of factory
workers carrying metal lunch pails, lines of miles of cyclone
fence around factories, special gates with yellow, flashing
lights strung over them to wink workers in and out.

Cage had been a wholesale grocer in Toledo. He'd worked
for a man named Vargo who owned a warehouse full of
groceries. The big warehouse always damp, wind rattling the
corrugated metal walls. Walking between straight rows of
tall stacks of boxes, the smell of laundry detergent, sugar,
flour, spilled from damp boxes.

In Ohio white winters turned gray as the Ohio sky.
Smoke, slush, gray twilights. Weeks of clouds, gray crowds of
people. Ohio seemed old, crowded, had been cleared,

planted, concreted, fenced. In Texas, Cage had found hot, cheap, dusty land. Land he could walk off in squares, mark with flimsy sticks and orange plastic tags that jerked in the wind. Miles of wild land, unused land, waiting. In Texas, big laughing Mexican men building streets, stopping to curse, joke, wipe the backs of dark, strong necks with big blue bandannas. Streets Cage could name, land he could sell to the same Mexicans who built his streets. Land cheap to buy, easy to sell. Cheap labor. Big billboards with his name on them in big red letters, his picture in the yellow pages. A small land office full of a green metal desk, a telephone, a fat phone book, some fold-up metal chairs, a coffee pot and paper cups, a free calendar from an auto parts company, a pretty blonde in a bathing suit arched back onto the fender of a new car like the deer Cage saw on cars every fall, the calendar stuck on the wall, certain days xed in blue ballpoint. *Now, Mr. Sanchez, let me drive you out to that lot we were talking about. The best view in this development.* Taking them in the big, air-conditioned Buick. Against the Texas heat, cool, quiet, smooth. June Boulevard, Ohio Lane, Texas Way.

Behind him now, Ohio was the past. But Texas, oh boy, Texas, he knew, was the future. And what a future he would build. Marrying June was just the beginning. He was going to be heard from. He was building more than houses, he was building a new life, making a place for June and himself.

He eased up on the gas, the car hesitated on top of an overpass, some kind of water running underneath, channel or canal, locks, something for tankers. The lights of Galveston stretched out ahead. He began passing billboards that named hotels, motels, restaurants, seaside amusements. The streets nearly empty, Cage making every green light. Mercury-vapor lamps arched overhead, dropping light over him and June in windshield shapes. June sat up, slowly scratched her cheek where it had been against his pants.

The hotel had a circular drive. Cage pulled around and

stopped beneath the canopy, June stretching, blinking against the brightness of the colored lights aimed up through a fountain in front of the hotel lobby, the water in the fountain turned off for the night.

Bellhop lifting the heavy suitcases out of the deep trunk, June's new initials in gold on her luggage.

Cage handed his car keys to a boy in a gold-braided jacket. In the lobby he stared through his reflection in the glass doors and watched the boy wheel the Buick into a parking place.

He remembered the beat up black station wagon at the Sinclair station in Blanco, the two muddy cowboys, Turk, and Jordan West's zombie son tilted back in the office. If they could just see him now. He had wanted to tell them. Almost told Turk that June had been his bride from the first night, if Turk knew what he meant. Wanted to clap the two ranchers on the back and laugh confidentially, if they all knew what he meant by that. Wanted to tell them all how much the Buick really cost, tell them how many San Antonio banks would fall all over themselves to loan him money, a few thousand for a car or a house or real money, big money, for a development full of new houses. Wanted to tell them about this hotel, tell them where he was taking Turk's sister. Not just a hotel room, you stupid shitkickers, a suite of rooms, a bedroom bigger than most of your houses, a big plush bathroom, a fancy dressing room with mirrors all around, and the carpets ankle deep and soft enough to lie down on. Soft enough for that, if they knew what he meant. He thought of all the things he'd like to tell Turk, names to call him, pictured himself beating hell out of all of them, the two smart-ass cowboys with their shit-eating grins, Turk who acted like he had a right to look down his fat red nose at Cage, even the gum-chewing, pimply kid sitting in the office in a country music coma. Beat them all to pieces and drive smoothly over their bodies in his new, quiet Buick.

"Look at that, June, a Caddy on one side, a Chrysler on the other. Just look at this place." He stood a few seconds longer at the doors, looking out at the Buick, newer than the Cadillac, sticking out beyond the Chrysler, at least as long, maybe longer.

15

CAGE AND June stayed in the executive suite, which was larger than the bridal suite. Every morning Cage called room service and had breakfast sent up. They had champagne for breakfast. The bedroom had a big television set mounted on the wall. It was mounted in a bracket that could be swiveled left or right, and the television could be seen from either of the king-sized beds and even from the bathroom which adjoined the bedroom. Cage watched the late movie while he lay in the big tub covered with steaming hot water. Every morning, as they ate breakfast in bed, June watched a cartoon show.

One wall of the bedroom had a huge window looking out on the Gulf, tinted blue against the south Texas sun which did not shine until the last day they were in Galveston. They never got down to the beach, without the sun there was not much reason to go, but Cage walked around the rooms in his socks and boxer underwear that looked like a huge bathing suit, smoking fat cigars he had sent up from the lobby, drinking champagne with ice in his glass, looking down at the deep blue Gulf through the tinted glass.

Cage took June dancing. A different place every night, the Cactus Club, the Three Palms, Blue's Sho-Bar, Longhorn Saloon, the Silver Dollar Bar-N Ballroom. There were waitresses in short fringed skirts and cowboy boots, purple bruises on their thighs; lights that made their teeth glow and June's bra shine through her blouse; colored drinks with cherries, orange slices, sprigs of mint, tiny colored straws to drink through; tiny dance floors; country music bands in sequins and string ties. During an intermission at the Silver Dollar Bar-N Ballroom, June got up on the empty bandstand and played steel guitar and lots of folks clapped. When the band came back the man who sang said June seemed to play about as well as the regular pedal steel player.

The honeymoon seemed to flip by like days on a calendar in a movie, pages flipping to make time disappear. They stayed out late every night, sometimes eating breakfast before going to sleep. Afternoons they spent snug in the hotel suite, making love, watching the weather over the Gulf, watching reruns on the big color-TV. Cage went from room to room sitting in all the different chairs. When he was a boy his mother wrapped tissue paper around coathangers for a dry cleaners in Toledo, and the few chairs in their house were always stacked with coathangers and heavy piles of tissue wrap. Trying to fall asleep he stared at shadows of the bundles of bare hangers against the living room wall where he lay every night on the couch. The house always smelled like other people's clothes.

Cage's daddy, a disabled vet from World War I, spent the last half of his life in a wheelchair, paralyzed from the waist down. He had survived the American assault in the Argonne Forest and had come home from France on one of the big ships carrying thousands of American veterans. Then he was run down by a streetcar only weeks before his discharge. At least the army paid his hospital bills for a while. He sat in the wheelchair and drank wine to ease the hurting in his legs.

109

The doctors all agreed that he was just imagining the pain, they said he couldn't actually feel anything from the waist down. Eventually, they severed his spinal cord where his leg nerves joined, but, unconvinced, he still suffered the pains.

Cage could not remember his daddy the way he had been before the accident with the streetcar. His mother slept in a different room after the accident because his daddy's moaning kept her awake, and, sometimes, his daddy would wet the bed while he slept. He had been trained at the army hospital to go to the bathroom only at certain times each day, emptying his bowels every morning, his bladder four times a day, but he felt nothing but the leg pains, and, sometimes, his body forgot its schedule. Cage didn't understand why his mother and daddy didn't sleep together like other kids' parents, and his mother told him that when he was older he would understand what his daddy had lost, and why it would have been unfair for her to sleep in the same bed with him.

Once, Cage had smelled something burning, a strong, sweet, singe-smell, and had found his daddy asleep in his wheelchair, his leg against a space heater, the blue gas flame slowly cooking his daddy's white, hairless calf.

Cage remembered the cramped frame house, the skinny backyard where no grass would grow and rainwater stood for days in dark puddles, the alley down which it seemed the loud red garbage truck was constantly coming. In front, the house was jammed up against the sidewalk, a telephone pole, the dirty street. Too hot in the kitchen, too cold at night trying to sleep in the drafty living room. Moving piles and piles of coathangers off the sofa, every night, to make his bed. The smell of soot outside, the smell of grease in the kitchen, the smell of urine in his daddy's room, the smell of his mother's lilac perfume in her room, her door always shut.

He remembered the dark space beneath the broken-in slat of the wooden front porch floor where he had stuffed rocks and sticks and a broken baseball bat and his flannel pajamas, trying to fill the hole.

He remembered the sound of his mother twisting tissue paper around coathangers.

He remembered the bathroom, handlebars in the wall and a special foam pad on the toilet seat for his daddy.

Trying to remember his daddy's face, all Cage could see was the vague shape of a man in a silver wheelchair in the alley behind that house in Toledo, sitting in the alley where the garbage men drove their trucks and emptied dented galvanized tin garbage cans, sitting in the alley in his wheelchair with a box of graham crackers under his arm, a jar of pickled pigsfeet in his hand, eating the pigsfeet, offering one to Cage, holding a dripping pink pig's foot out, his arm extended in the alley to Cage.

When Cage and June made love, Cage sometimes saw this image of his daddy. Something about the color of the pink pigsfeet in the big jar of clear liquid was obscene, but erotic, and Cage would take June's ear in his mouth and bite. Deep in June's ear Cage's tongue tasting something sour, and Cage could not get rid of the image of his daddy and the dripping pigsfoot, the extended arm on the faceless body.

Cage never told June about his daddy in the alley, but when he sucked her ear into his mouth June held him tighter, until he would have a violent orgasm, bucking against her like he was having convulsions.

They never talked when they were making love, but Cage talked a lot afterwards. He would run his hand over June's body, describing what she felt like, his hand sliding smoothly down her side, over her hip, down her thigh, knee, shin, ankle, like a bannister worn smooth, night after night, the same hand moving slowly up, gently down.

They would lie on damp sheets listening to music from the radio, the music always slow and sad, always there in the

111

background sounding far away, a little tinny. Then Cage would take out June's clothes and dress her. He would invent new ways for her to wear her clothes, new combinations he thought up for her. This blouse with this skirt, this scarf tied not around the neck, but around the waist, like this.

16

Sunday nite

Dear Cage and June,

Thank you for the nice postcard. Galveston sure looks pretty but I know you are glad to be home and enjoying your new house. I wish Turk would take me someplace sometime. Lord only knows what he does with his money. He mowed the grass at the cemetery three times this month and has been getting work at Jordan's station all summer and already says hes spent his money. Now hes down in the valley at some chicken ranch and probably making a salary plus expenses but he doesn't ever tell me his business thats for sure.

I don't think its ever going to cool down. We had 96 today and its still in the 80s and ten at nite. The t-v said they got a shower at Johnson City today but we didn't get a drop. Is too bad you all have had rain the whole time down there.

Did I tell you that Mrs. Webb who lives in the Hillview Apts. has a cancer? Those are the new apts. They built back in behind the school. Naomi said if she died, Mrs. Webb she meant, I could sell my house and get her apt. Mrs. Webb's apt. She has air cond.

113

and central heat and comes furnished but I don't think I want to leave my old house, hot as it is and cold in the winter. It needs painting and the roof leaks so bad I probably couldn't sell it anyway.

I had roast today, leftovers for supper. Silly to cook for just myself, but I did anyway. There was more fat than meat. I mashed potatoes and made gravey, had some snap beans and maccaroni and cheeze. The beans were real good.

Dr. O'Connor is still at the hospital in Temple but I called his office and the nurse gave me a salve that stopped that awfull itch I had. It isn't well but is better.

When you all get time, please come get me and take me to see your new house. You all are all I have to be proud of. I tell everyone what Cage said about getting me a new waterheater. That would be real nice. You all sure did get the new house decorated fast, but I tell everyone Cage gets things done fast. I'd get Turk to bring me down when he gets back but he is scared his car is fixing to go out on him. Lord only knows what that'll cost.

I guess I better close now, it's time for an old woman to go to bed and get some sleep if I can between hearing the hiway trucks and worrying about being here alone all night. I have got so old and slow I don't do much else but sleep and worry. Come see me as soon as you can.

Love,
Eunice Momma

17

WHAT TURK smelled was a strong mixture of barnyard and ammonia. Over fifty thousand laying hens and each one with a skinny gray mountain of chicken shit under its cage. Inside, the dark hen houses reminded Turk of pictures he had seen of Carlsbad Caverns, the tall, pointed mounds of chicken shit like the icicle-shaped stalagmites. The Plantation Egg Ranch was southwest of San Antonio, between Cotulla and Dilley. The gray wooden hen houses hunched close to the ground, like doodlebugs balled together when a big rock is rolled away. A fancy new house with a redwood-fenced patio and pool sat beside the hen houses.

It was hot on the egg ranch. The tin roofs and wire cages held the heat, and the few trees that managed to grow in the dry dirt were short and scraggly and gave little shade. Most of them had been cleared away by a bulldozer to make room for more hen houses.

He was always, it seemed, working in the heat. Pumping gas, cutting grass in the cemetery, working for the highway department clearing right of ways. In the summer dust, pulling limbs, cutting out cedar, itchy, thorn stuck, cut by

Johnson grass, picking up hot beer cans and broken bottles. Dinner in shade they made by tilting the bed of a dump truck up against the sun, sitting underneath, eating sun-warm roast beef sandwiches Momma packed in a paper sack, listening to men tell stories about women they had known, black fingernails and dirty thumbprints on white, white bread, talking with their mouths full, spitting crumbs when they laughed. Mexicans, across the highway, together, under a short live oak, asleep through most of the break, whispering their Mexican words when they were awake. Mexicans could sleep standing up, just like horses and mules. He couldn't believe some of the stuff they brought with them to eat. They had ways, weird ways, looks they gave each other like they all had some big secret. He couldn't figure Mexicans at all, but something about them made him nervous, a little scared, maybe—angry, for sure.

Now he was working with Mexes again. Hanging curtain near Cotulla in the dust. It was Mr. Lovejoy's job. He had sent Turk in the panel truck and had given him money to hire Mexican help. The first day they put up over a thousand yards of curtain, and when he drove back in to Cotulla he rolled the windows down, pushed the panel truck for all it was worth, trying to blow the smell of chicken shit out of his clothes.

Turk spent that night lying on top of the blue chenille spread on a soft double bed at the Red Arrow Motor Court in Cotulla. He jerked awake as often as he managed to fall asleep, flies dancing down his leg, his mind jumping with the effort of trying to go blank. He tried it with the window open, loud cars racing down the gravel road to the A & W Drive-In, someone pitching a squeaky, plastic beach ball across the square of dead grass in front of the motel as if there was a swimming pool, soda pop bottles clunking down through the big red Coke machine outside his room. He tried it with the window shut, the half-curtains drawn across the

116

bottom of the window, and he could hear the bedspread peel off his sweaty shoulders, the folds of the sheets leaving a pink pattern on his skin, and the noise of the flies was louder.

Finally, near midnight, he gave up and took a shower, the pipes moaning and knocking like knees in the wall, the water changing suddenly from warm to cold, the bar of motel soap squirting out of his hand to slide around on the metal floor of the shower stall. His arms ached, sore from the sun, tired from nailing nylon curtain pockets on the ends of hen houses; his fingers ached from working nylon cord through grommet holes, nylon cord through little silver pulleys, nylong cord around heavy stone weights to pull the curtain up and let the curtain down. The rolls and rolls of black and gray curtain that kept out the wind in winter, the sun in summer. The curtain that made daytime dark, fooled hens into laying more than once a day, their days and nights shortened by the curtain.

He put his clammy clothes back on and left to hunt a cup of coffee in Cotulla.

Outside, a white cat, fat as a Christmas turkey, sat on the dead grass and stared at him. He clapped his hands and stomped his feet at the cat, but it just sat and stared. Whoever had been tossing the beach ball had disappeared. Mr. Lovejoy's panel truck was pink in the light of the neon Red Arrow Motor Court sign. Turk wrote his name in the dust on the back of the truck. The cab was littered with empty half-pint milk cartons and bread crusts and smelled like sweat and piss. The night air was hot, still. Hammers, boxes of nails, bolts of curtain slid around in the back of the truck as he pulled out of the narrow parking area. The A & W was dark when he drove by, but several cars were still parked under the curb service canopy, nosed together like they were conspiring or whispering jokes.

Downtown Cotulla, what there was of it, was as empty as a town in a science fiction movie where all the people have

117

been evaporated by aliens. South of town a Texaco was still open, and, adjoining the Texaco, the Snazzy Pig Cafe. Over the café door, a big plywood cutout of a pig painted pink, GOOD BAR-B-Q in black across the pig's back.

The Snazzy Pig was empty except for the waitress who sat in one of the red booths by the front windows smoking and staring out at the highway. Gentleman Jim Reeves was in the jukebox, singing, *tell that man there with you, he'll have to go.* A sign taped to the cash register, IN GOD WE TRUST, ALL OTHERS PAY CASH. The waitress waited until Turk sat down at the counter before she slowly got up and came around to take his order. He watched her pour his coffee into a heavy white mug beside a pyramid of little cardboard boxes of cornflakes. He tried to blow the stack of boxes over, without blowing hard enough for her to notice what he was doing. The cornflakes didn't budge, but his cheeks ached like he'd been blowing up balloons. The coffee was bitter, but at least it was hot.

Jim Reeves quit singing and Turk said howdy to the waitress who said nothing. He watched in the mirror as she walked back to her booth. She wore thin, black flats and walked on the balls of her feet, making her calves flex a little with each step. She saw him looking at her in the mirror when she lit a cigarette, and she stared at his reflection until he lowered his head to his coffee.

He wanted something else, but didn't really know what. He wasn't particularly hungry, but he took the menu, a heavy red plastic cover over it, and read the columns of barbeque plates, hamburgers, chicken fried steak. One thing for sure, he didn't want *chicken* anything.

The café was hot with silence and fluorescent light. He slowly spun the round rack of post cards on the counter. He picked one, a busy street scene of Mexico City. He looked at the postcard, wondering what made the city look foreign. Maybe it was all the little cars, or the fountain that the streets fanned out from. In the mirror he saw that the waitress was watching him now. He wondered would she run and block the door if he slipped the postcard in his pocket and started to leave. He imagined himself wrapping his arm around her and carrying her right on out the door she was blocking, her legs kicking up and down like a scissortail, her arms swinging, sharp fists pecking his face and chest. She was in this empty, silent heat with him, this waitress with her cigarettes and blank face staring out the window at the empty gravel parking lot, the Texaco, the empty, narrow highway, and he wanted to talk to her. They were in this silence together, and he was burning to talk to her, to tell her, tell her—what? To say they should not sit alone and apart in this empty café, the Snazzy, Snappy, Jazzy, Sassy Pig. To tell her he was alone, she was alone, they could spend the night together. It ought to be that way. He would tell her her calves were nice, good, full. That he had watched her skirt ride up the backs of her good thighs and they should not be alone as long as they were together in the Shabby, Sad Pig Cafe. The pig, the pink pig café. Pink pig, pink pie, pink eye. To say she had pretty, pretty eyes. Pig, prig, plink, prink, pink, prick. To please, to please let him put his pink prick, to put it in her pink. Between her good, good legs. To kiss her lips, her pink, pink lips, her blank face.

The screened door opened, and a Mexican family came in. A man, a boy just walking, two girls in identical white dresses, a woman.

The man was big. Round shoulders, round elbows, a big round head, shiny black hair combed straight back. He looked like the men Turk had hired to work with him at the egg ranch, thick, dark, secretive. Maybe he *was* one Turk had worked with, they all looked alike to Turk. Like this one, they all had big teeth, strong-looking big white teeth, and they all showed their big white teeth when they smiled, which they did most of the time they were not sleeping. This

119

one had been smiling, showing his big white teeth, since he had come through the door, smiling and nodding his head, that Catholic necklace they all wore, to protect them or something, jerking out from the neck of his shirt.

The children, all three, dirty, barefoot, staring at everything, their bare legs dark and shiny as polished wood, their eyes round and white as the smooth wet bottom of Turk's empty coffee mug.

The woman, long black hair she lifted up off the back of her neck, raising her arm, bent at the elbow like a dark bird wing, hair feathers under her arm. A dark wet patch of hair under her arm Turk saw for a second like a mouth that opened to speak but did not, the hair under her arm a dark secret she would never tell. And fine dark hair on her legs. It made him surge with anger and excitement, the black hair under her arm and down her legs, like the fast, flying language they used. Words that ran together, twisted together like vines and tree limbs, curly black words, coiled and shaped like iron balconies on rich houses in San Antonio, words as slick and shiny and hard as wrought iron. Turk had tried their strange words, words they made on their tongues, quick and darting, warm and wet, and his tongue had twisted, grown large in his throat. The woman rolled the strange words off her tongue, plaiting the words into meanings, twirling sentences like a lariat.

He had seen them plenty of times, women like her, her dark skin, her long dark hair, her black dress curved off her shoulders over the tops of her brown breasts that shook gently as she lifted the little boy into a chair. She sat, watching the top of the table, her legs close together, held back beneath her chair, her thighs hidden beneath the table, beneath the heavy dress. He had seen the old ones too, their hair knotted back in dull, gray buns, skin greasy and thick, breasts resting on bellies, understraps hanging off soft round shoulders. This one was already getting thick in the ankles.

She lifted her hair off her shoulder, gave her head a short shake like a horse flicking off flies.

The man read the menu out loud, quietly translating the words to his children. They stared at the fluorescent tubes in the ceiling. The woman watched the top of the table.

The waitress was taking her time. She stared into the window, took a long, slow pull on her cigarette, watching her reflection, making up her mind. She finally ground the cigarette out, making slow circles in the ashtray, holding the smoke until she stood up. She smiled at Turk, gave him a knowing look, let out a long white cloud of smoke. Now the waitress knew she shared the silence with Turk. Now she knew.

The Mexican woman lifted her hair off her shoulder. The skin where her hair joined her scalp was pink. Under her arm, under the dark hair there, her skin was pink. The skin up under her black dress, Turk knew, would be pink, between her thighs, pink.

In Sally's apartment he sat naked, the pink print of his elbows on his knees as he leaned on his stomach watching Sally, naked on her bed. Her pink body, pink painted nails, pink nipples, pink cheeks, pink lips. Pink panties, pink bra, pink slip, pink nylons lying on the floor. She had pink mosquito bites on her back, in her closet the insides of her shoes were pink. Pink bedspread and rug, pink bathroom, shower curtain, pink toilet and tub. Inside her mouth, in her nose, in her ears, inside in between her legs, she was pink. Out in the cemetery her last husband had a pink granite tombstone.

It made him furious. If they can't talk American why do they come here?

His anger caught in his chest like a cold breath that begins to burn and ache in the throat. He watched the Mexican woman in the mirror lift the plastic rose from the vase on their table and hold it over her breast for a moment, her lips

121

moving, some Mexican mystery she whispered, the man
leaning his dark forehead against hers. Turk saw a sharp line
bulging the man's pocket, a knife or a razor, he knew they all
carried blades, and he felt his hand slip over the stainless
steel knife he'd unrolled from his paper napkin. His anger
took him back to Sally and a Saturday afternoon when he
was driving her car and they were backed into by a Mexican
man in the parking lot of the Handy Andy grocery near her
apartment. Sally had said to forget it, it was only a scratch,
the Mexican's car was hurt much worse. Turk had yelled and
yelled, first at the Mexican, then at Sally. And Sally said he
was acting crazy, for Christ's sake, acting like he was scared
of them or something, for Christ's sake. She said he was just
like her last husband getting so mad and he'd better watch his
step or he'd end up dead too, with a heart attack.

Turk knew better than that. He wouldn't die like that,
like her last husband. Taking a crap. They found him sitting
straight up on the toilet. The landlady, opening the apartment door for the TV repair man, Sally at school teaching
little Mexicans to say *the quick brown fox jumped over the lazy
dog.* He wondered if they called her on her pink telephone. She never cried. All through the funeral, she never
cried. Turk knew she would cry if it was him, he knew she
would.

Now the waitress knew there was a kinship, knew she and
Turk were together now in the Snazzy Pig Cafe. She sure was
glad he hadn't left before they came. Her name was Claire,
and her chin sank softly in like a worn doorstep where she
kept touching one little pimple. She thought they only ate
tamales and things anyway. She was only working temporary, until her friend got out of the army, where he was now,
up at Fort Sam Houston, and she got this job from a friend of
his worked on the base, though she'd like a San Antonio job
better, this one had a free room over the cafe, and her friend
didn't like her in a big city where so many men could chase

after her. She was from Tunbridge, near Rugby, North Dakota, which was the geographical center of North America, but she guessed Turk probably hadn't ever been there had he? Her daddy had a farm near Tunbridge. When she turned eighteen she moved into Rugby to live in a city. She had a job there, a good job in a grocery, a supermarket chain, and lived in a nice two-story house walking distance from the supermarket, but when she told her old boyfriend she didn't want to marry him, he beat her up real bad. The second time he came round and beat on her she yelled and yelled until her landlord heard and busted in. Her old boyfriend busted both her landlord's arms, her landlord was a kinda old guy, and then her boyfriend told her he'd be back in a day and to be ready to go. Well she knew this guy in the army who was leaving for Texas who said she should come with him, so here she was. She liked the supermarket better, but she was seeing new places and wanted to stay down here and go to college or business school if she could save up enough money.

Turk gave Claire some money for the jukebox, and she played "House of Blue Lovers" and "I Cried a Tear," "Jack Newman, B3, and Ernest Tubb, J6. I play them all them time," she said. She brought the Mexicans their hamburgers and laughed at that, "What about their tamales?" she whispered to Turk. When the Mexicans left, Claire showed Turk the two quarters the man left under the edge of his plate. "Hey Turk, think I oughta wash these off before I touch 'em?" She talked the whole time she cleared their table.

At 1:30 Claire shut off the coffee maker and locked up. Taking a couple of six-packs of Pearl they headed back to Turk's motel room, where Claire gave him tight little kisses, holding her lips hard against his, and let him run his hands over her breasts and thighs until her blouse was wrinkled and her skirt was damp with his sweat, but she wouldn't take her clothes off. He thought she must have a bad scar or a birth-

123

mark she didn't want him to find. Sally had a scar across her stomach from some operation she had had and she was always trying to hide it from him. Claire dozed off, drowsy from the beer, which had gotten warm, and Turk thought about screwing her while she slept. He had heard stories in the army about men screwing sleeping women, even women who were dead, according to a guy who had driven an ambulance for a while, but he didn't really believe those stories. He set his half-empty can of beer between Claire's legs and stretched out beside her on the bed.

The next morning the can of beer was still upright between Claire's legs and they both laughed at that. He dropped her off at the Snazzy Pig on his way to the egg ranch. Her face was puffy and her clothes were a mess. She didn't have to work until afternoon, so she went up to her room to sleep and Turk sat down to breakfast. The café was crowded with men in straw hats, khakis, levis. A wrinkled old man with a tuft of white hair growing out of each ear served Turk pancakes, ham, and coffee. As he climbed back into Mr. Lovejoy's panel truck, Turk saw that the shades were pulled down in the windows above the café. Parked in front of the café in the morning sun, the truck seat had gotten so hot it burned his back and the backs of his legs, and he wrapped a piece of cardboard around the steering wheel until he got some air stirred to cool things off some.

At the egg ranch the owner asked Turk how the job was coming along, and Turk said fine, if these spics would just keep working and quit fooling around he could be done in four days. The owner told Turk he'd built the new house and swimming pool last summer for his wife and daughter. Said he had to be close by all the time to kick ass, Mexicans being not only lazy as niggers, but, give them half a chance, they'll steal you blind to boot. Turk watched the owner's daughter through the open gate of the redwood fence, sixteen or seventeen and long blonde hair, in her swim suit lying down by

124

the bright blue pool. She looked like a girl on a billboard advertising milk, slender and tan and healthy. Turk asked the owner how they could stand the smell of all the chickens and the piles and piles of gray chicken shit, he'd nearly gagged the first day he spent hanging curtain. The owner frowned, told Turk a man got used to the smell, told Turk, after saying the job had to be done in three days at most, that smell was the smell of success.

That night at the Snazzy Pig the old man with hair in his ears told Turk that Claire had gone up to Fort Sam with her boyfriend, down on a two-day pass, she'd be back the next day. Turk played a quarter's worth of pinball and drove back to the Red Arrow. He parked and locked the truck, took the distributor cap with him. In case some Mexican tried to steal Mr. Lovejoy's truck.

The picture postcard of Mexico City lay on the table by his bed. He filled in Sally's address, wrote her he was on his way back from Old Mexico and would stop by in a few days. Then he picked up the phone on the dresser and asked the desk to connect him with long distance. He placed a call, person to person, for Mr. Turk Marrs in Blanco, Texas. He told the operator this was Mr. Clint Hunter calling and gave her Momma's number. He could hear wind in the telephone, then it started ringing. Momma answered, who is this, she said. The operator said a Mr. Clint Hunter was calling long distance for Turk Marrs. Momma's voice rose, said Mr. Marrs was not at home just now, she'd be glad to talk to Mr. Hunter. The operator asked when Mr. Marrs would be in, was there another number? Momma didn't know, wasn't sure, she could take a message, though. Turk hung up. He pictured Momma in the dining room, the three bare bulbs bright on the tablecloth, the room warm, empty, the refrigerator humming, his alarm clock ticking if she hadn't let it run down, and he knew she'd be awake for hours wondering why Clint Hunter, Clint Hunter who owned one of the

125

biggest, richest ranches in the state, and who raised prize bulls worth thousands of dollars each, and who had United States senators and Hollywood actresses come down to barbecues on his ranch, why a man like that wanted to talk to Turk.

He was tired but wanted to mail the postcard to Sally before he went to bed. There was a stamp machine in the motel office and a mail box on the side street.

Walking waist high in dust, the neon arrow shooting continually over his head at the stucco row of rooms, he wondered where all the dust came from, and knew it would never settle, but would sift forever through the heat, filming over windows, windshields, headlights, eyes. Down here the heat and the dust were part of the air, air he could see but could not see through. And he guessed the world down here maybe looked better for the dust, the dust covering up the Red Arrow Motel and the dirty parking lot at the A & W Drive-in and the wrinkled old men walking from beat-up, rust-gutted cars and pickups into the Snazzy Pig Cafe. There was a fine layer of dust over his hands covering the raw spots he had rubbed there working with the curtain, and he could feel the grit along the edges of his gums. And he thought about Claire and last night and knew that being with her could never be personal, never be special or lasting. He would blow out of town with all this dust and leave her in the Snazzy Pig waiting for the boy at Fort Sam to get another pass. He knew the only special times he had ever had had been with Sally, the only secrets he had ever shared, the only unspoken conversations, had been in Sally's bed, the sheets burning his elbows and knees, the pictures of her husbands face-down in her dresser drawer, his own white back, moving, alive, reflected in Sally's dresser mirror.

18

CAGE CLOSED the deal with Texaco the day after he and June got back from their honeymoon. He had hoped for something like this when he bought the house and lot, actually two big lots, at the entrance to the new subdivision. He had 1.8 acres at the entrance to Moonview Estates. A builder he knew told Cage about the house before it ever went on the market. A couple had bought it from the builder, then gone into bankruptcy right after the house was completed, before they ever moved in. Cage got it for a song, he told June, and she could decorate the house any way she wanted. With the money he'd saved on the deal she could have the best interior decorator in town come in if she wanted. The house sat to one side of the large lot, leaving the southwest corner, the corner of Moonhill Lane and the new access road to the new expressway that looped the city, wide open. It was a prime corner and just what Texaco wanted. They could catch traffic from the new loop as well as regular customers who would be building in Moonview Estates and wanting a dependable station nearby to keep their Oldsmobiles and Pontiac station wagons gassed and washed and greased. Cage had known all along what a prime corner he was getting, and he told the folks from Texaco, "Its a prime corner, and you're getting in ahead of the zoning commission; you'll be set and if you're lucky they won't let Gulf or Humble in." The Texaco people showed Cage drawings, an artist's concept, of the station. They would build it out of Austin stone, to harmonize with the area, and put nice little flower gardens along the curb and a big redwood planter-box to hide the rest room doors. It would be open twenty-four hours a day. The bright red star would light up Cage's side yard at night, discourage prowlers.

"Got more," Cage told June, "for that little piece of front lawn than I paid for the entire two acres. You could just call the lot our house sits on free land, free and clear."

The same day he closed the deal he applied for a Texaco credit card for himself and one for June.

"Mighty convenient," he said, "having Texaco for a neighbor. Not to mention the grass I won't have to have mowed."

19 THREE DAYS after he mailed the post card of Mexico City to Sally, Turk nailed the last curtain pocket on the end of the last hen house he planned to look at for a long time. The owner gave him a check made out to Mr. Lovejoy, and Turk left Cotulla. He stopped at the Red Arrow Motor Court just long enough to pick up his few things and pay his bill. Later, he wished he'd taken the time to shower and change his clothes. He drove with the windows down, trying to cool off and blow the smell of chicken shit and sweat out of the panel truck. The sun was going down on his left, and as he drove through patches of mesquite the sun seemed to be racing along with him, darting deep red between the short trees.

Near Devine he was wishing the truck had a radio when the red light came on beneath the speedometer. By the time he stopped at a station the temperature needle was off the edge of the gauge. He filled the radiator and then made some phone calls and got lucky and found a guy at a truck stop garage just a mile north of Devine who had a rebuilt generator he said would fit the truck. The man let Turk use

129

his tools to put the generator on the truck, but he charged enough for the generator that Turk figured he paid high rent for a couple of wrenches and a crowbar. He watched for the red generator light all the way to San Antonio, seeing it and the sun bright in his mind's eye, but the dash stayed dark like the sky.

By the time he got to San Antonio it was close to midnight. It had taken him nearly four hours to get eighty miles. On the new San Antonio expressway he thought about June and Cage, wondered if they were out there somewhere among all those little lights, and if they were there somewhere, were they awake or sleeping, did they think about him, sense his presence nearby? If he knew where their house was, he could go there. He could walk through their house while they slept, bash Cage's face in with a hammer, one of the hammers in the truck, smash him right in the moustache, cover him with a sheet of leftover chicken curtain. Make June get up and make him coffee while they waited for the police, explain to her that he did it for her own good. Explain that he was her brother, that she was his little sister, and just because they didn't know each other didn't mean that blood didn't count. Tell her it was thicker than Cage's money. Then he was approaching the exit ramp for the highway to Austin, had to decide whether to go see Sally right now, wake her up tonight, tell her he had come to know something about himself and her, something he felt about her in Cotulla with Claire, or go back instead to the Blanco highway home. Something he knew now, something he hadn't thought out in words yet. Something, he thought, and his lips moved, forming the word, *something,* I have to talk about with Sally.

He took the exit for Austin, then pulled onto the access road and stopped on top of a hill. All around him was the darkness that held the spread of all the little lights of the city. Some of the lights moved through the darkness, some winked on and off, but all were silent. He felt like no one knew he was there, watching, eavesdropping with his eyes. He pulled on the emergency brake, switched the lights off. The engine still running, he got out and stood in front of the truck, his reflection in the windshield staring back at him as if he were still sitting behind the steering wheel. He stood there, staring at himself, thinking of all the quiet weight of the truck, the brake holding the truck on the hill. He moved his arm until its reflection disappeared below the bottom edge of the windshield, imagined the reflection of himself easing a finger around the gray handle that could release the brake. He lifted his arm, pulled it down like he was putting the truck in first gear, made his reflection grip the steering wheel, prepare to run him down. As he stood there, outside himself, watching himself, he realized he had never really believed in the future, had never thought of making the future turn out any certain way. Just as he had always felt he couldn't remember the past with any certainty, he felt he could not forsee the future either. The future was not something to do, it was something that did to him, and the past was what it had done. There had always seemed to be no way to escape that, no way to change what would be done to him.

But, with Claire, in the Snazzy Pig Cafe, in his room at the Red Arrow Motor Court, he had seen something for the first time. With Claire he had felt something about Sally. With Claire he had wanted to touch Sally, to be with *somebody*, not just *anybody*. Far away from her, with Claire in Cotulla, he had seen Sally closer. With Claire his lips and his arms and his hands moved and touched and his mind thought about it while it was happening, how hard and slippery Claire's lips felt, how dark his own arms looked against her pale skin, his own hands strange and unfamiliar as they moved over Claire's different body. With Sally he never thought, *my lips are on her,* when they kissed. With Sally his lips and his mind moved together, he stayed inside himself

131

and looked out at her. With Claire he seemed to be outside, beside himself on the bed, watching. Kissing Sally he felt a surge of some kind, a connection being made. He saw the connection, but he didn't understand it, the seeing was with his body more than his mind, an understanding in his body, like the good feeling when he met a big semi on a dark highway and blinked his headlights and the big truck blinked back. It was a connection that didn't need to be thought about, didn't have to be understood. With Claire he felt separated from himself, into two selves, one acting, the other watching, and the Turk who was watching was never sure what the other Turk might do. He was even a little afraid of the other Turk, afraid he might not let the Turk who was watching back inside, afraid of what he might do next. Like tonight, standing on the road watching the other Turk in the windshield of the panel truck. What would happen, he thought, if that Turk let off the emergency brake and rolled over this Turk, drove on down this hill and back onto the expressway. Would anyone know the difference? When that other Turk, that reflection of Turk, sat across from Momma eating supper, would she see the difference? Would Momma sense that she was sitting across from a murderer, a man who had run over her son in a panel truck and left him behind in the darkness? And Sally, would Sally hold that other Turk in her arms and never know he was not Turk?

He walked up close to the truck and leaned against the front, stretching to touch his reflected hand in the windshield. He could feel the heat of his trip rising off the metal beneath his chest. When he flattened his hand against his hand on the windshield the hand inside the truck disappeared. He was one self again. He climbed back into the truck and the dome light came on and he saw green bug blood on his hand.

He took the road to Blanco. He was afraid of losing all these feelings. If he went on to Austin and woke Sally and tried to talk about these feelings, tried to explain and understand, he might lose the feelings. He would hold the feelings tonight, he would drive to Blanco feeling this way, would lie in his bed and have all these feelings until he fell asleep.

Tomorrow he would call Sally. He could take her out to eat, get dressed up. Somewhere new, somewhere they had never been. Somewhere they had candles on the tables. He pictured the scene, like the Zale's Jewelry commercial on television, a man's hand reaching across a white tablecloth to take a woman's hand, the woman's hand small with long shiny nails, a ring on one finger, the candle dancing in the diamonds on the ring, people around them at other tables smiling, everyone looking nice, happy.

He went over in his mind how it would be, what he would wear, what they would order for supper, how he would be special to Sally and she would realize he knew about things he had never known about before.

As he drove on to Blanco he got sleepy, and it was hard to keep the feelings. Tomorrow he would think this all out again. He would go over it again on his way to Austin to see Sally, and when he got there he would have the feelings again. He would leave Blanco early tomorrow and drive slowly to Austin and get this all out in his mind, all clear and good.

20

TURK OPENED his eyes. He couldn't remember getting in bed. His room looked close and soft, like a room late at night softened by the light of a television, and for a moment he thought it was still night, that Momma had left the TV on, but this was the soft blue light ahead of sunrise.

He lay inside his body, waiting to feel the excitement in him again. He thought about Sally. He was going to call her, going to see her today, take her out to supper tonight. Something had happened, he was different today. Inside his body felt good, and he got up and slipped into his pants. Carrying his shoes and socks, his shirt held under one arm, he went into the kitchen to dress. He heard Momma breathing heavily in her sleep.

Outside, trees were still dripping from an early morning thunderstorm, the wet grass darkened the big round toes of his work shoes. His old Ford started first time and didn't make a sound in the gravel as he slowly backed out of the yard onto the side road.

There was no traffic. Too early. When he got downtown

the streetlight at the intersection of the highway and the courthouse square went off. There were no cars at the Bowling Alley Cafe. Sudie must have overslept. What time *was* it? He had waked before his alarm and punched it off without looking at the time, and his watch had stopped during the night, still showed midnight. He wished his car radio worked.

He pulled around behind the Bowling Alley and put the car out of gear. Holding one foot on the brake, he stood out on the other foot and pissed onto the pavement, steam rising from his puddle.

Then he headed back toward the house, enjoying the cool air through the open car windows. Jordan's car was still parked at the Sinclair station, he could see the rear end, jacked up, sticking out beyond a cedar tree that blocked his vision of the side of the station. Turk had been promising Jordan for two weeks he'd put new brakeshoes on the car. Getting the wheels pulled was as far as he had gotten before leaving for the egg ranch job down in the valley. Now rust was collecting on the metal parts he had exposed. His rags and tools, tools that belonged to the station, still lay up under the car, its rear poking up like someone bent over for a rectal exam. Turk thought he could pull in right now and finish the brake job. But it was pretty near sunup, he'd just get started and it'd be time to open up the station, time to go get breakfast.

He drove on past the station, watching his reflection in the green glass front. That was the same Turk, the familiar Turk flashing by, his arm out the car window dark and muscular, he looked young and strong. He felt good. Hell, he could finish Jordan's brake job by noon easy, probably even have time to wash his old Ford before tonight, maybe give it a wax job, too. The sky was getting lighter, pink and orange outlined the hills to the east, one last star was visible. He started to make a wish on the star, Sally was always doing that, then

135

he decided he didn't need any more wishes, he was different. He was going to make his own changes, he didn't need any help from the stars. Today was going to be special, he could feel it everyway. The Ford was running good, the road felt fast. He drove on. He passed houses with drawn shades and closed doors, newspapers sticking out of mail boxes along the highway, news from San Antonio and Austin, news of the world. A Rainbow Bread truck passed him going the other way, into town. The fresh bread would smell good inside the truck. Turk had done that once, driven a bread truck. Not a bad job, good as most, better than some. He grinned at himself in his rearview mirror. The day felt like days when he was a kid and woke knowing he didn't have to go to school, days when they went fishing years ago, days when Armon had been taking them somewhere. Him and Momma and June and Armon, all going down to the river years ago. Picnics, fishing, it all seemed a lot simpler back then. But, hell, he was too young to start thinking about the past as the good old days.

Thinking of a picnic reminded him how hungry he was getting. Sudie would be at the café by now. He turned around in the middle of the highway, saw himself again in the mirror. Was that really him? He did look kinda different, looked better. He seemed as different looking to himself as Armon seemed when he looked at old snapshots and tried to remember him. One thing he knew though, one thing for sure, this morning he looked good. He could feel how good he looked. And he knew how to look at a woman in a certain way. Any woman. It was a special look he knew how to give.

Sudie would be at the café looking for him to show up, and he'd kid around with her. They'd be alone for a while, her stacking little boxes of cornflakes, stacking doughnuts in the glass display case, putting coffee and water in the coffee maker, him sitting at the counter, leaning toward her on his elbows, the muscles in his arms hard. The two of them, watching the coffee drip into the glass pots, the smell of his ham and eggs on the griddle, talking and laughing in the empty café before even the cook showed up, Sudie herself cooking his breakfast. He might play something on the jukebox, they might dance. No, he wouldn't play anything, they would just sit there in the morning quiet, listening to the grease sizzling and the low hum of the Dr Pepper cooler and the coffee dripping.

He passed Momma's, the kitchen light he'd left on for Momma, yellow in the side window, Momma probably still sleeping didn't even know he was gone. He stopped to let a girl walk her bicycle across the highway. She gave the bike a push and swung her leg over easily, never broke her stride. He liked her, she was young and healthy. Like him, up early, afraid she might miss something.

The soft yellow light just ahead of the sun was coming over the tops of the low trees, yellow sheen along roof edges, yellow etching the dinosaur's back on the Sinclair sign, the sky beer colored. Turk pulled across the highway on an impulse and drove over to Jordan's car at the station. He got out to look at the electric clock on the wall over the shelves of maps, fan belts, boxes of wiper blades.

At the double garage doors, he stopped. Two men were inside the office, their backs to him. One had his shirt off. They were pulling maps off the shelf, letting them spill onto the floor, where one had fallen open and Turk saw a maze of yellow and red and white lines. Mexicans. They had grease-black hair, dark trousers. A third man stepped into Turk's vision carrying a new battery, hefting it up onto the metal desk where Turk's red baseball cap lay beside his coffee mug. This third man reached up and grabbed the transistor radio tied to the light cord, cut it down with a long-bladed knife. It was like watching a show on television, seeing the three men moving inside the glassed-in office, silent, the volume off. Turk stepped back out of sight, behind the corner of the garage wall.

Quickly, but quietly, he walked to Jordan's blocked-up car, slipped his ring of keys out of his pocket and unlocked the passenger side door, eased it open. Kneeling, he folded the front seat forward and slid Jordan's shotgun off the back floor and out the door. It was in a canvas bag he unsnapped and reached inside, the handle hard, solid, cool. Holding the stock, he let the gun case slide off, slip down the double barrels, whispering like a woman's dress. He broke the shotgun open as he walked. Two shell ends filled the barrels, coppery as new pennies. He cocked the gun back into place, let the safety off, circled around behind the station to the office side.

The three men were still inside, stacking tools and oil filters on the desk with the battery. Through the plate-glass wall, painted dinosaur green, Turk could now barely hear fast Mexican music from the transistor radio. His mind was moving fast, he felt strong and sure.

He braced himself, his left foot planted against the office wall, his left arm flat against the wall, the shotgun, heavy, firm in his right hand. Slowly, without a sound, he brought the shotgun back, his head swiveled, turning back, keeping pace with the shotgun, the barrels blue. Looking towards the highway, away from the office, his right leg back with the shotgun, aimed away from the office, he paused. Across the highway he saw the light on in the window at Momma's just before he pushed off with his right foot, swinging the shotgun and his body into the glass wall, into the office.

At the river with Armon, bringing back his rod, arching back, bait dancing at the end of the rod, casting sidearmed, swinging the rod back beneath tree limbs, casting with his whole body, watching the line spin out onto the green water, catching the sun on the bait, the bait on the sun on the river, circles moving out from the spot of sun on the water, out to the bank where his toes grip the edge and he feels the first wide ring of water from his bait.

Back in high school, swinging the heavy bat back, bringing it back to cut with all his strength after the coach scratched his head to say take a ball, bringing it forward, batting at a ball he can't see, the heavy bat pulling him behind it, pulling him into infield, some girl's red dress or blue blouse in the corner of his eye as he swings.

Down in San Antonio, back when Armon took him to the circus, inside a huge white tent, animal trainer, lion tamer, whip back, arching, body following whip, curve imitating curve, air moving away from his body, whip and body coiling, cracking, through the flaming hoop, into the jaws of the lion.

All the slow swinging of his life. Swinging tools for the highway department, cutting limbs, grass. Swatting at flies in the hot office of the Sinclair station. Beating rugs for Momma out back, rugs hung over the clothesline, clouds of dust, dust particles catching the sun, the wire rug beater making designs in the rug, pulling him into the colored pattern.

Swinging a shotgun, hurling buckshot into a green field, green glass grass, his reflection in glass.

Dance. He pirouetted on his left leg, his followthrough perfect. The glass fell away from the barrels, he squeezed both triggers the moment the double barrels hit the glass, pulling him in behind the gun, through the shattered hole in the wall. The glass exploded, the shotgun exploded, he was showered with blood, cut by flying glass and bone.

Turk lay on top of the shotgun, the barrels hard against his cheek. His right eye burned, the right lens of his bifocals shattered. The only sound was blood dripping onto a roadmap near Turk's ear out of a hole in the back of the man who lay across the desk above him.

The other two men were on the floor beside Turk, one on top of the other, arms clasped, legs spread, like they were dancing together. The one without a shirt was on top, most of his waist shot away, splattered on the walls and ceiling. Turk had not heard any of the men cry out, had heard nothing but the sound of the explosion and the steady dripping of blood.

Like sieves, cans scattered around the office poured oil into the blood that covered the concrete floor, filling the small office with the strong smell of oil. Turk got to his knees and crawled to the door from the office into the adjoining garage bays. There was no one outside, no cars passed on the highway.

How long had it taken? It might have been two minutes or thirty. How loud was the shotgun? Did the glass walls muffle the explosion? The light was still on down at Momma's, but the sun was up now, just over the tops of the hills.

In the garage he pulled one of the wide, heavy overhead doors open about half way, and, taking off his shoes so he wouldn't track blood, went out to his car and drove it inside, then closed the door again and slipped his heavy shoes back on.

On his knees, he began jacking up the front of his car, using the hand jack from the trunk. In the hubcap his face looked tired, but not scared. He wiped his face on his shirt sleeve. He couldn't stop his right eye from bleeding, but he could still see with it. He hadn't looked at the clock in the office, he still didn't know the time. In the hubcap his face was small at the center of the circle, got larger around the edges, near the tire. He looked like someone seen through his bifocals when he had them off, held them out to squint through them, looking for fingerprints, smudges.

His car jacked up high, both front tires off, he went back into the office for the shotgun. The stock was sticky, bits of matted hair and blood stuck to the barrels. One eye stared up at him from the face of the Mexican boy who lay, alone, across the desk, his other eye hidden beneath his head, which was twisted queerly, looking back over his shoulder, resting on Turk's baseball cap.

Avoiding the clock on the wall, not thinking how it had surely stopped with the shotgun blast, hit by flying shot, bone, intestine, glass, oil can, Turk grabbed the man on the desk around the waist and dragged him to the wall and leaned him into the exploded opening.

The thick glass stuck out around the hole, jagged, like green teeth in an opened mouth. The glass teeth caught in the man's shirt, hooked into his back and side, held him in a sitting position, his head slouched onto his chest. Turk looked down at the top of the man's head. Like he's taking one of those siestas, he thought. Then Turk held his hand out, palm down, fingers spread, and placed it gently on top of the man's head. The dark hair was cold, wet.

"Amigo," Turk whispered, "I had to do something."

He picked up his baseball cap, wiped the bill on his thigh, put the cap on. Half the mirror from the front of the cigarette machine was in pieces on the floor. Turk saw himself in the broken half still on the machine. He stared at himself, one eye bloody, oil smeared across his forehead, his lips wet and shining. His cap was on crooked, and he reached to straighten it, but he touched the cap in the mirror, not the cap on his head. "You've got the wrong head, Turk," he said. His hand left streaks of blood, oil on the mirror. Fingerpainting.

swinging the rod back beneath tree limbs, casting with his whole body, watching the line spin out onto the green water

He saw the transistor radio on the desk. It had been covered by the body of the dead Mexican. He turned it on, shook it, but it wouldn't play. The Coke machine had stopped running too, but he leaned down and unplugged it anyway.

141

A truck went by on the highway, a man Turk knew, the horn tooting in a friendly way. Turk waved from inside the office, didn't know if the man saw him or not. The truck whined into a higher gear and passed Momma's, where the light in the kitchen window had gone out.

Turk slid beneath his car, loosened the bolts around the oil pan until it slipped off at one end, the gasket tearing and peeling like old skin, thick oil still warm from the engine pouring all over his chest. He pulled the shotgun under with him and rested it in the crook of one arm, and, with his other hand, pushed at the jack.

the heavy bat pulling him behind it, pulling him

The jack leaned, but would not slip. Turk rested a minute, trying to remember something. He hadn't even called Sally. She still thought he was on his way back from Mexico. She'd probably have his postcard by now. Whatever it was he had had last night, driving home from Cotulla, was lost. But he felt good, even now, he felt good. He had done something important today, he was different now. The soft ache of the shotgun's kick felt good in his arm. He felt strong. Going through that glass wall had been like going through outer space, entering a dream, passing through his own reflection like someone diving through a magic mirror in a kids' story. His eye was bleeding but didn't hurt, and his mind, Jesus, was going so fast.

He had to hurry. Someone, anyone, might show up any second. Momma must have heard the shotgun. She'd never figure out why Mr. Clint Hunter called him long distance. He didn't have much time left.

What time was it?

He wrapped his hand around the jack, the metal was cool, nice to touch. His elbow jerked a little.

whip back, arching, body following whip, curve imitating curve, air moving away from his body

142

He thought of Armon, tried to picture him. Already buried by the time Turk got home, he never got a chance to see what he looked like, had to remember from years before, he'd left for the army and when he got back they had buried Armon. How could he know what his own daddy looked like? There were pictures in a scrapbook somewhere, but he couldn't trust pictures. There were pictures in that same scrapbook of Turk, but he knew they were not right. Those people, the people in the pictures, were gone, had left, disappeared into the camera the way he had disappeared into the glass-walled office this morning. What had happened to the person in that scrapbook that they said was his daddy? Where was the person in the picture they said was Turk? Why had he never told Sally about the connection between them? He could have asked her to marry him. Why hadn't he gone to Austin to see her last night? Why did he wait until he was out of time to tell her? But, what could he have said, what exactly would he have told her? He had never had much to say. There wasn't anything to say.

He tried to think back over his life. He had always heard that your whole life passed before you when you were about to die. He thought of June, remembered her wedding. Someone might have shown him a picture in a scrapbook, a snapshot from June's wedding, and said, There Turk, there *you* are, but he knew it would not have been him. Everything was just as it happened, continuous, like showings at the Lone Star picture show, the present, That was what counted. Not the past squared off in some pretty picture, not the future dreamed up in some fine plan, just doing things right now. This second, this second.

How long since he shot the gun? He couldn't remember pulling the triggers, couldn't remember the noise of the shotgun, couldn't remember the faces of the Mexican men. And if you couldn't even remember it, how could you be sure it had happened? He couldn't fix any picture in his mind, everything jumped around.

Swinging tools for the highway department, swatting at flies, beating rugs for Momma

He tried to remember Momma's face, she almost came into view, then something got in the way, the Coke machine, his dark green shirt hanging on his bedroom door, the dark shape of his shoes on wet grass. His mind was cluttered, he couldn't clean it out, couldn't hold it still. Things kept jumping in front of his eyes. He couldn't remember Sally, couldn't remember the way her back looked when she lay asleep on her side. He thought the pictures, Sally's pink bathroom, her shower curtain, her shape shadowed behind it, but he couldn't see them. How could he be sure he had ever seen them, that anything had happened? The past was a made-up story no more real than the future he had thought out last night that would never happen now.

Swinging a shotgun

In a clutter of mental snapshots Turk saw the hiked-up rear of Jordan West's Chevy, the bare brake drums hanging down, naked, like sex organs, some secret Turk had exposed, the promise he had not kept.

Sudie would be looking for him later, expecting him to come in for coffee. He felt the safety pin, the coins pinned in his shirt pocket.

He could have done that brake job by noon, gone home for Momma's dinner, had coffee with Robert Allen when Jordan's boy came by after school, washed and waxed his car, and left early for Austin.

his reflection in glass

He was not surprised, was not afraid when he pushed the jack out from under his car, but he was unhappy about Jordan's brake job.

The jack clanged against the concrete. Turk's palm came up beneath the car, his arm on the floor, bent at ninety degrees like a waiter carrying a tray over his head, the bones in his wrist snapping as the car settled onto his chest. His lungs filled with blood, quickly hot, like a bad chest cold or inhaling his first cigarette. When he died, Turk was thinking of motor oil.

21

SNOW WAS blowing in the window, piling up on top of her, her legs freezing but unable to move beneath the weight of snow covering her. Then the gas space heater exploded, shooting burning pieces of metal like a roman candle. The explosion woke her, her bed covers, even the bottom sheet, wadded around her legs and feet, the fan humming back and forth across her bed.

"Middle of summer," she said out loud, "and I dream a snow storm."

She got up and threw the quilt over her wadded sheets. She went to her dresser and sat heavily, peering into her swollen eyes.

"Turk," she called, "you up yet, you lazy thing?"

She pulled a comb through her short gray hair and slowly worked her arms into her flannel robe. She hated her fuzzy houseshoes, she had two pair on the floor of her closet, one pair Turk had given her and one pair YCola had given her. YCola, she pronounced her name Y-C-ola, was an old woman who lived two houses down from Eunice and Turk, towards town. She was, Eunice always said, "An ole biddy,

146

full of gossip, rich as cream, and just plain mean." Eunice
had always suspected YCola had gotten the fuzzy houseshoes
herself and didn't like them any better than Eunice did and
that was why she had given them away. Eunice found her
favorite pair of shoes, her only comfortable ones, bought two
sizes too big they didn't hurt when her feet swelled up, and
carefully she laced them all the way up. Later in the day the
laces would be undone, clicking against the floor when she
walked.

The kitchen light was on, Turk must already be up, she
thought. She bent to light the gas oven, calling Turk again as
she leaned her head down to watch the blue flame run the
long U above the broiler.

"Turk," she hollered, "come get your coffee."

Coffee water on, the broiler door left open for the bread
she would toast, she went to hurry Turk, on her way to the
bathroom. But he was gone, his bed unmade, the cap left off
the toothpaste.

Eunice pulled down the shades in his room. It was pretty
cool now, but it would be hot as the hinges of hell in another
hour or two, once the sun got fired up good. She went to the
bathroom and sat down gingerly on the edge of the cold toilet
seat. She was not entirely sure Turk didn't have some disease
she might pick up from the toilet seat. He sure scratched
a lot.

Passing back through his room, she made his bed and
sprinkled talcum powder lightly over the spread. Talcum
powder seemed clean and fresh. She pulled the wick up a
little in the green Air Wick bottle she carried from the bathroom to Turk's bedside table.

She walked around the house, pulling shades, slapping the
backs of soft chairs, bed pillows, the sofa bed, dust particles
floating in the crack of sunlight that had just started coming
through the edge of the front window.

Back in her bedroom, she stood before her mirror holding

her robe open, her blue gown pulled up over her breasts, held up under her chin while she looked at herself. Her white skin hung in loose grins under her arms, under her breasts, looked like the skin on a chicken ready for the oven, the shape of her belly pooching out like the bulge of a chicken breast. She let her gown slip down over her breasts, belly, thighs, drew it tight around her hips and waist. The doctor had told her it would not be a bad idea for her to put on a little weight. She thought maybe she had gained a few pounds. Later, after Turk came in for his breakfast, she would go down to the washateria and weigh herself.

She decided not to make her bed until later, she needed to change the sheets, so she left it and went to pour the boiling water into the coffee pot.

The sun was well up now, she flipped off the kitchen light. Outside she heard a big truck honk, go grinding up the long hill.

During the night she had heard lots of thunder and been waked once by lightning, but now everything looked very pretty, still wet from the rain, shining in the early morning sun. The skies were clearing, it would be another hot one. She was glad she didn't have to go out. She didn't have to go to San Antonio to see the doctor for two more weeks. He had told her she looked fine, he wanted a blood sugar test on her sometime soon, but there was no rush. She was sure she had cataracts on her eyes, but he told her she was just nearsighted, he said she probably just needed her glasses changed.

She had just sat down to drink her coffee when the phone rang. She listened, three short rings, it was hers. Not that it mattered. Lucille Waters would listen in anyway, she always did.

It was Naomi Phelps calling to see if Eunice had any news about Gracie Tucker.

"What about Gracie Tucker?" Eunice had not talked to

Naomi since June's wedding and was upset that something had happened to Gracie and no one had bothered to tell her about it.

"Why Eunice, I would've called you myself, but I thought sure you knew. I was calling you to find out how she was getting along."

"Wait just a minute, Naomi." Eunice went and turned off the flame under the coffee, carried the telephone to the big rocker, the cord stretched taut across the end of the sideboard, "Now, what happened?"

"Well, three days ago she had real bad chest pains and was just real sick. Two nurses at her house kept in touch with Dr. O'Connor over the telephone and he told them what to do for her, but she didn't get much better so they took her on to San Antonio last night in the ambulance. Carl went to stay with her and Betty is going for him this morning to take him to work and then she'll drive back to San Antonio to stay with poor old Gracie. Betty's supposed to talk with Dr. O'Connor later today, he's never at the hospital until after Carl has to leave for work and then he's gone time Carl gets off in the evenings. Dr. O'Connor is feeding her through her veins and says there ought to be a change any day now, for the good or for the bad. He says it could go either way."

"Well, doesn't he know what's wrong with her?"

"Seems like everything in her just collapsed. He says her veins are just caved in, her muscles just wore out. She's stove up real bad, and I don't see how she can live but a few more days. I was down there yesterday and she looks terrible and she can only barely talk and is unconscious most of the time. She asked for Carl but he was gone to work by the time she came to."

"And glad he was, if I know Carl Tillison."

"He did go down to the hospital."

"Naomi, when it gets close to the end all the buzzards

come home to roost. I may be mean, but he'll be right there when her money is divided. She's got more money than the government and no one to leave it to but him and Betty."

"It sure is costing a lot to take care of her. If she hangs on much longer down there she won't have much left time she dies."

"Carl's probably already got her house up for rent, that's why he wanted her in the hospital I bet, get her insurance to pay her bills and he makes money off her house. Then, if she doesn't die, he'll put her away in the rest home."

"She's way up in her nineties, Eunice. You wouldn't want to live alone if you were that old. You're lucky, you've got Turk. Some of us don't have anybody. They're real nice at the rest home. The rooms are all carpeted, have TVs, private bathrooms. I'm plum tired of having to fix my own meals then having to eat them alone. I just might get myself over there in a few more years. You're just lucky having Turk stay with you."

"You know I can't count on Turk, no telling what instructions Sally might give him. She could tell him to move off to Timbuktu and he'd start packing. Besides, it'd be a relief to quit cooking and cleaning for him. What little room and board he gives me is a drop in the bucket, that's all. I wish I was on welfare, and I would be if I could get on."

"Well,"

"Listen Naomi, it's not getting any better. I was down to the Red & White last week, thought I'd make a pecan pie for when Cage got here, well, let me tell you, pecans are up thirty cents a sack. I didn't have enough money to get what little bit of milk and butter and Kayro syrup I needed, ended up making a lemon pie from lemon Jello. Jello is about all a person can afford. And our electric bill was higher this month than ever since I've lived in this house. And the water and gas was nearly double last month. I'm having them

150

check my meters. I wish I could read those things, I know they're stealing me blind."

"Oh, I know it, it's all a person can do just keeping her head above water. Buddy had to have his car worked on last month, they said they couldn't fix it in Johnson City, he had to take it to a man in Stonewall. The man kept it four days and charged him over two hundred dollars to fix it, and it would've been more if Buddy hadn't found some used parts in San Antonio."

"Where did Buddy get two hundred dollars?"

"Well, Eunice, I imagine he did like everybody has to do these days, he's paying it out on time, that's what."

"Did you hear that YCola's son-in-law paid to have her bathroom done over? Nine hundred dollars, I heard. And Lord knows *she* doesn't need any more money."

"I think she had loaned him that money when he married Cherry. She just spent it when he paid her back."

"Well I'll declare there's no one owes me any, it's the other way around. Nobody to leave me any either. But I do think Cage is going to pay for me a new hot water heater."

"Eunice, I forgot to tell you, Olivia's son, the one lives in Baton Rouge, sent her a round trip ticket on the airplane from San Antonio. He's gonna pay for her trip and they're gonna keep her with them for a month."

"Naomi, I guess you and me just have each to comfort the other in our old age. At least we have our minds. I think Olivia is going crazy-sick. They say she talks to Auntie and Papa like they were still alive. And—I hope Lucille Waters isn't listening in, if she is she'll have to cut the phone off when she hears this—last week Dot told me Olivia was running around neckid. Neckid as a jaybird, *not a stitch* of her clothes on. You know, Naomi, I wouldn't be one bit surprised if that's why they're flying her to Louisiana. She might not ever come back."

"I heard she's done that more than once."

"Um-um. I feel so sorry for her."

"I guess it's like they say in the Bible, the strong and the living just have to go on carrying the load for the sick and the infirm and the dead that leave us behind. When it's my time to go I'll sure be ready. Least ways I'll be getting out of here and on to a better place."

"Truer words, Naomi, truer words."

"Oh Eunice I better run along. If you need any tomatoes, I got lots of nice ones. My niece in Johnson City sent me some nice fresh vegetables yesterday. All kinds of fruit, too, bananas, apples, cantaloupe. Some squash, turnips and greens, and snap beans. The cantaloupe are those little Mexican cantaloupe, but they're real sweet."

"Will you bring me some? I love cantaloupe and we never buy any cause it gives Turk heartburn. If you can't come, maybe I can get him to drive me over this afternoon, but getting him to take me anywhere is like pulling teeth."

"Maybe I can right after dinner. I'm going to visit old Mr. Knoll, he's still down with that broke hip. It's not too far from the Knoll place to your house, but it's so almighty hot."

"If it ain't burning hot it's freezing cold. Guess these northerly breezes that thunderhead brought in this morning won't be enough to keep it nice today. It was 98 yesterday in San Antonio and supposed to top 100 today. Maybe it won't be that bad here, but it's already feeling like a scorcher coming on."

"Yeah, seems like summer lasts longer every year. Wouldn't surprise me if it lasted through Christmas this time, I'll call the minute I hear anything on Gracie. She certainly has my prayers."

"Do, Naomi. I don't seem to have any news for you. I better go do my housework and see what's happened to Turk. He still isn't back for his breakfast."

152

Eunice hung up, her ear warm from the telephone. She leaned back in the rocker wondering what had become of Turk and took the first sip of her morning coffee, wincing at the taste, it was stone cold.

22

CAGE answered the phone. Pearlie Fulcher, Sheriff J. J. Pearlie Fulcher, calling from Blanco. Cage had trouble hearing, he and June were watching a television quiz show, the balding history professor from Providence, Rhode Island, trying to come up with the right answer, the concentration music was loud, loud.

Turk was dead. Found by a woman stopping for a Coke at the Sinclair station. "Also," the Sheriff said, "three Messkins. Must of surprised him. He managed to shoot, blew one clean through the wall. Kinda messy. Haven't figured how he got the gun, need an I.D. on it, probably Jordan West's but we can't locate him." Sometime this morning. They'd had Eunice up to the hospital in Johnson City, but she'd be brought back home pretty soon. Naomi Phelps had stayed with her, but she had to leave to visit another friend in the hospital in San Antonio, and someone said they should get June up here to be at the house when Eunice arrived.

Cage pictured June, in their new den, eating Hershey's Kisses, the light of the television on her face. He realized he

154

was shaking his keys in his pocket, saying, yes, yes, they'd drive right up.

In the den he sat back down in the red recliner, waiting to tell her. He didn't know what to expect, didn't know how she'd react. He'd never liked Turk, but this, this might be hard.

The quiz show was almost over. He picked up their paper plates, empty beer cans, watermelon rinds on the bar divider between the kitchen and den. Lazy dinner, afternoon television, television louder when the thermostat kicked the central air conditioning off. Their new house, orange brick, double carport, patio, sliding glass doors. June's breadcrust on her plate, neatly peeled off her sandwich, an empty brown square of crust on her plate. Cage put the ham back in the refrigerator. It smelled sweet, was sticky, cloves sticking like buckshot into the skin, a diamond pattern in the ham fat, like the wrinkled brown skin on the back of Turk's neck. Making room in the crowded refrigerator for the big ham, Cage's finger stuck in the soft stick of margarine, he licked it clean, cold and greasy in his mouth.

In their bedroom, quietly getting their sunglasses, he shook the change in his pocket into his palm, pulled it out. One silver dollar he let slide back down into his pocket, the rest he dropped coin by coin into a blue plastic Planter's Peanut Man on his side of the new mahogany dresser. He'd sold a lakefront lot to a man who worked for a vending machine company. The man sent a Peanut Man bank every month with his payment. Cage had three Peanut Man banks full of change on the floor of his closet. He was going to fill enough of the banks with change to take June to see the Chicago Bears play football in the fall. He'd figured how they could see six football games in Illinois and Ohio on a three-week trip.

He walked slowly down the hall, listening to the soft electric crackle of his socks on the wool carpet, the man on the late movie last night, in rubber socks, walking to the electric chair, the camera following, tracking the feet down the corridor.

He opened the door to the living room. Closed off to save on air conditioning, the living room was hot, smelled like sizing in a fabric shop, reminded Cage of the dry cleaners in Toledo. He shut the door behind him, the cold air shut off behind him, the voices on the television shut off behind him, the memory of the hiss of heavy steam pressing machines deep in the hot brick building of the dry cleaners rising like steam in his mind, the hand-lettered sign over the cleaners' door: Let Us Be Your Clothes Friends.

June had decorated the house. The living room walls were a soft, warm color the paint chart called rosebud pink, the thick carpet, chocolate brown. Against the wall were stiff, mahogany chairs upholstered with pink seats and pink, heartshaped backs. An imitation crystal chandelier hung, suspended from the center of the ceiling. The lady at the lamp shop had been right, he really couldn't tell it from the real thing. The overstuffed sofa, soft velvet stripes, pastel blue, green, yellow. Matching green drapes were drawn across the picture window, behind a tall, skinny lamp. Cage felt like a stranger in the living room. Dust covered the dark mahogany coffee table. He felt like he was in a furniture store, in the showroom window. Living room, they did no living here. If he drew the drapes he imagined he would look out at downtown buildings, cars, buses, people walking back and forth in front of the big window, stopping to look longingly in at the lovely furnishings on display.

He silently turned the doorknob, cracked the door back to the hall, listened like a TV detective. He heard the muted music of the television, the bonus question was being asked, the show would be over in a minute or two. He ran his finger across the top of the little end table by the door, wrote his name in the dust, wrote JUNE beneath CAGE, saw his face reflected in the lines his finger left in the dust.

When he finally told her about Turk she didn't say anything. Then she just nodded, said she had to dress, said she couldn't go in shorts.

He sat on their bed while June changed her clothes, and he rewrapped the elastic bandage he wore around his right shin. He had varicose veins from standing on the concrete floors of grocery warehouses in Ohio. Beneath the wide legs of his pants his legs were surprisingly thin and white. If this bandage is flesh colored, he thought, then I really am a white man. The veins were purple. Office supply, typewriter carbon, mimeo ink, indelible pencil purple. Veins grew up his legs like vines, winter trees, cracks in glass, blue lightning.

June sat before her mirror, tweezers nipping at her eyebrows. He quickly ran his electric razor over his face watching the stubble like dark snow float into the lavatory. Soft buckshot, he thought, and sloshed aftershave lotion on his face so he could feel the sharp sting. Her pink Lady Electric on the shelf where he replaced his. He zipped her dress, imagining the red tracks the metal teeth would make down her back.

June's car, Cage drove. The disappearing blue sky turning into cloud, the whole sky going white, bright like a light bulb, and as hot. June's new Thunderbird, Silver Mink, the sun white, star-white, on the hood, silver-dollar silver. Chrome and ice-white inside, air-conditioned cold, air-conditioned quiet.

She asked him again, all the sheriff had told him. About bodies, blood, the kick of the shotgun, the sequence.

"What else? Tell me Cage, tell me everything."

"There was something. A missing thumb. Two were shot off, they only found one, didn't know for sure where to fit the one they found."

June held her thumb up like a hitchhiker. He could see

157

that it might become a joke, "The Case of the Missing Thumb." Sherlock Holmes, Perry Mason, the late movie.

The speedometer, one reason Cage had bought June the Thunderbird, registered up to 140. The drive to Blanco took forty-five minutes by the clock in the dash. Coming down the hill to cross over the bridge he hit a jackrabbit. He swerved to miss it, but the jackrabbit swerved too. The right front tire bumped, softly, very quietly. A good heavy car. A good solid-feeling thunk that didn't lose the rhythm of the road, the speed. June made a soft laughing sound deep in her throat, said nothing.

An old Studebaker met them on the bridge, the driver touching the brim of his Stetson, nodding to them. Did he know about Turk, did he know who they were, Cage wondered. A white-haired woman stopped sweeping her front walk when they passed, stared openly at them, holding her palm over her eyes against the glare. And her, did she know?

June wanted to go to the Sinclair first. There were still several highway patrol and sheriff's cars, a television news car from San Antonio was just driving away.

Sheriff Fulcher was there. "Three am-bu-lances," he said. "Three am-bu-lances and we still didn't have enough for everyone to have his own am-bu-lance. Put two of the Messkins in together. Beats all I've ever seen."

Sheriff Fulcher stopped and lowered his voice, told June in a slow monotone how sorry he was about her brother, that just about everybody in Blanco County knew Turk and they sure never would've thought something like this would've happened to old Turk. Then he filled them in: Turk had been taken to Johnson City where a doctor at the hospital had pronounced him dead, of course he was dead before that lady ever found him, but it had to be official for the state. He should be on his way back to Blanco right now. They would take the body to the funeral home, then deliver it to the house after it was prepared for the services. Eunice was wait-

158

ing at the funeral home now. Naomi Phelps was there too, waiting for June. None of the Messkins had been identified yet, Sheriff Fulcher reckoned they were all at the morgue in Johnson City. One of Jordan West's boys had come by and identified the shotgun, it was Jordan's all right. He'd gone fishing and wouldn't be back till late, he still didn't know about Turk. They should go on over to Eunice's, the sheriff would try to come by later for a word with her himself, in the meantime tell her for him how sorry he was.

Some boys were searching the pavement around the station yelling that they were going to find the missing thumb. As he got in the car, Cage heard Sheriff Fulcher tell them that the one who found it could ride with him in the squad car to take it to the morgue in Johnson City.

23

THEY PUT Turk on the dining room table. They had tried the old sideboard first, but it had leaned and creaked with the weight of him. The big table was fine, and there was enough room for the glass punch bowl June's ex-boss had given her for a wedding present and Eunice especially admired.

Four rows of metal folding chairs in the living room faced the double french doors into the dining room, the table with Turk on it scooted up against the doorway. The french doors, with their small panes of glass reflecting the ceiling light, opened out into the living room, Turk's coffin was tilted up enough for June to see his forehead and the end of his nose catching the light.

Was that really her brother? How had he come to this?

Cage on her left, his collar tight, his face red, a little triangle of toilet paper stuck to his neck. How had he nicked himself with an electric razor? He looked as stiff as Turk.

Turk's suit, bought yesterday for the funeral, tight across his chest. What did they do, split the clothes open down the back? Easier to dress them that way, when they're so stiff.

160

Like doll clothes really, just fastened around the hard neck. Cage cut his neck. Nicked his neck, neckid nick on his neck. Coffin, coffee in the kitchen, coughing. Coughing up blood, coffee break, break neck, neck broke, dead throat, blood goat.

There is pow'r, pow'r, wonder working pow'r
In the precious blood of the lamb.

They'd left soap under Turk's fingernails, little white crescents, crescent moons. His hand was stuck over his chest, slipped under the edge of the new suit coat like he was reaching for something in his pocket. Cigarettes? Wallet? Handkerchief? Business card? Pistol? Shoot with your eyes closed.

Momma on her right, June could smell her new black dress. Momma looked smaller, older, looked lost in the high collar and wide sleeves. The dress looked like a choir robe. Momma had dark bags under her eyes and she had streaked her makeup with crying all morning. She looked like pictures in *National Geographic* of hundred-year-old, wrinkled, wise native women, someone from high in a remote mountain village. June almost expected her to throw up her arms and begin chanting and wailing some strange native dirge.

Someone at the front door was telling people to view the body now. Single file. Down this row, take a good hard look, nod to Eunice, back up the other side.

June wondered if the back of his head would leave an oil stain on the satin pillow, a small dark circle like the one on her carport.

Why hadn't Sally come?

Had anyone ever slept in a coffin? Beforehand? Had anyone made love in a coffin? Hadn't she read something about that, something she read in a magazine at the beauty parlor? Satin sheets. Sperm color. Coffin come. Have to lie doubledeck, no room for side-by-side. Someone told her once that Mexicans bury standing up. Were the three Mexicans being buried today too? Were they already in the ground, standing up down there? Would their legs rot and their bodies crumble to their knees? Would their necks rot and their heads fall into their hands?

Brother Bailey stood in front of Turk in his coffin, head bowed.

There on stage, spotlights on the glass panes. He turned to the coffin, the lid up. A piano recital, the lid up, exposing the shining wires. Bailey lifted his arms, moved his mouth.

Would you o'er Satan a Vic'to'ry win?

There's pow'r in the blood, pow'r in the blood

The little brace folded with a click and the lid dropped shut, locked tight. You're about a half quart down Missus, better get it checked next time you fill up.

Silver handles curved around the corners of the coffin like grins, chrome trim, bumpers.

All rise.

Every head bowed and every eye closed, *Dearly Beloved, we are gathered together*

Did the dead really turn over in their graves? Did Turk have his face down now, deep in his small satin pillow? If he arched his back would the lid pop open?

Where was Sally?

Brother Bailey raised his head. A whisper, *Be seated please.* Cage coughed, his arm softly bumped her shoulder. A truck whined by on the highway.

For a thousand years in Thy sight are but as yesterday when it is past, and as a watch in the night.

Why was everyone so quiet? He couldn't hear, the lid was shut. Satin insulated. Soundproof satin, soundproof room.

Thou carriest them away as with a flood; they are as a sleep: in the morning they are like grass which groweth up. In the morning it flourisheth, and groweth up; in the evening it is cut down, and withereth.

From his empty room, Turk's alarm clock ticked. Bare floors carried dust and sounds. Turk's shape still lay on his bed, the empty mattress sagging from an old weight. Turk sleeping through everything as usual, snoring, clock ticking.

For we are consumed by Thine anger, and by Thy wrath are we troubled.

Coffin bomb. His body had already begun the slow explosion. Inside. Ticking. Time bomb. The coffin sliding around in the belly of a bomber, falling smoothly out of the bomb bay, hitting the earth with a soft thud, a dud, sinking deep, dirt falling in on top. A mound. A dud. A slow fuse. To lie, ticking, dormant. God will lean down and see the mound and dig in with His huge white fingers and Turk will go off in God's hand like an old firecracker.

The days of our years are threescore years and ten

Cage on her left, Momma on her right. Behind her the hush of held breath; buttoned collars and knotted ties; combed hair; lowered veils; soft white gloves and folded hands; polished, heavy, motionless shoes, side-by-side on the floor.

Where was Sally?

for it is soon cut off, and we fly away

Folded tight in the warm coffin, Turk was growing wings. Damp coffin. Dark cocoon. Thin, moist, transparent wings, growing in folds in the crowded, satin chamber, accordion folds, folded and packed like a waiting parachute.

So teach us to number our days

The light reflected on Momma's leg, making her stocking shine. Did she feel the light on her leg? The sting of the white circle of light a magnifying glass made. Sitting in the dirt, Turk holding the round glass, Armon's gift. June watching Turk's eye, large, rounded, through the thick, round lens. The sweet death smell of singed hair, soft sun-bleached fuzz on June's small leg. The mystery of magnification, looking close, the fiery death of a grasshopper on a rock, wings moving, clear and bright in the sun. Suddenly smoke came out of his body before he could fly, watching him die, smell-

163

ing him fry, watching Turk's fingerprint on the glass, watching Turk's eye. *Four and twenty blackbirds baked in a pie.* Had it been so many years? And now. Turk was in there now, the lid was locked. Men were lifting, carrying his box.

The hearse and limousine, new Cadillacs, so black they turned purple in the sun.

June and Cage sat on each side of Eunice on the wide back seat. Buddy Wilkinson, who'd taken over the funeral home when his daddy died, stood by the front door watching them loading the casket. The driver of the limousine was the high school football team's fullback, the driver of the hearse played halfback and defensive end. June had seen their pictures in the San Antonio newspaper. The fullback had the engine running, the air conditioning on high. The end of summer, the hottest time.

No one spoke. They sat listening to the engine and the fan blowing the cool air into the limousine.

While they waited, people were walking slowly out of the house to their automobiles, pick-up trucks. Slowly, like they were ashamed, a few people drove into position behind the limousine, their headlights turned on in the bright sun.

No one spoke. June listened to the metal sounds of the coffin being loaded in front of them. Turk would be first in line.

Don't ever laugh when a hearse goes by
For you may be the next to die

When had she first heard that? At school? Was it Turk she had first heard sing it?

They'll wrap you up in a big white sheet
And drop you down about six feet.

So loud, over and over in her mind. She thought Cage and Momma must hear it coming out of her ears, escaping through her nose, gurgling out of her mouth. The chorus was laughter, loud giggling, school kids yelling and teasing and giggling.

164

Buddy Wilkinson nodded to the boy driving the hearse, it moved smothly away from the edge of the yard onto the highway. Then he slid into the limousine and nodded to the fullback and they slipped quietly in behind the hearse. Like a football play, June thought, the halfback leading off with the ball tucked in behind him, the fullback following in case he fumbled.

Approaching cars pulled over to let them pass. Honoring the dead. Keeping their distance.

No townspeople on the sidewalks to tip their hats, bow their heads. Blanco was empty. They went through the first intersection, the purple reflection in the green glass of store-fronts, an oil slick on glass ponds. The sun burned deep into the black back of the hearse, oily rainbows down in the metal.

When you get old and think you're sweet
Take off your shoes and smell your feet

The same tune, same loud chorus of giggling. A woman in a convertible, drinking a Coke, out-of-state license plates, waiting for them to pass. Staring, tipping the bottle of Coke up in the sun.

Lots of water, for the end of summer, in the river. Soft circles of shade along the river. No one fishing. No one pic-nicking.

Cage smiled at her, squeezed her arm. Momma cleared her throat, said nothing.

They stopped. The cemetery still a half-mile up on the right.

"What is it, what's the matter?" asked Eunice.

Buddy Wilkinson got out, one leg on the hot pavement, one still in the cool Cadillac. His door window was a green square against the sky.

"Mexican funeral," he said.

As he said it, June saw the coffin stick out of the side of the hearse, then emerge, carried across the highway in front of

165

them by six figures, black against the bright sunlight. She thought again of the three Mexicans. Could it be one of their funerals? But they were probably still in the morgue in Johnson City, waiting to be claimed. She leaned over to Cage's side and saw the line of people moving slowly up the road from the colony.

"It's old Gertie," Buddy Wilkinson said. "You know, they didn't even embalm her. That's how those people are." He was back inside the limousine, his door shut. "Guess we'll just have to wait till they get across."

"I didn't know Gertie died," Eunice said.

Buddy Wilkinson spoke without turning to face them, "Say she was just full of tumors. Dr. O'Connor finally got her to let him operate. Found one big as a avocado. Just sewed her back up."

No one said anything.

June had been hearing stories about Gertie since she was old enough to listen. They called her Iron Gertie, because she came around to do people's ironing. She was from Old Mexico and always acted like she didn't understand English, but folks said she spoke plain as anybody when she wanted to.

The color of the old pennies she carried tied in a knot in her handkerchief, Gertie gave off the smell a rifle barrel left on a man's hands after he'd been hunting. Her hair was tied in a knot too, hard and black as Easter's muscles before he got killed, shiny as a chicken snake, smooth as the skin on an eggplant. Easter was an old black man who did odd jobs and lived with Gertie commonlaw. Over and over, June had heard the story, how Easter was working on the railroad and got himself coupled in half by that big snapping turtle hookup on the cars.

After Easter got killed, Gertie moved into Boardhouse, the old post office out at the colony. Mexicans didn't have to live in the colony any more, not since June was too young to

166

remember, and most of the old houses and few stores were deserted, so all the children Gertie took in had the whole colony to roam. June had always been fascinated by the old settlement, a few miles from town. She had heard stories about the sundown laws that made it illegal for Mexicans to remain in town after sundown, and had heard scary stories about lynchings and beatings. Long after the sundown laws had been wiped out and most of the scary stories forgotten, the colony where the Mexicans lived together seemed to hold secrets in the dark grains of the weatherbeaten board buildings. Gertie had just moved in to take advantage of the free rent, and no one had ever questioned her squatter's rights. She had well water and kerosine lamps and cooked on a wood fire. Dr. O'Connor had been one of the first white people to visit Gertie in Boardhouse, and he said she had one wall done up with wanted posters and one wall stamped all over with FIRST CLASS in black and AIR MAIL in red. He said she served all those kids refried beans through the stamp window and the kids practiced safecracking on the combination dials on the row of brass mailboxes that divided Boardhouse into two rooms. Dr. O'Connor had been known to spruce up his stories some, but June always liked the picture of Gertie's adopted kids all lined up at the stamp window for their suppers.

The fullback revved the engine and they began moving again. June turned and looked behind them at the pairs of yellow headlights. As they drove past, Gertie's funeral procession stopped, the short line of people standing in the ditch along the highway.

Gertie's coffin was wooden, unpainted. Six men in shiny black suits held it, looking light as a leaf, on their shoulders. Each man rested the box on his inside shoulder, each held his inside arm beneath the coffin, three on each side, locking arms with the men opposite them, forming a cradle the coffin rode on. Each man seemed to bow his head as Turk's hearse

167

drove by, each held his hat, black hats, stiffly out from his dark, shining forehead, in his free hand. Six straight arms, each out and up at the same angle, six dark suit arms, six white strips of shirt cuff, six dark hands, six dark hats, six dark faces covered with sweat, expressionless.

"That's for Turk, June. It's for Turk," Eunice said. "They're taking their hats off to Turk."

"Like soldiers in drill," said Buddy Wilkinson.

June watched behind them as they drove on to the cemetery. Gertie's six pallbearers had not moved, her mourners stood in the ditch waiting for every car to pass.

June was still looking out the back window when the limousine turned off the highway into the cemetery and the sun hit her directly in the eyes. Those men, those six dark skinned, dark suited, dark hatted men, were holding their hats, not off to Turk, were holding their hats against the Texas sun.

In the shadow of a row of cedar trees, they stopped, the heavy limousine shuddering, then the engine stopped. Buddy Wilkinson waited a minute, then slowly got out and opened the door for Eunice. As they walked into the sunlight, going farther up the hill, June heard the squeak of the rollers as the coffin was slid out of the hearse. Jordan West and Robert Allen were the only pallbearers June recognized. Momma had made up the list with Buddy Wilkinson's help. Below, close to the bottom of the hill, car doors were slamming. People started slowly up the incline behind them, keeping a respectful distance, men taking long strides over rocks and weeds, women walking carefully in high heels.

Cage helped Eunice, had an arm around her shoulder. He hadn't said anything this morning when he and June were dressing. She was glad for the silence.

They'll wrap you up in a big white sheet
a big white sheet, a big white sheet

168

They reached a raw mound of dirt where Buddy Wilkinson was directing two boys who were hurriedly setting up more metal folding chairs. The same chairs from the living room? Had they run up and down the rows folding them up, loaded them on a truck, into another hearse, then raced around behind the square, over the new highway bridge, and gotten here ahead of them, just in time to set the chairs up again? June wanted to run back to the house and see if the chairs were gone, the living room empty.

Turk was on a kind of scaffold over the hole, and people were crowding into chairs, leaving the first row empty for Momma and Cage and her. When she sat down June thought the seat still felt warm. Was it the chair she had sat in back in Momma's living room?

June wanted to scoot her chair back, afraid the edge of earth around Turk's open grave might give way. She looked down the hill they had walked up, looked for Gertie, but couldn't see over Turk's coffin. She stood up so she could see and Momma grabbed her arm, Momma's face jerking up at her, small and white under a black hat. June stepped behind Momma and held Momma's shoulders.

Below, the little dark line of Mexican people moved slowly into the cemetery. Gertie's coffin was just a little shape, a brown pellet on the road, almost lost in all that space.

June wondered if Gertie wore the same striped rebozo, even now, inside the hot box. The same striped rebozo June had always seen her wearing, winter and summer the same, every time she had ever seen Gertie. Built like a fat, dark snowman, her round body balancing her round head, Gertie reminded June of African women she had seen in movies, carrying jugs and baskets on their heads.

Brother Bailey was on stage again. Talking very softly. June could barely hear what he was saying. No one on the back row would be able to hear him. He mumbled. Probably, June thought, he preached like that too, and then wondered why he didn't save more souls.

Everyone was standing to sing. Not Momma. Momma was going to sit and listen. What was the song? "The Old Rugged Cross?" That was not right, that was an Easter song. She knew that song.

stood an old rug'ed cross
a big white sheet, a big white sheet

She pictured the people grabbing a big white sheet, all holding it by the edges, flipping Turk's body up into the air, catching him on the sheet, bouncing him higher and higher, the sheet billowing up after his body, jerking down when he hit, sagging with his weight, then arching up again, the people holding the sheet, heaving, singing.

a big white sheet, a big white sheet

June looked again for Gertie. Getting closer, Gertie's coffin looked like one of the fat cigars Cage sometimes smoked. She felt Momma's shoulder blades beneath old, loose skin, and squeezed until her knuckles were white and Momma whispered to stop, it was hurting her. In the heat, June smelled the dirt. In the heat, she smelled Momma's new dress, remembered the smell of the bathroom when she was a little girl, the smell Momma left in the bathroom, stronger than the Air Wick sticking up out of the bottle, the strong smell of the rolls of gauze in the wastebasket that Turk had thrown at her and called, on the rag.

It was almost over. Bailey was reading the Bible again. He did *that* loud enough.

For whosoever shall call upon the name of the Lord shall be saved.

At the bottom of the hill, Gertie's coffin floated above a short cedar tree. Dr. O'Connor had said Gertie had had the tumor in her side a long time. Gertie said she'd been born with it. Dr. O'Connor told how Gertie was so fat and sore

170

she had to sit sideways on the bed and bend her knee up and reach down sideways to buckle her shoes. He told how old Gertie couldn't get going in the mornings without those kids of hers. He said they pulled her underpants over her shoes and up over those big legs and huge hips, while she worked a dress down over her big round head.

June wondered how Gertie managed to make the four miles she walked every day from the colony to Blanco and four miles back after she was done with her ironing.

Turk's last song, "Nearer My God to Thee." Softly.

June remembered Gertie's eyes, black as the blacktopped road she always walked to town.

At the bottom of the hill Gertie's coffin rested on a big rock. The Mexicans were taking turns with two shovels, everyone was digging some, the men, the women, the girls, the boys. Gertie's children were all there, most of them orphans people had brought by asking if Gertie could take them for just a little while. They squatted and knelt among the wooden crosses and aluminum grave markers in the part of the cemetery set aside for Mexicans and for colored people.

Momma stood up when Turk's casket was lowered into the ground. No one had cried yet. The straps were pulled out and the pallbearers tossed in flowers from their lapels.

Some people were already leaving, most were lined up to hug Momma, say something to her. Most spoke also to Cage, to June. The boys who worked for Buddy Wilkinson stood a short distance away, having a cigarette, waiting to finish the job and go home. After she and Cage and Momma started back to the limousine, June watched the boys roll up the artificial grass, so green against the rocks and caliche dirt. They folded the chairs and took the silver scaffolding Turk had been lowered from, but they left the grave open, the dirt in a pile beside it. June didn't see anyone who looked like a gravedigger. No shovels but the two moving steadily at the bottom of the hill, digging Gertie's resting place.

Dr. O'Connor just sewed her back up. Tumor big around as an avocado. Hard, dark green. The bulges of body, big cheeks, wide, flared nostrils, bulging knot of black hair, breasts, belly, huge thighs and calves pulled in tight behind smooth, worn knees, her excess flesh tucked and held behind those knees like stuffing pulled into the shape of a star beneath the button in a mattress. Gertie should have had a coffin at least as big as a double bed. Did all the air go out of her when she died? Did they lay her, coiled up upon her shriveled self, in the corner of her coffin?

Buddy Wilkinson had the air conditioner fan on so high in the limousine that June couldn't even hear the dirt and rocks under the big tires, and she felt as if they were riding on air, slowly floating out of the cemetery. Then they were back onto the paved road, the huge car shot out from under the shadow of the hill, and June winced at the sun, still high in the sky above the hills that were everywhere.

24

Wed. nite

Dear Cage and June,

Thank you all for the letter and nice check. Things are so high it is hard to get by. My electric bill was overdue this week and I got a notice in a red envelope. I think they do that so everyone in town will see that red spot in your box and shame you into paying. And my gas has gone up too. With Turk gone I miss the little bit he gave for the house running money. I can't believe he's gone and don't know what's to become of me now.

Well, here it is October and soon to be cold again. It will be Halloween and Mexican kids all over raising cane. Sometimes I get scared here all alone. If I was up to it I'd dust flour all over me and scare wits out of those hoodlums. That little Malone boy— he's those Irish people's kid, immigrants or something, they just moved to town—he's a devil and runs with that awful tomboy girl Sherry Smith. They ought to be put in jail.

I needed to go to the eye Dr. Thurs. but cancelled my appointment. I just didn't have any way to go without Turk to drive me. They said they will take me the day after Thanksgiving, the Dr.

173

will be there until noon. So I'm going to count on youall coming here for Thanksgiving and then running me over there the next day. I can't believe Turk has been dead over a month already and won't be with us Thanksgiving.

Thank you Cage for paying for the sidewalk. I hated to be the only poor one on the block without one. They layed it real nice and it will be good this winter to keep out of the mud. Hope you got home the other nite o.k. in that fog. Guess we'll have lots more bad weather before it gets good again. Jordan West came by today and said they had a shower down at Little Blanco but it was sunshiney here. I spent the whole entire day alone unless you count Jordan West coming by for five minutes. Can't get anything but snow on our old t-v and the paper didn't come. I can't see to read anyway. I can't see period. I poured hot grease on my thumb and made 2 big blisters and today burned the thumb on the other hand. The handle broke off the broiler on the cook stove and I worked and worked to try and fix it and couldn't. I must be just getting old. Ha!

A drunk Mexican with a load of pipe ran through that new Schonhauer Cafe at Fredricksburg about three oclock one night last week and simply tore it up. It was damaged about $6000 but didn't hurt the mexican. If it was eating time probably 25 or 50 people would be dead and cars tore up where they park out front.

I hope you can read this. This lite is so bad and I can't see for beans.

Come see me for I am all alone now.

Love,
Eunice Momma

25 JUNE SLEPT late, sometimes until noon, and by the time she woke up Cage would be gone, out at the property selling lots. She never ate breakfast when Cage was not home, but had instant coffee and smoked several ciga-rettes. She had started smoking after Cage asked her to marry him, but no one knew. She hid cigarettes in the toes of shoes, wrapped the shoes in tissue paper and kept them in shoeboxes in the back of her closet.

Her slow waking-up ritual was a great pleasure, and she prepared for it every night when she went to bed, carefully arranging each object on her bedside table. The clock radio with the luminous dial she turned catty-cornered so she could reach the knob and switch it on without opening her eyes. Her compact and lipstick, the lipstick upright on top of the compact, on top of the radio. A cup holding one level teaspoonful of instant coffee between the radio and the bed, and beside the cup, the Traveller's Percolator, a gift from Cage. Allowing for evaporation, she poured just over one full cup of water into the little pot every night. In the morn-

175

ing she plugged it into the side of the radio. Beneath the edge of the radio she carefully hid two cigarettes to last until she was ready to get out of bed.

After her first cup of coffee, she went into the guest bathroom that was seldom used, sat on the toilet, and smoked, reading the funnies and the sports section of the morning paper. Since Turk's funeral she had watched the sports pages for news or pictures of the Blanco High football players who had driven the hearse and the limousine. Finishing the newspaper, she flushed her cigarette butts down the toilet, and shook perfume into the toilet bowl, bathtub, and lavatory. Then she went back to her own bathroom to soak in a deep tub of hot water. She sprinkled bath oil over the water and watched the rainbows light made on the oil slicks and slowly soaped herself. After her bath she always dusted herself all over with Johnson's Baby Powder.

She had her second cup of coffee sitting across from herself in her dresser mirror. Blue beneath her skin, a small vein was visible in one breast, and she ran her fingers slowly along the line, imagining the miles of veins running through her body, like wires holding her together, the hot current of her blood charging her body with energy. She ran her hands along her collarbone, feeling the flesh sink in on each side of the ridges of bone that slid in from her shoulders to the center of her chest, forming an arrow that pointed down between her breasts.

Carefully, she shaved beneath her arms with Cage's old silver safety razor. He had bought her a Lady Electric shaver, like his new electric, but she liked the feel of the thick shaving cream and warm water beneath her arms, liked the soft sound of the blade moving across skin. She liked tending to her body, the different motions she had to make, her different smells, the way her hair grew thick in the folds of her body, beneath her arms, between her hips, between her

176

thighs. She wondered why hair did not grow damp and thick between her fingers and toes, behind her knees where her legs hinged. She took her heavy gold comb and carefully combed her dark pubic hair, combing away from her body, down from her navel, in the direction of the arrow of bone between her breasts. She ran her hands down each leg, held one leg at a time up off the stool, feeling the weight of each leg in her arms. She pulled on her stockings. She always wore them, they made her legs feel firmer, silkier. Sitting naked, except for the nylons, legs spread, knees bent, feet hooked behind the back legs of the dresser stool, she pulled the cold comb through the curly, dark pubic hair, watching the curls straighten, then slowly float back into place, the comb making gentle swells in the hair, dark waves on dark water. She parted the thick hair down the middle in line with her navel, and combed it out to either side. She slipped the comb deep into the hair, flat against her skin, and pulled it straight up, electricity in the comb drawing the hair up and out, leaving it puffed up and full, a bush, a soft porcupine, a pillow of hair. She held the comb up by her face looking in the mirror at two dark hairs caught in the teeth, how much darker than the brown hair framing her face. Because, she thought, it grows in darkness, the cave, the cellar, the dark room, the damp, deep room.

She made thin black lines over her eyelids and brushed her lashes darker, thicker. The lipstick she used was the color of her skin, the manufacturer called it Natural Love Shade. It made her lips look wet, coppery, with a silver sheen. The delicate creases of skin, parallel lines that ran up and down, close together across each lip, tiny cracks in her skin filling up with the coppery color, copper shining through silver like the edge of a new, mint silver dollar. She painted her fingernails and toenails the same satin silver. She wore no jewelry but her wedding rings and a single strand of real pearls Cage had given her. All her dresses were expensive. She never wore a hat.

In the Thunderbird the radio was always on. Rear speaker, a soft, bass voice behind the backseat talking about a new Hitchcock movie opening downtown staring Cary Grant. She backed down the driveway fast, the underside of the Thunderbird scraped the pavement when it dipped out of the drive into the street. The voice on the radio changed, a new voice started talking about a man, a teenager, in Nebraska, who had been sentenced to the electric chair for killing eleven people.

Summer was over, the days were getting shorter, darkness came earlier, it was turning cooler, but June wore no sleeves. Sunlight through tinted glass colored the soft hair on her arms. Through windows rolled tightly up she heard only deep noises, heavy, muffled noises: thick, fat tires on concrete, an invisible airplane above the clouds, a power mower several houses away rolling smoothly over someone's lawn.

Driving, she felt free, aimless, but still in control, on her own, on the move, exploring, driving, driving. The powerful automobile responded quickly and smoothly to her small foot on the accelerator, turned easily with one hand on the steering wheel. Weighing a hundred pounds, she was moving this machine that weighed two tons. Locked and belted inside behind posts and sheets of metal, dark squares of thick glass, she felt disguised by the automobile as she moved anonymously around the city.

She drove down to the new loop, maneuvering the Thunderbird easily through a detour, between the orange rubber cones marking the construction area. As she dipped beneath an elevated span of the expressway, she saw a man riding a jackhammer. The noise sounded slowed-down, a record played at slow speed. The man held the silver handle just below his waist and moved up and down, this too, slowed,

178

like a slow motion film of a bronc-buster trying to hang on at a rodeo, every second worth more money. It was the movie scene of a man pushing the T down into the box, followed by the dull, distant explosion of a mountain, gray, black, brown, smoke and earth filling the screen, coming right at her. Or, science-fiction, the man weightless, the jackhammer a giant electro-magnet jerking along the metal floor of the spaceship, the man holding on, his legs, body, floating—space pulling at him. Or, he was the TV doctor, struggling with the huge hypo, he had to get the needle through the thick skin of the Incredible Fifty-Foot Man who was waking up, the needle skipping off the huge, bulging arm like a ricocheting bullet off a steel wall.

June left the scene behind. Left behind the fast new expressway, the rows of arching mercury lightpoles, the new suburban office buildings of clear glass and shining metal. Left behind the red, white, and blue billboards: Vote For Frank "Bud" Holcomb, Let Bud Bloom For You In City Government—a giant daisy splashed against a grinning picture of Frank "Bud" Holcomb. She got off the expressway and drove down into the crowded, dirty parts of town where wooden houses seemed to lean together to keep from falling down, built up on ridges on each side of the narrow streets, each house holding its dirty skirt up above its ankles, its bare feet standing in the street against the curb covered with empty cardboard boxes, RC bottles, and beer cans, popsicle sticks. The people, porch people, sitting, rocking, staring. Old, old women, fat in sagging porch swings or rocking chairs so small they looked to be taking bites out of the heavy buttocks the fat women stuck into them. Young women, hair in big blue curlers or phosphorescent-looking silk scarves, holding babies, diapers stark white beneath dark, bowling-ball bodies, hanging like fat ticks to their mothers' breasts.

She passed little grocery stores, bars with the front windows painted over, names like Paradise, Goddess, Sunrise,

179

Silver Moon. Sometimes the narrow front door of a bar would open, quick flash, jerking frame of film, a dark, laughing man in striped pants or brightly colored shoes dancing— in or out?—caught in some twist of his body, his long fingers curling around something, a cigarette, a knife, a straight razor? June looked in opened doors, always dark, a dark moment, a shadowy blink. Maybe the hint of colored lights, little lights like Christmas tree lights, a pinball machine, a jukebox, or a bubbling electric beer sign. Sometimes a woman's leg, bare to the thigh, then lost in darkness, bare flesh hanging off the edge of a stool, colored light swimming up the skin. Sometimes the colored arches of men's backs bent over a pool table in a cone of yellow light, the serious huddle the shape of a upturned bowl, a Jello mold.

They always stared. Sometimes they whistled, yelled at her. June never answered, never went inside, but she sought out these streets, drove off a wide, fast, clean street, down into these bumpy, close, warmer streets where her heart beat faster and she felt heavy beads of sweat hang, break, and trickle down her side, down the space between her breasts, the back of her jersey dress stuck to her skin.

She went shopping downtown, pulled the Thunderbird into a cool, dark parking garage, rode a tiny elevator up to the big department store. The middle of the week, no one in the men's department, the Stag Shop. Just June and the clerk, a young man, probably a college boy working his way through school, looking uncomfortable in the suit and vest and shining cuff links which stuck out of his coat sleeves. June dawdled, ran her hand over material, slipped her fingers into cool pockets lined with satin. She bought colored shirts for Cage, ties to match, a bright red silk handkerchief to stick out of Cage's coat pocket like a fat, flapping tongue. The young clerk recited sales talk, blended wool, very durable, all season weight. June asking him to try things on for her, turn around so she could see the back. He, nervous as a pent up horse, backing into the rack of suits, stepping on his own polished shoe. His thin, blond hair parted perfectly, combed carefully, like he'd just stepped into the men's room and slicked it down. His skin smooth, no beard, his lips dark and puffy. Touching his soft cheek when she held a tie up against his collar. Wanting to put a finger to his full upper lip, imagining her fingernail would tear a little hole and sink into air under his skin, like a pastry. Charging it all, signing her name slowly, his hand leaving a moist palm print on the thin carbon paper of the charge pad.

Imagining him inside the Thunderbird with her. Slowly rubbing his hands from his thighs to his knees on the dark wool trousers, the smell of new clothes on the back seat, the windows sealed. Letting her dress ride up to her thighs, leaning across him to get her sunglasses from the glove compartment, brushing across his shoulder, the material tightening across her breasts as she stretched out her arm. Music, behind the backseat, Ray Price singing "I Wish I Could Fall in Love Today."

The boy put the charge slip into a gold cylinder, snapped it shut, and slipped it into a pipe that ran up into the ceiling.

Maybe he lived with his mother in a hot little apartment over a grocery store, his father long gone, his younger sisters in school, his mother taking in ironing. He was no college boy, he had to work to support his family. She would help him. She would take him home in her big car. They would stop at a curb service drive-in for a hamburger and beer, the metal tray at the car window, laughing and drinking beer until the blue neon lights came on, neon buzzing, Elvis coming from the jukebox inside, speakers hung outside under the canopy they parked beneath.

Feeling lighthearted, good from the beer, she would drive toward the cramped apartment where his mother and three sisters lived with him. Lights on all around them, headlights and streetlights racing by in bright, liquid lines, the Thun-

181

derbird a molten shape of silver, June and this blond boy in a time-lapse photograph. They would not talk while she drove. She would drive very fast and very sure.

She would park in a dark alley and they would walk across a dead strip of grass, under sagging clothesline wires, and up rickety, wooden outside stairs, come through a rusted screened porch cluttered with empty milk bottles and a mop dripping gray water, into a tiny kitchen crowded with a porcelain-topped table and four wooden chairs. She would follow him down a little hallway, a linoleum runner on the floor, past his mother's room, a glimpse of her through the cracked door, barefoot and in her slip, her face hidden by her hair, her forearms shining with sweat.

In his room, right next door to his mother, they would hear the soft bump and squeak of her iron moving back and forth on the ironing board, and June would undress, let her expensive dress fall on the dusty floor. His ears red, goose bumps on his thin legs, she would lie on top of him in his narrow bed and make love to him, quickly but gently. Then, while he slept, she would slip out of the bed and dress, the ironing in the next room stopped. She would leave money, a lot of money, beneath his pillow, like the tooth fairy. She would be his fairy queen. She would visit him in his dreams. She would never see him again.

Carrying the bags of Cage's new clothes, June rode to the top floor of the department store to the Ranch Room, where she had the fruit plate lunch and looked out at San Antonio. She sat a long time, smoking and looking at the rooftops of buildings.

Cage would not be home until late, way after dark. Business had been real good lately, more people had been coming out in the evenings after they got off work. Cage thought the billboard was finally paying off, that and the ad he'd put in the paper.

June drove to the Greyhound bus station. She liked to go to the bus station and watch people coming and going. She sat at the horseshoe-shaped counter and ordered a cup of coffee. Next to her a woman swung a huge purse up against the counter and started looking over the menu. The waitress came to take the woman's order.

"Is your hamburger fresh?"

The waitress shrugged, said she guessed so.

"I must keep up my *strenth*," the woman said. She said *strenth*, not *strength*. Maybe a foreigner, June thought. "And your milkshake, is it nice and thick?"

The waitress was chewing gum. She shifted the gum to one side of her mouth and grinned, showing the gray wad between her teeth. "Thick shakes is one thing we got for sure," she said.

The foreign woman turned to June as if June had been part of the conversation all along. "I got to keep up my *strenth*," she said. "For the long trip. I am going to California, you know. My son is out there. Went right after he got home from the war. He does something to TVs. He wrote they have their own swimming pool in the yard." She ordered a hamburger and a pineapple milkshake. She took a hand mirror out of her huge purse and inspected her face, then smiled at June, "I do hate riding the bus, do you also?"

June pretended she didn't hear, took a drink of coffee, the bright overhead light floating on top, lowering her head until it blocked the light out, the coffee dark and bottomless again.

The woman leaned over, June heard the rustle of her skin in her clothes, smelled her powder and perfume. She put her hand on June's arm, fingers wrinkled where the skin ended at the tips of her fingers, as if she had been put together at an upholstery shop, the skin gathered at the ends of her fingers, her bright red fingernails red thumbtacks holding her skin in place. "Where," she asked, "are you going?"

June put a quarter on the counter by her half-empty cup and went into the waiting room. She heard the woman rustling in her clothes again, thought for a minute she was going to follow her. The woman's hand left a burning feeling on June's arm. In the mirrors that lined the walls of the coffee shop June could see her, turned halfway around on her stool, her legs still facing the counter, her trunk and head facing June's back, her mouth open, arms hanging, like a ventriloquist's dummy.

The waiting room was crowded, warm. June found a space on one of the long wooden benches, like church pews, and watched some soldiers playing pinball, butting their bodies against the machines, the bumping and binging echoing with the noise of luggage being moved about, doors swinging open, banging shut, the nasal voice from the wall speakers announcing arrivals and departures, a steady line of people disappearing through the terminal doors.

A copy of *Time* magazine lay on the seat and June picked it up. It was folded open to an article about highway safety. The page was full of small print and small black and white pictures, the slick paper smelled like a beauty parlor. There was one large picture of three cars after a bad smash up, one of the cars cut completely in half, the roof of another sheered off, and she could see a blurred body on the seat. The third car was flipped over, upside down on top of the front half of the car cut in two. In the photograph the street was black, shiny. There was one other body partway visible through a shattered windshield, one leg sticking into the edge of the picture. At the top of the page was a red box with large black numbers printed inside, predictions of how many Americans would be killed in traffic accidents over the Thanksgiving and Christmas holidays. Thanksgiving was not long off. Cage and June would drive to Blanco. Maybe they would be in Cage's Buick and a giant truck would drive right through them, cutting the Buick in two, splitting it right down the middle, Cage on one side, June on the other. She read the numbers inside the box again, thinking they were not such big numbers, not too much to expect from such a big country. She would remember the predictions until after the holidays and see if the records were broken.

An old man using a cane, a white cane, a blind man, came slowly across the waiting room and stopped in front of the men's room. June remembered the blind man she used to see on her way to work at Texas Cut Flower. But this blind man was much older. Could he be the same man? Had that much time passed without her noticing? No, it had been less than a year. Had something awful happened to him and suddenly aged him years? Had his sightless eyes seen something that made his hair turn dry and white, his body shrink, his skin fade and wrinkle? June remembered a story in Sunday School, when she was a girl in Blanco, about a painter who searched the streets for a man to pose as Jesus at the last supper. Finally he found the perfect model for Christ and painted him into the picture. Months later, when all he had left to paint was Judas, he searched again for the perfect model, and again he found him. In his studio, when he completed the painting, he showed it to the dreadful-looking man who had become his Judas. The man broke down and through his crying managed to tell the artist that he was the same man who, months before, had been Jesus. The blind man stood, waiting, until a man in a Greyhound uniform opened the door and helped him into the men's room. June wondered what the old blind man might have touched, what shapes had he felt through his questioning fingers, what had his skin told him? She wondered what he looked like without his clothes, whether his skin was marked in all the places where he had taken some knowledge in. Did he have heavy folds of skin all over his body, secret, dark creases, white hair growing out from under the folds of skin, out of his stomach, down his back, growing, like grass where seeds were spilled,

185

from all the secret places where the blind man had touched something and learned its secret? Were the tips of his fingers padded with soft, white hair, smooth and quiet when they moved over surfaces? She could let him touch her, run his hands over her body, feel what she looked like, learn what secrets her skin held. The more he touched her with his old hands the more he would wish he could see, would wish more than ever that he had eyes. June would leave a dime for him in his metal cup.

She sat a long time watching the door to the men's room, but the old blind man still did not come out.

She got up and walked over near the entrance to the coffee shop. The foreign woman was still at the counter, bent over the pineapple milkshake.

Near the pinball machines was an automatic photograph machine. Twenty-five cents for four photos. June got change, a handfull of quarters, and stepped into the booth. There was a stool to sit on, a mirror to look into, directions printed below. She dropped a quarter in, a blue light came on, the mirror flashed, quickly, four times, and four photographs came out in a strip, like stamps from a stamp machine. Four little faces of June. She dropped another quarter in, and each time the blue light came on she made a different face and got four different pictures. Pulling the curtain to the booth completely closed, she turned the back of her head to the mirror and took four photographs from behind. She stood up, the top of the mirror cutting off her head, framed her chest in the mirror and took four more pictures. It was hot in the booth, but she kept taking pictures. She lit a cigarette and took pictures of herself smoking. She kept stuffing the strips of photos into her purse. Feeling through the material of her dress she unhooked her bra, a soft looseness inside the dress. She unbuttoned the top two buttons of the dress, reached in and slipped the cups of the bra up over her breasts and slid the bra up like a necklace under her chin, to hold it out of the way. Unfastening more buttons, she spread the dress apart, leaned close to the mirror, and took four photographs of her breasts. She stepped forward, pressed against the cold mirror, nipples hard, the light flashing again. The pictures were blurred, her nipples two dark spots.

She looked out the corner of the booth where the curtain closed. No one was paying any attention, the pinball machine was still blinking and ringing, people were dozing on the wooden benches, waiting, others hurrying back and forth lugging suitcases and packages.

She slid her half slip and panties down over her hips to her thighs and pressed her abdomen against the mirror, leaning up on tiptoes, the muscles in her legs tight. Like those boys pushing up against the pinball machine, like making love, she thought. The machine whirred softly like an x-ray machine, and when the photographs came out June almost expected to see what was inside her. There was a dark spot near the top of each little picture, her bellybutton, and a dark, blurred area near the bottom, where her pubic hair began.

Her body peeled off the glass surface of the mirror with the sound of a bandage coming off, and she pulled her slip and panties up and sat on the stool buttoning the dress with one hand while she pulled the bra down over her breasts with the other. She left the bra unhooked and slipped out of the booth and walked to the women's room. No one seemed to notice. The women's room was empty. She hooked the bra back, rinsed her face with cold water, dabbed dry with a paper towel. She reached in her purse for powder and lipstick. There were the strips of photographs, curling together in her purse as if they were alive.

In a toilet stall she locked the door and sat, her dress stretched across her lap. She took out the strips of photographs. They reminded her of strips of bacon, and she pictured them each wrapped around a piece of meat or a ball of

187

cheese with a toothpick poked through them, a toothpick through her mouth, the back of her head, the middle of her chest, forced through the knot on her belly. One by one she unrolled the strips and looked at them again, and then began tearing them into tiny pieces. She tore them all into confetti except the strip of the back of her head and the strip of her blurred belly and pubic hair. Searching in her purse for all the strips she found the appointment card from the gynecology clinic. Folded in half, it was dirty with pencil lead, powder, and lipstick, but, unfolded, the inside was clean and white. There was the appointment date, months past, and the telephone number she was to have called about her tests. She tore the card up like the photographs and flushed all the bits down the toilet. The tests and the x-ray machines and the doctors couldn't tell her what was inside her any more than the photo machine could. The two rolls of pictures she hadn't torn up were wrapped like rings around her finger, hidden by the fist she made.

The waiting room looked the same, Mexicans and soldiers mostly, some colored people, a few students. People sitting, staring at nothing, reading magazines and newspapers, sleeping, time passing and standing still at the same moment. June went back to the empty seat on the long bench and tore one of the small pictures of the back of her head and one of her belly off the strips and slipped them each inside the *Time*, placed them next to the picture of the three-car collision. The body on the seat of the wrecked car was still there, still bleeding down both tiny legs. She shut the magazine. Now, she thought, is the body still bleeding in the picture? She jerked the page open again, there was the body on the seat. And there was the back of her head resting just under one of the wrecked cars, and her own bare belly visible beside the bleeding body on the seat. She shut the magazine again. It was like the light in the refrigerator. Did the light go off when you closed the door, or did it go on and on, lighting up

188

the milk and butter and limp brocolli? With the pages closed
did the three cars right themselves on the shiny pavement,
rev their engines and repeat the accident, over and over the
tearing of metal and flesh, the cracking of glass and bone,
tiny shards and splinters? She had heard about holy cards
that really bled, and she knew a Catholic girl in school who
told her she wore a picture of Jesus around her neck until she
got a passion mark on her breast where his lips were. Maybe
her own small head was even now hurtling backwards into
that wreck inside the dark, closed pages of *Time*. Even now
her soft and naked belly might be soaking up blood where it
ran from the body on the seat.

She hurried to a phone booth and stuck two more pictures
into the coin return. Let them crawl up into the telephone
and listen to people talk, let them even escape out into the
telephone lines and cross the country, entering houses and
offices, speeding under the still feet of birds, through thick
trees, night and day moving long distances, listening and
being heard.

The next two she tore off and stuck into the silver cup of
the blind man who had positioned himself against the wall by
the terminal doors where people passed to board the buses.
She saw herself bob up and down in his dark glasses as he
nodded his thanks and reached two long fingers into his cup
like a priest dipping for holy water and pulled the pictures
out, rubbing them between his thumb and forefinger, slowly
snapping them into his inside pocket, beneath his worn jacket. Soon, she thought, she would be next to his skin.

The last two pictures she carried in her fist, through the
double swinging terminal doors to the ramps where the buses
waited. She found a bus that was empty, the motor running,
doors open. Inside it was dirty, the seats smelled like sweat
and smoke, hard thumbprints of chewing gum were stuck
along the bottoms of the windows. Near the back of the bus
she stuck the tiny photos up in a crack between the up-

189

holstery and metal frame of the armrest of an aisle seat. She sat in the seat a minute, looking through her reflection in the tinted window at a man loading suitcases into the bottom of a bus at the next ramp.

She stepped off the bus and walked outside, around the rear of the bus, where she stopped and waved goodbye. Then she went out the back drive to the station to the street and walked around to the Thunderbird. The air was cool, the sun gone, city lights coming on in the sky. A nice time to be leaving, the long dark night stretching ahead. Sweat under her arms, across her back, between her legs, was cold when air moved through her dress.

Cage would be home before long. She would catch the expressway to the loop a few blocks from the Greyhound station and take it almost all the way to her house. She would be there, taking her bath, when Cage got home. He would take her out to supper somewhere fancy tonight.

26

Dear Cage and June,

Was so glad to get your alls letter. I'm o.k. I know Cage hates this weather. Can't think many folks would want to get out and look at lots when it is so cold. We might get a snow this winter. I'm afraid to open my gas bill I have had the heaters on so high. They found those Massey sisters froze to death Sunday. Eddilee and Pollysue, do you remember them June? Their place is over toward Banderra and the rain washed out that dirt road and then the ice storm like to paralized things around here, Lord how fast the weather can change when we get a blue norther blow in. Lord knows how long since the gas truck got in to them and filled their tank. They found them sitting up in bed, both in the same bed together. I guess the poor old things were trying to stay warm. They were both bad off anyway, so many things the matter with them, Eddilee had heart, high blood pressure, and old age for

191

both. Yesterday only hit up to 34. If it keeps up we'll get rationed gas.

I get so lonely. Was sure glad you all came Thanksgiving. I still have the wine. I might drink a glass tonite to ward off this cold. I started to make a choclate pie today but since I'm not supposed to eat sweets I'll wait untill you come again. Are you sure you want to come get me and bring me there for x-mas? It seems like an extra trip when you all could just stay here. I know Cage is a good driver but you can't trust the other people. There's Mexicans running up and down the hiway drunk as skunks. A little 12 yr. old boy got runover downtown last week. A carload of mexicans drunk and speeding came through and ran him right down. They put them all in jail but what difference will it make when there's so many of them left. You should have seen the funeral. They called out school and the school busses went right in the funeral and his little classmates carryed the coffin. The football team is dedicating their games to his memory. When they came down the hiway I just cried. It reminded me of Turk's funeral, of course.

Thank you all for the nice check—I sure can use it. Since this weather keeps me inside I just might go buy a pattern and make you a nice apron June, would that be allright, for a x-mas present I mean? If I can see to stitch anymore.

Giant is going to play at the Lone Star. I haven't seen a movie in 20 yrs. except on t-v and with my old t-v you don't see much. I guess I'll have to wait for Giant to be on t-v too. Hope it does while I'm still around.

I think I hear it doing something out there now, sounds like sleet.

Did I tell you about the Dillard boy? He's in trouble again, they may put him in reform school this time. His poor mother. June didn't you have a date with him to something in highschool?

Well, I thank you all for your alls letter and for the nice check. I hoped to get some x-mass shopping done before x-mas but if this nasty bad weather keeps up I'll just have to stay in. Going to the Dr. and keeping warm keeps me about broke. I guess you all are proud Cage made his deal with the Texaco people, I know the money comes in handy, it costs so much to get by. I even miss the little bit Turk used to give me. Too bad he didn't have more insurance. Write me and come see me.

Love,
Eunice Momma

27

IT HAD been a good year for Cage.

"Damn good year," he said. "Business couldn't be better."

He had a new tin roof put on Eunice's house, her Christmas present, that and one of the plots he bought in the Blanco cemetery. One for Eunice, one for June, one for himself, three in a row in the new section of the cemetery near the western property line. There was no space left close to Armon, but Turk was just a stone's throw, behind a cedar tree. Eunce was delighted, she had worried that the cemetery might fill up or be bought out before she had enough money saved to buy her own plot, and she had fretted that she might end up all alone down at the Twin Sisters cemetery. She was glad June and Cage would be right by her. Cage was glad too, he had saved a bundle compared to the cost in San Antonio cemeteries.

June's Christmas present was harder to pick out, it had to be something really special. He wanted to show everybody how pleased he was with his new wife. He went to jewelry stores and looked at diamond broaches, necklaces, bracelets. They seemed so small for the money, hardly worth it. He

194

even drove up to Dallas—he wanted to see a man there anyway, about investing in a new shopping center—and shopped at Neiman-Marcus. The saleslady suggested a fur coat. He looked at sable, chinchilla, mink, and finally bought a full length mink, dyed black. It would, he thought, look sharp with the silver Thunderbird.

He also decided to take June on a vacation after Christmas. A second honeymoon, he told her. January would be a great time to go. It was his worst month, because of the weather, and he knew he would be busy in spring and summer with the new Arroyo Lake development. He had gotten in on the ground floor on that one. A big recreational property, it looked like a cinch, and there were some big money men interested, all they were waiting for was the dam that would fill the lake they were having dug. He knew those lakefront lots would sell like hotcakes once they got the water—he'd already sold four on the promise of water and the artist's drawing of the new lake and clubhouse.

While he was in Dallas buying June the mink coat he got tickets for the Cotton Bowl, New Year's Day, and decided they would drive up for the game and fly to Las Vegas from Dallas right after the game for their vacation. Lucky for him the man who was interested in the shopping center knew some men in Dallas who got Cage forty-yardline tickets even though the game was already a sellout.

Cage had always wanted a Cadillac, and he thought he might just buy himself one—a Christmas present from Cage to Cage. He figured it would be a good business investment, especially if the big money men really got into the Arroyo Lake deal. He didn't want them to balk because he looked like a piker. He looked at Cadillacs in Dallas, Austin, and in San Antonio. One salesman asked him if he was sure he wanted to put that kind of money into a car, and Cage told him he reckoned he had enough cash on hand to buy two or three Caddies if that was what he wanted. Of course he would never pay cash for anything expensive because he thought that having lots of payments and making them on time kept his credit good and helped him make business deals. As he told June, "We don't want to get our capital all tied up, we might need that money in a hurry someday."

The week before Christmas, Cage surprised June, drove home for lunch in his new car. In the end he'd bought another Buick, from the same dealer in Temple where he'd made such a good deal on his other Buick. He got a steal again, his trade-in was less than a year old. "But," he joked, "the new-car-smell was gone so I knew it was time to trade again. It's the biggest Buick they make," he told June. "Rides just as smooth as a Cadillac, and I actually think it's better looking."

The new Buick was bright yellow. June called it taxicab yellow. Cage said there weren't any taxicabs cost so much. June told him he'd better watch out, it'd be easy to spot. Said he'd better not try sneaking around on her because she'd go cruise by all the bars and whorehouses and see where he was by spotting his big, yellow taxi. Cage just grinned from ear to ear.

Driving her slowly around the block, she was still in her nightgown and slippers, he talked nonstop, "It was a demo model, driven by the owner of the dealership himself, only got four thousand miles on it, perfect servicing there at the dealer's, and I made such a great deal on the trade-in. Just a goddamned steal. Not only do I happen to really like the color yellow, but it's a good color for safety, you know I read that most wrecks happen at dusk or dawn because people can't see good enough then. They're even making underwater divers' gear this color of yellow, I think they call it safety yellow, so if you can see it underwater imagine how well you can see it on the highway."

June imagined a big semi homing in on the yellow car, bright target, some evening just at dusk. She imagined the

196

color of blood on the bright yellow dashboard, catsup and mustard. She imagined the big semi splitting the long yellow Buick right down the middle, the two halves curling off like a banana peeling. She imagined Cage sitting upright, dead, in this bright yellow coffin. Parked in their driveway the car seemed to glow at night, like a yellow porch light for keeping bugs away.

28

CAGE SAT alone in the small trailer that was his office at Arroyo Lake Estates. Through the one window he watched puffs of diesel smoke that seemed to rise out of the earth, as if he was sitting on the slope of a volcano that was slowly coming to life. Then the huge chain treads of the yellow Caterpillar inched up out of the ground. The man operating the machine was just a dark spot from where Cage watched, and inside the office Cage could not hear the whines and groans of metal and rocks and dirt. The Caterpillar paused, level with the horizon, then dipped down again, crawled slowly and silently out of sight, leaving only its occasional smoke signals for Cage to watch.

Weekdays were always slow. He had straightened out the desk, stacked the real estate contracts in the lower left drawer, thrown away all the memo pad sheets that were covered with figures—down payments, finance charges, monthly amounts. He had sharpened all the pencils in the top drawer. Now he was building a city on top of the green desk. The green desk top was grass. He folded and tore carefully with a plastic ruler edge the strips of white paper he was using for concrete. A planned community, a brand new, ideal city. He made radio and television station transmitters with straightened paper clips that stuck up into the sky over his city. The tallest building was the empty box his new stapler had come in, and the stapler itself was an enormous parking garage just off the expressway which arched over a midcity lake—a dark blue rectangle of commemorative stamps he had picked up that morning at the post office.

He bit off a new pencil eraser and set it at the end of the city, near his expressway. Their house, June and Cage's. And in their house was their bed and June was sleeping there now. They had colored sheets on their bed, yellow sheets, green sheets, sheets with little blue flowers on them, even sheets with pink and white stripes.

When he was a boy in Ohio he had never seen any sheets but white, white and stiff from the line beside the house, cold every night and stiff like the crust of snow that covered everything outside.

He thought of June in that house in bed, thought of her sleeping there alone, her arms wrapped around a pillow, holding a pillow lengthwise against her body as if it were another body. He thought of all the dresses hanging in her closet, all the shoes sitting side by side on the floor of her closet. All the dresses different, the shoes, different, all different. Like the colored sheets, all different. Sheets, dresses, shoes for every occasion, change them every day if you want.

This was good. He was out of Ohio for good. Texas had a brand-new feeling, like the new house by the new expressway and all June's new dresses and shoes and the new sheets stacked in the linen closet, some of them still in their plastic wrappers. He was going to have a good life, give June a good life, there was easy money here and new things and all this unused land that he would buy and sell. And, one day soon, June would sit by him in a new Cadillac that would take them elegantly to dinner parties at big houses where maids would open heavy doors and take their coats. He would buy her a lovely dress, a blue dress the color of his postage stamp lake, and he would wear a tuxedo with a pure white coat, a red rose in his lapel, a rose from June, from her own rose garden. She would straighten the studs in his shirt, help him fasten the cuff links, all gold, his initials cut in gold, her fingernails long and polished, her fingers soft, fast, sure.

Tonight, on his way home, he would stop at a dime store and buy a little box of stick-on stars and he would make a Texas flag to put on a pencil flagpole over his city on the desk. For now, he carefully moved the buildings and expressways and lake into the top desk drawer.

He walked around outside the land office. The Caterpillar was silent, out of sight down in the trough it was digging in the earth. The sky was clear, the sun warm. It had been a cool weekend, especially the nights, but now it was almost like spring again. He had never known weather like this, warm in December. He kicked at the ground with his heel, made wedge-shaped holes with his shoe. When his daddy died they had trouble burying him, the ground was so hard frozen. They almost had to wait for a thaw, but the cemetery had some kind of digging machine that did the trick. His daddy, stiff before he died. His daddy, dreaming of the war, dreaming of two good legs, remembering a café in some small town in France, remembering walking on cobblestones, feeling the uneven pavement beneath his feet. His daddy died in his wheelchair, his head bowed, chin on his chest, his shirt unbuttoned at the top, a two day old beard, the smell of sweat and piss. He wet his pants when he died.

Cage held his hands over his mouth, cupped his hands like a mask over his face, breathed out, smelled his hands, his breath. Cologne and toothpaste. The way clean people smelled. A smell of newness, a tight, creased smell, like the mixture of cologne and sizing in his new shirt, a hard, slick smell, like the perfect knot in his tie.

He knelt down to watch a fat lizard sunning himself on a rock. The lizard was the color of the rock and did not move. Cage watched the swell of the lizard's throat slowly pulsing. He poked at the lizard with a stick, it darted off the rock onto the hard, white caliche, then shot into a dusty bush. Cage followed the lizard, walking like a frog, squatting like a movie ambusher. He thought of the rifle in the land office, for rattlers, one of the salesmen had brought it out. He remembered the blood at the Sinclair station, the holes in the glass, thought about Turk's heart being crushed under the weight of his car.

The lizard was balanced on a skinny limb deep in the bush, his weight making the tiny branch sway slowly up and down. His mouth was open, a spot of pink giving him away. Cage thought of June, the way her body smelled like baby powder. The thick hair between her thighs, the dampness, the pink and soft skin where he touched her, slipped his fingers in, his wedding band slipping back and forth over his knuckle, wet from inside her body. There was a little slip of soft skin along the lizard's neck that seemed to glow pink, as if the skin there was translucent and the lizard's pink tounge and throat were showing through. That was the place where boys rubbed to put a lizard to sleep, hypnotize, mesmerize, paralyze. The lizard's long mouth was open, a pink slit, dark inside. Would it bite? He poked at it with his stick, it did not try to run. Was it frozen with fear? Afraid to run, afraid of staying still. He could kill it so easily, just one swing of his arm, one jerk of his wrist. If he left and got the rifle to shoot it to pieces, would it still be there in the bush, waiting, when he came back with the gun? Somehow he felt that it would. He reached slowly into the bush, his four fingers pressed together and opened slightly from his thumb, in imitation of the lizard's slit-open mouth, a claw, a clamp opening to close.

He grabbed the tail. The second he touched the skin of the lizard his arm jerked back, a reflex action, his arm jerked out of the bush and a chill ran up the back of his neck. He had the tail, the lizard was gone.

The tail hung from his hand like a guilty child hanging its head. It had let the lizard get away. When he tried to drop it, the tail stuck to his thumb and he had to shake it loose. It lay on the ground like a living thing, and he quickly kicked it into the dead grass under the bush.

Back in the trailer he washed his hands and slowly ate a sack lunch June had fixed the night before, the sandwiches still cool from being in the refrigerator overnight. He spent the afternoon going through the files of people he had sold lots to, saying their names outloud as he alphabetized the folders. He wished June would call to see how he was, and he started to call her, but didn't. He would wait until dark and see if she called him first. He made a list of things he hoped she might get him for Christmas, and he planned a trip they might take one day to Acapulco, or, even, Rio de Janeiro.

Nobody came to see a lot all afternoon, and he did not call any of his prospects, even two he had promised to call, because he didn't want his line to be busy in case June called. Not until way after dark when it started getting cold in the office did he lock up and head home.

Driving out to the paved road he saw two deer. They were standing side by side in front of the huge, yellow Caterpillar parked off the dirt road. The headlights hit them and they did not move, their eyes shining like the glass eyes of trophy heads in a hunting lodge, and they looked like a painting of deer and not living things. The Caterpillar might have been some prehistoric ancestor the artist had painted in behind them, its long, flat face resting on the ground. Cage wanted to see them move. He honked his horn and blinked the lights but still they were still. He turned the car lights completely off, then on again. When the lights hit the Caterpillar the deer had disappeared, without a sign. All the way home he

202

kept thinking he had no way of knowing for sure that he had even seen them at all.

As he neared home he got to thinking that June must have been out Christmas shopping and that was why she didn't call to see what was keeping him so long. She was shopping for his Christmas present, and he wadded up the list he'd made of things he wanted and pushed it out the vent window as he went over an overpass. He turned on his radio, which he seldom remembered to use, and kept time to the music with his fingers, the music from some movie he couldn't remember, just music with no singing, his wedding band clicking out the tune against the steering wheel.

29 JUNE PICKED out the Christmas tree, a tall, skinny fir, dyed pink. It was so tall Cage had to cut a foot off the top, and still it touched the ceiling. Cage went to three shopping centers and finally had to go to Kresses downtown to find enough pink bulbs to cover the tree. June said pink on pink was very soft and pretty, rich-looking she said, like her pink moonstone necklace on her pink taffeta dress, or like thick pink frosting on a pink cake. Cage said it looked real pretty, and real, well, Christmasy, he guessed, was the word.

The Buick dealer had given Cage a Christmas album with TEMPLE BUICK stamped in red on the cover, and he played it over and over while he sat in the living room drinking eggnog and watching June decorate her tree, singing along with Bing Crosby, *Just like the Christ-mas-es I used to know,* whistling with some children's choir on "Rudolph the Red Nosed Reindeer." The last song on the album was a loud choral group doing "Deck the Halls with Boughs of Holly," to which Cage always sang, *Deck the Halls with Boston Charlie,* and laughed out loud.

204

Christmas Eve they were going to get Eunice in Blanco and drive her back down to San Antonio to spend Christmas with them. It was a warm, sunny morning, Cage had had his new car washed and told June he'd like to drive her and Eunice out to Arroyo Lake Estates on the way back from Blanco, when he got a call from the police that they had arrested one of the salesmen Cage had hired. The police had stopped him for speeding, and he was drunk and had nearly five thousand dollars in cash and one of Cage's business cards in his wallet. Cage figured the money belonged to Arroyo Lake Estates. The police figured it did too, and they wanted Cage to come down and answer some questions, maybe take them out to the sales office at the property.

He hated to go on Christmas Eve. "Looks like they could just keep that boy on ice until after the holidays and then investigate."

June said it really didn't matter, she'd go get Momma and surely he'd be back in a few hours. He insisted she take his new Buick. She said she'd rather go in the Thunderbird, she hated to drive his new car, but he said for her to take the Buick, it was all cleaned and nice for the ride.

Driving to Blanco the only thing June noticed different about his new Buick from his old Buick, besides the color, was the smell of after shave lotion in the new one. She wondered if this was the smell of the salesman who had used it as a demonstrator. Alone in Cage's car, she felt like there was some other man riding with her, some man who smelled like spice cake and rum sauce.

Momma was ready when June got there, waiting for them. She seemed disappointed that Cage wasn't with June, but not for long. She soon started in on the new manager down at the Red and White, whom she said she hated worse than rat poison. She was tearing into him when they crossed the river, leaving Blanco, and still ripping when June turned onto their street by the new Texaco, its strings of bright green and red plastic pennants flapping like Momma's mouth.

Thank heavens Cage was back home already, he could help listen to Momma. He was outside, riding the Lay-Z-Man Ride-N-Mow over the dead grass. When it was warm he liked to get out in the yard and play at yard work. Whatever Cage started, the yardboy had to finish. When he saw them turn in, he waved and drove the mower across the lawn to the driveway. When he waved, a dark figure against the sun, June saw Turk riding the tractor, mowing Blanco cemetery grass.

Christmas Day was sunny too, even warmer than the day before. They all slept late, they had opened their packages the night before. June had told Cage she didn't want to spend her Christmas cooking, so he had ordered an already prepared dinner, turkey and dressing, candied yams, sweet peas, cranberry sauce, and pecan pie. All June had to do was stick everything in the oven and set the timer. It all came in tin, throwaway containers for heating.

While they waited for dinner to heat up they walked around the house inspecting June's rosebushes. Eunice stayed inside, listening for the timer, peeking into the oven every few minutes.

The roses had not done well, and Cage knew they would not come back in the spring. He snapped off a dead twig, pulled off a brown thorn, flipped it onto the dead grass. He needed to have a good sprinkler system put in. The lawn was a smooth, even brown, unbroken by trees or shrubs. It looked like a golf green painted brown. He shook the change in his pocket and fondled the gold money clip, June's Christmas gift, his initials in flowery letters on the face of a replica of a Roman coin. He wished she had had some special

206

message engraved on the back, but there were only the initials. Still, he liked it, he liked it a lot. It was a good sign, a money clip, showed she had faith in him, in his success. She liked the mink coat. He was glad of that. She was not hard to please, she seemed to like everything he bought her, she never complained when he had to work late and on weekends, didn't seem to mind the long days at home alone. She seemed almost glad when he told her they would have to postpone the vacation, the second honeymoon, to Las Vegas, and it was her idea to sell the Cotton Bowl tickets.

"We can watch the game on TV and see all the other bowls, too. It would be too hard to get back from Dallas in time for your meeting in Austin."

He had gotten a call from one of his partners in Arroyo Lake Estates that the big fish, as he put it, were ready to fry. He said even the governor was interested. There was talk of widening the highway that went past the property. A meeting had been arranged for the day after New Years, in Austin. The governor was interested.

June said she would call a radio station that had a regular For Sale or Swap program and sell the Cotton Bowl tickets.

She liked football games on television as much as, maybe more than, he did. She knew the names of all the teams, coaches, her favorite players, knew all the records, kept track of yards gained by each player during every game she watched, wrote everything down on the telephone pad. Her Colts were doing much better than his Chicago Bears. It made him smile, picturing her, small in the big den chair, yelling for hulking football players. She told him when he met the governor to see what he could do to get a pro team going in Texas. "You know," she told him, "there might be enough money in a football franchise for Texas to interest those big shots you're dealing with." He reminded her that next fall both Dallas and Houston were supposed to have

207

teams, that Dallas might have two, one in the NFL and one in the new AFL. "I want one here, in San Antonio, my own team," she said.

Watching her walk in front of him, so small and fragile inside the long, thick mink coat, he realized how much he loved taking care of her. He resolved to have a landscape service come out first thing in spring and replant the entire rose garden. He didn't care if he had to replant it once a year. He remembered a poem from school, about roses, *My love is a rose—a red, red rose. My love is a red, red rose.* June was his rose, a rose of Texas, the Rose of San Antone, and he had come all the way from Ohio to pick her.

He knew he was happy.

Not many men have something this good and decent, he thought. And such a good future yet to come. He ran his thumb over his initials on the gold money clip in his pocket and felt a knot begin to grow in his throat. In the dead crinkle of the grass he heard the tissue paper his mother had wrapped around coathangers and he felt his eyes getting wet. He remembered the photographs and magazines they had found in his father's dresser after he died. Filth. Why did he have to have such filth in the house, in the same house with his wife and his son, why did he? His mother had cried and Cage had torn every filthy picture into tiny pieces, little naked thighs and backs, lewd little faces, tiny bare breasts and bellies, torn into flakes of color he flushed down the toilet.

That salesman the police had arrested, stealing money from Arroyo Lake Estates, from Cage and his partners who had given him a job and offered him the chance to make a success of himself, that same man had always been talking about women like Marilyn Monroe and Bridget Bardot. Cage should have fired him for the way he talked. Why did some men want smut like that?

Cage took June's hand, cool, smooth. She was watching the traffic on the expressway, fast, made small by distance. Her hand was as smooth as the glass reindeer he'd bought her for the Christmas dinner centerpiece. She was as fragile, as quiet, and even lovlier, he thought, than those delicate deer.

"Merry Christmas, June," he said, and he squeezed her hand. He wanted to say, "Merry Christmas, my Rose of Texas, my San Antonio Rose," but he only said, "Merry Christmas," again.

She laughed, shook her head a little, as if she was just waking up, and kissed him on the nose. "I love the coat, Cage, I love it."

When they got back inside, the buzzer was buzzing and Eunice was asleep on the living room couch, the pink lights on the tree shining on her forehead. Cage liked Eunice, felt good that he had given her the new roof. It was so easy to make women happy, but so many men didn't seem to understand. Cage stood in the hall while June took food from the oven. He waited until he got over the hard spot in his throat, the sting in his eyes. The last time he had cried had been in the men's room at the movies when he took June to see *A Night to Remember* and brave men put their wives and children in the few lifeboats and stayed behind on the sinking *Titanic.* And the last time before that had been back in Ohio when he was a boy himself. Somehow, he thought, June had made him see things again in a new way, a way that would let him be moved to tears, something he had not been able to do since he was a little boy. It was one of the ways she kept him young, he thought, and what more can a man ask of life? A man's home, now he really understood it, is his castle.

That night Eunice went to bed early and he and June stayed up and finished the last of the eggnog. Then June put her radio on low, and when he came out of the bathroom from brushing his teeth she was lying on top of the bed wearing her new mink coat, and nothing on underneath.

Two days after Christmas they drove Eunice back to Blanco and stayed until after supper. When they got back home that night they had a Christmas card in the mailbox from the governor. Cage put the governor's Christmas card on top of the television and they sat in the den and each had a big mug full of strong eggnog before they went to bed.

30

Saturday p.m.

Dear Cage and June,

Can't believe X-mas has come and gone and I am almost a year older. It is good Cages business is doing so good. I better start watching for his picture in the paper or on the t-v news. Has he met the Governor yet? June who would have thought it that you'd marry someone so important? And thank you all for the check. I finally got a new bedspread, you'll have to come see it. My old rash is back and I am out of salve and haven't bathed since Wed. I itch so bad.

They are opening a pool hall downtown. All this town of hood-lums needs. I saw the beer permit notice on the door when I went down to get me some Kayro syrup. I hate worse than sin to use that Red and White with their nasty smart alek mgr. I thought I'd make a nice pecan pie in case you all came up but my pecans are all dry rotted, so its just as good you didn't come yet.

We had a right smart thunderstorm yesterday. Did you get any in S.A.? Felt like spring with the limbs blowing down but besides wind it wasn't much to talk about in rain. I'm ready for hot weather and glad of today's sunshine even if it is cold as a frog.

211

June do you remember that Smith boy, Ran I think he was called, who came around her when he was a kid selling Watkins products? He went off to Virginia or somewhere up there and I heard he was going to make a Dr. and come back here to Blanco. I can't figure why a young Dr. would come here unless he just wants the practice patching up cuttings and gunfight holes from that pool hall. He won't have any slow spaces here. Dear Jesus everone is either old and sick or young and crazy wild—you knew they arrested both those Garrett boys?

I am just an old woman with no one to tell her troubles to. I remember Armon's going like it was yesterday and Turk's just was. I hope I live to go with Cage over to the Governor's Mansion someday.

I'm getting so sleepy I best go put the coffee heating. Guess there's reason in doing what the Drs. tell me but reckon I'll be plane ornery where my nitetime cup comes in. As old as me and a good cup of coffee when youre alone and cold is as good a pleasure as is.

My kitchen is getting a stink I haven't burned the garbage out back and haven't carryed the sack out from under the sink all week. Its too windy to burn and I can't bend to pick up my sack and tote it without popping my backbone. Expect it to be sitting here overflowing with mold next time you come unless my bones loose up.

The new roof is so good. It shines like silver in the sun and doesn't leak the least bit. Guess I'll say goodnite.

Love,
Eunice Momma

31

JUNE RODE in back of Earl Dodge's new Cadillac watching the sunlight on Earl Dodge's elbow. Earl was driving, Cage sat up front with him, talking. Earl was one of the developers who opened up Mesa View, a big resort community near Austin, and he had written Cage about helping develop Arroyo Lake Estates. He was taking Cage and June out to eat, but first he wanted to drive out and get a look at the property. He was just in from Amarillo, drove all night, where his brother Jes owned a modular homes outfit.

"Though I'd hesitate to call these homes modular or pre-fab. What they are is factory assembled units ready for on-the-site installation in less than a week and as well made as any fine home. Most of the units we put in at Mesa View cost a good $30,000 and all run over a thousand square feet."

Earl had the car's heater on high but still rode with his window all the way down, his left elbow jutting out. June watched the little blue alligators woven into his short sleeved shirt crawling in blue lines up his shoulder. On his muscular arm, so tight in the knit shirt it looked swollen, fine hairs curled softly together, bleached almost white by the sun.

213

They pulled off the highway onto the dirt road, and Earl pulled up near the Arroyo Lake Estates sign. "Nothing like the beauty of a pretty gal to sell the beauty of lake property." he led June over in front of the sign and stood back squinting, taking a picture of her in the January sun, her shoulders and head sticking up out of the deep blue lake painted on the billboard, the word: RESORT sticking out of the side of her neck.

Down the dirt road to Arroyo Lake Estates they passed the Double Diamond Ranch, a bright yellow sign hanging off the gate: EXOTICS.

"Bless me, Cage, you got a strip tease ranch going here?"

"No," Cage said without joining Earl Dodge's laughter, "The Double Diamond is a hunting ranch. They bring in all kinds of antelope and buffalo from Africa and charge big game hunters to shoot their trophies. Hunters come from all over, stay in the Double Diamond Lodge. They've got their own airstrip—even got a helicopter to taxi people back and forth from the San Antonio airport."

"Hope all that shooting won't scare our buyers off."

June watched to see if Cage reacted to Earl Dodge's use of *our*. After all, she thought, he's not in on the deal yet. At least not as far as June knew.

"They don't hunt this close to the lodge, and there's another ranch in between our property and theirs," Cage said. "We might make them into an asset. I've been talking to the owners about renting the use of their airstrip, and maybe clubhouse privileges for our clients—at least until we get our own pool and clubhouse up."

"June, this hubby of yours don't miss a bet, does he?"

Cage turned to look at June and she smiled, he smiled back. Earl Dodge was drumming the fingers of his left hand on the roof of the Cadillac. June wished he'd turn on the radio. There was a song in her head, Bob Wills, "When You Leave Amarillo, Turn Out the Light." She hummed the

214

tune until they came to the entrance to the property, and Earl Dodge stopped tapping on the roof.

Cage started to get out to open the gate, but Earl Dodge had the car in Park and was at the front bumper before Cage could get his door open. June watched the man walk, arms swinging at his side, long, almost bowlegged stride, kicking up soft clouds of dust nearly as high as his waist. He wore red ostrich skin boots and corduroy jeans so tight his legs bulged in them like his arms in the knit shirt. He looked swollen, all over. He had a big white cowboy hat tipped back on his head, and he occasionally tapped the brim with his ring, a big gold high school ring with a purple stone, which he wore on his first finger.

As they drove deeper into the property, Earl Dodge talked about work he had done out in west Texas, building earth dams.

"Jesus, this is a goldmine. Cage you can sure pick 'em. Dam us up a few of these draws, make some nice little lakes—not just Arroyo Lake but Arroyo *Lakes*. More lakes means more water for lots to front on, right? Bring down a few of Jes's lake houses, hang those babies off the edges over our lakes—man. Come summer, folks from Dallas and Houston be getting in line to buy these tracts." Cage was grinning, turned to wink at June. "You know Cage," Earl Dodge talked on, "the government will pay most of the cost of the dams, all we do is say it's for water conservation."

The Cadillac bounced and swayed over the ruts and holes in the road and when Earl Dodge bounced, his hair, which was chopped off even across his wide neck, brushed up and down over his shirt collar like Cage's moustache brushed up and down over his lip. When Cage was talking and Earl Dodge was nodding, June pretended the back of Earl Dodge's head was Cage's face, the strip of Earl Dodge's pink neck Cage's lips making the words.

Cage was pointing at a clearing in a grove of spindly live

215

oaks at the edge of a bluff. "You suppose you could get us over there, right out by those live oaks, see if we could get a shot of the highway, get a snapshot with that camera of yours to show how convenient the tract is to the San Antonio highway? No, never mind. Forget it Earl, I must be crazy—this new Caddy doesn't deserve that kind of rough treatment. I'll get it later on. I probably should buy a Jeep for riding around these rocky hills."

"What kind of treatment, man? A few rocks, a little high grass—hell, that's why I bought this baby, have the power when I need the power."

He gunned the big car out across the open pasture, swerving back and forth around small cedars and big rocks and June let her head fall back against the upholstery and closed her eyes.

She relaxed, her legs floated apart beneath her skirt, her heels touching on the floorboard. The air between her thighs was cool, her ankles were warm against the back of the front seat where the air came out of the heater. It was like soaking her feet in warm water, the heat near the carpeted floor. They drove over a tree limb and she felt it scrape beneath her feet. When the car stopped she felt the cool air from Earl Dodge's open window stop, smelled dust, heard the soft click of the camera. With her eyes closed Earl Dodge and Cage sounded far away, seemed to drone, their voices ran together with the faint sounds of cars and trucks passing over on the highway.

Her arms and legs felt heavy, dead. She wondered if she would be able to move them if she tried. She wondered if she could open her eyes. She felt bloated, weighted, anchored to the seat and floor of the car. She tried to make her mind think something fast inside her still body. A paddle ball on a rubber string, whap, whap, whap, the paddle batting the ball, the string jerking the ball back. Under her lids her eyeballs jerked back and forth, but she did not move.

216

Off and on for the past few days she had been having cramps and feeling like her period was about to start, but it was not near time. The car was going slowly up a hill, there was a low whine in the engine. June imagined that she was bleeding, blood running out onto Earl's fancy upholstery. A pain came up into her from beneath the car, sharp and thin like a wire, like a child's drawing of electricity—jagged and bright colored, but then it stopped short, seemed to be grounded somewhere under her stomach.

She held her breath, afraid the pain would come again and afraid it wouldn't. She wanted to feel it again so she could tell where it was hurting, so she could describe the feeling. Not a stitch, like pains were often named. She had a sense of what it meant to feel that, a stitch, a stitch in your side, but how could she be sure? How could she know what someone else meant, what someone else felt? Maybe the pain she had just experienced was not actually painful. Maybe it was a common feeling for other people, some kind of muscle spasm, a normal jerking inside her body, like a heartbeat. Maybe most people had that bad a feeling all the time and didn't consider that a pain, didn't think that was a bad enough hurting. What if it hurt like that every time her heart beat?

Or, maybe it was severe pain, worse than a hot bullet hole, worse than glass and metal cutting and smashing in a car wreck, worse than the most painful pains given in a hospital. On TV people got shot and kept walking, kept talking, kept shooting back. She had seen a news film of a woman after a head-on collision who talked into the microphone while her legs were cut out of the metal with a blow torch. And in hospitals people had arms and legs sawed off, lungs and kidneys taken out, then they sat up in bed eating cubes of Jello and making jokes about their pains. Maybe she was immune to pain and what she had just felt would have killed anyone else. A pain bad enough to hurt someone immune to pain would be a killing pain. The warning pains would not have

217

been strong enough to hurt her. What if she had missed the signs of some disease and now she was having a killing pain but didn't realize it and she would die in the back of this car while Cage and this stranger, this Earl Dodge, talked about the clubhouse and common park for the property owners in Arroyo Lake Estates.

"Here, along the river, Cage, we oughta have a little park for everybody who buys a lot, so folks who can't afford lake frontage can come sit around by this river. That would be a big attraction, we could advertise every single lot as a waterfront lot."

"Isn't it pretty along here? That's Bexar Creek, but I don't blame you calling it a river, it is nearly big as a river. Why don't you get a shot of those waterfalls there."

"Cage, it may not be a real river, but it looks clear and nice enough that I'd just love to stop and shuck these clothes and go skinny-dipping if it was summertime. Fact is, I would do just that if it was a little warmer today and June wasn't out here with us."

They were crossing a low-water bridge over the creek and the water was high enough from weekend showers that it was running several inches over the concrete. June still had her eyes closed. She could hear the tires in the water, the sounds of fluids in her body. The slap of water against a whitewall. A thick cramp below her belly. She listened for her blood to start running, expected to feel it warm beneath her thighs. She was being rolled down a hospital hall on a narrow cart, the little rubber wheels squeaking regularly. A nurse leaned over her, squinted down at her, the nurse's face hidden by a green surgical mask. Tubes stuck out of her, draining off blood and urine and thick poisons. Then her blood began to flow out, gushing out of the tubes onto the floor, steadily pouring out until the little wheels were covered and she could no longer hear them squeak. She was slowing down, getting bogged in her blood. The nurse was leaving, crawling

218

up a ladder to the floor above, her uniform stained red from the waist down. June felt the blood slopping over the edges of the pad, floating her up off the cart, up toward the ceiling.

She opened her eyes. Through the rear window of the car, clouds tinted green, blue-green sky.

They were stopped on top of a rocky knoll surrounded by dark green cedar bushes. Earl Dodge was leaning out his window with the camera, laughing, telling Cage these damned little ole pictures cost nearly fifty cents apiece. He told Cage he figured he owned at least a good part of the Kodak company. June saw him in the rearview mirror, a round, smooth pock mark on his temple. When he dropped the camera on the seat beside him and saw June watching in the mirror, she winked at him, imitating him with the camera.

The cramps had passed, she had lost the pain, the feeling she could not describe, could not understand. There should be some way of really knowing. Some machine they could hook up to both patient and doctor which would let the doctor share the pain and know it better.

Heading out of Arroyo Lake Estates, going back to the highway, they met a pickup on the road, a rancher who owned four thousand acres adjoining Arroyo Lake Estates. Cage had been talking to the man for months about selling part of his ranch, if the development went as well as Cage thought it might. The man was willing, so long as his neighbors didn't find out that he was selling to a subdivider. Cage wasn't sure whether the man might be just telling him that to jack up the price. The pickup stopped and Cage told Earl Dodge to wait until he spoke to the man. June leaned up against the front seat, and she and Earl Dodge watched Cage walk over and shake hands with the man, who had climbed out of the truck. The man had a wide-brimmed straw hat he kept slapping against his leg as he moved his mouth, talking, chewing tobacco. He nodded to the woman and boy still in the truck cab. Cage's arm disappeared into the truck,

219

the boy dropped his head a couple of times, the woman, a fat woman in a blue print dress, smiled and nodded.

Earl Dodge told June he thought he ought to meet this man too, said to please excuse him. She was left alone in the car, the engine idling, the heater still on, blowing warm air against her ankles.

The pantomine was repeated, the man slapping the hat, spitting his tobacco, smiling, nodding. Earl Dodge grabbing the man's hand and shaking so hard June saw the man stumble a little. Earl Dodge's hand going into the truck, the boy's lowered eyes, the woman's smile, her slow nodding head. The rancher and his boy and the fat woman never looked at June.

With Earl Dodge and Cage back in the car there was a good deal of waving as the truck, two-toned with dust, drove on by.

If she had been sick, if she had bled, if she had started dying in the back of this car out on the rocky edge of a dry arroyo, would Earl Dodge, stranger tight in his clothes, have pulled open her blouse, unfastened the belt on her skirt, slipped her lacy blue bra loose? Would Cage have been able to help her, would Cage have known what to do? Would Cage have stood shaking, watching the stranger tear her skirt off, trying to stop the blood running down her legs? She closed her eyes again, felt under her skirt to make sure she had on the tiny black underpants, was glad she had not worn a slip.

After the rocky dirt road, the highway was fast and silent. Cage reached over the seat and patted her knee. She held his hand, pushing with a long fingernail at his cuticle.

32 THE END of January, the beginning of a new year, a new decade. Cage was busy with Arroyo Lake Estates, he talked of million-dollar figures. June had left the Christmas tree up. It had dried out, pink and brown needles made a circle on the carpet and the pink dye had taken on a strong mildew smell. Whenever June came into the closed-up living room it smelled like she was opening an old, junked refrigerator. Still she did not take down the tree, and Cage was too busy and excited with his work to pay much attention. They had canceled indefinitely the vacation trip to Las Vegas.

Some nights, when Cage was out at the property or somewhere in a financial meeting, June sat in the pink living room with the pink tree lights the only lights on in the house. A spider had made a web from the ceiling to an upper branch of the tree, and June sat in one of the straight-backed mahogany chairs and watched for the spider. She didn't know how the spider attached its web to the smooth, flat ceiling. The web was always the same, looking in the pink light like the angel hair on the Christmas tree, but she never

221

saw the spider. She wondered where the spider went, why it never seemed to be safe in its web.

Other nights she had restless energy and drove around. She liked to go out to the airport and watch airplanes land and take off. She pretended she was waiting for someone, and she stood at the passenger gates and stared at people. She went out onto the observation deck and waved at the row of round windows in a departing airplane, warm yellow lights, looking for faces in the windows, like looking into the little glass window of her oven with the oven light on, watching something cook. Sometimes she cried a little, dabbing at her eyes with the silk scarf she waved over her head at taxiing airplanes. In the airport lobby she picked up copies of airline schedules, planned imaginary trips. She put coins into vending machines that sold airplane flight insurance. She took out twenty-four-hour policies on her life for hundreds of thousands of dollars. She made up names for herself, Honey Gold, Kitty Calhoun, Starr Young, Hortense Vandergeld, Lana Love. Then her beneficiaries were Rex Lancaster, Mac Traggert, Kirk King, Judson P. Vandergeld III, Price Power. Once, twice, she had coffee with other wavers and weepers, made up stories to tell them. Her husband was an actor, he wouldn't move her and the babies, twin boys, to Hollywood, wanted his sons to grow up in Texas. Perhaps they had seen her husband, one of the soldiers in *Battle Hymn?* He had helped produce *Oklahoma,* even though it was a rival state, she laughed. He was the one with the longish hair, a tiny scar at the corner of his mouth? Usually people remembered the scar. Yes, she had met Bill Holden, Jimmy Stewart—just like other men. Or, she was saying goodbye to the only man she ever really loved, it was awful, and here she was telling a stranger all her troubles. Worst of all, he was married. To a woman in South America where he ran a banana plantation. He was not South American, but no one could run the plantation like he did, so many people depended on him, theirs

222

was a selfish love, she knew it could not, she knew it should not, endure. Usually she cried when she talked with strangers at the airport. They were always inviting her to come visit them, people from San Antonio, people from other cities, other states. She had corners of napkins and ends of matchbooks stuffed in her purse with names and addresses scribbled on them. One man, an accountant from Houston, took a later flight so he could buy June a drink and try to cheer her up before he left. He wanted her to come to Houston with him, and she promised to think about it, promised to call him collect the minute she changed her mind. He would buy her ticket, pay for everything.

June was surprised at how easy it was to make people believe her stories, or at least act like they did. How easy to make herself part of other people's lives. She wondered how often the man from Houston thought of her. She knew he wanted to kiss her, so she let him, once, before he got on his airplane. She like to imagine him with the taste and feel of her on his lips as he streaked toward Houston thousands of feet above the earth. She thought how he was ready to buy her a ticket, take her places, thought how they could have gotten on an airplane together and disappeared into the clouds, could have landed in some foggy, mountain country to lead new lives, a different world somewhere. She wore her mink coat up on the observation deck and hoped really warm weather would not come too soon this year, she didn't want to have to quit wearing the soft, heavy coat.

33

THE SUPPER dishes were in the dishwasher, it was running smoothly. The television was on, "The Loretta Young Show," Loretta was just coming through a door, twirling around in a full skirt which bowed out then settled like an umbrella opening and closing. June didn't like the skirt. Cage was tilted back, sleeping, in his recliner, his shoes neatly side by side on the floor, his pants unbuckled. June saw him and Loretta reflected in the sliding glass doors of the den. Beyond the darkness of the backyard she saw a line of lights moving slowly throught the reflection of Cage's head, traffic on the expressway. Beyond that, a few lights of downtown San Antonio.

She got quietly up and walked down the hall to the living room door, opened it to the smell of mildew, flipped on the pink Christmas tree lights, closed the door behind her. The spider web was gone from the brown tree top. She got her mink coat from the living room closet and put it on. Slick lining inside the sleeves was cool against her bare arms, the edges of fur soft on her neck and calves.

Lying back on the soft couch, she slipped her right arm out of the sleeve, pulled the coat around her like a blanket, the empty sleeve flopping across her stomach reminding her of the times she played one-armed lady when she was a girl, holding her hidden arm tight against her side. As she moved her arm beneath the coat she watched the outside of the coat, trying to move her arm in a way that it wouldn't show on the outside fur. It was like being in a tent or under a heavy hump of covers, trying not to be seen, making love under a blanket on a hayride right in front of the chaperone. Her arm moved slowly, the rest of her frozen, stiff. Her arm going down her side and over her stomach.

Staring at the pink light closest to the top of the tree, she began to see spots. She tried to picture Cage, the reflection of him in the glass doors in the den, but all she saw were Armon and Turk. Armon and Turk, looking just alike near the top of the Christmas tree. She couldn't remember if they really had looked alike. The only dead people she knew. But there would be others. Soon enough there would be others.

Her hand was warm on her stomach through the silky material of her dress. She worked buttons open and pulled her slip up into accordion pleats across her stomach. Her fingers walked on her skin, nails making a light scratching sound, and moved under the elastic band of her panties. She imagined goldfish going under a ceramic archway down to the bottom of the bowl. Her fingers lay still in the curls of her pubic hair and she pictured the goldfish hiding in the dark foliage of underwater plants, thin green fronds floating, gently swaying against gills and fins. June lay still, her only motion an occasional little twitch in one of her fingers, some tiny muscle that quivered like the barely perceptible ripple in the tailfin of a goldfish, and the slow, even movement of her chest as she breathed.

The faces of Armon and Turk moved in the red and blue spots she saw when she closed her eyes. Identical Armons and Turks, moving up and down and around and around. Armons and Turks, faces hanging on the Christmas tree when she opened her eyes. Alike as the pink Christmas tree balls, each in its cardboard square, lined with cotton in the box that came out of the storage closet. Like the photographs of Armon and Turk that Momma got out of the cedar lined trunk. The Christmas balls, the old snapshots, were always the same. Held, unchanged, Armon and Turk, made the same age by death, were always the same.

From the top of the tree Armon's face grinned down at her just like the time he tricked her when she was little, hanging himself, and scared her half to death. His jokes, fooling around with death. He hadn't been satisfied with scaring June. *Go get Turk, and don't you tell.* Turk, so much older than her, didn't fool as easy. He grabbed the swinging body so hard Armon laughed and gave himself away. Turk sent her to the store for a bottle of catsup, blood for Armon's lip, and then went with her after Momma, both trying not give the trick away. *Momma, Momma, hurry. Daddy's killed himself dead.* And Momma, laughing, *Again? How'd he do it this time, with a gun or a knife or poison or some wild critter?* Momma said to tell Armon he better get himself resurrected faster than Jesus and get home, all of them, for supper. *And if he's wastin good catsup for blood you bring that home, too.* They glared at Momma all through supper. Then, while she did the dishes, they sat around the table and made a pact to trick her good. Armon had a trick card he said would do it. He pulled it out of his inside coat pocket and laid it on the oilcloth:

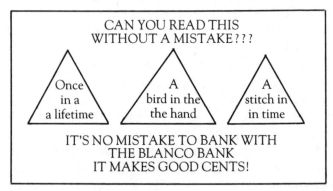

CAN YOU READ THIS
WITHOUT A MISTAKE???

Once
in a
a lifetime

A
bird in the
the hand

A
stitch in
in time

IT'S NO MISTAKE TO BANK WITH
THE BLANCO BANK
IT MAKES GOOD CENTS!

And he winked at June as he called Momma from the kitchen, *Eunice, can you still read?* And Momma came in, a cup towel in one hand, and glanced down at the card on the table. *Once in a lifetime, a bird in the hand, a stitch in time,* she reeled the words off and they started laughing. Finally, triumphant, one at a time, they read the phrases. *Once in a a lifetime,* read Armon. *A bird in the the hand,* read Turk. *A stitch in in time,* read June. Armon told Momma she should learn to read between the lines, and Turk said she should look before she leaped. June, feeling strange being united with Armon and Turk against Momma, said nothing. Momma went back to her dishes, but then she yelled that at least she didn't stutter and repeat herself when she read. Then Armon slapped the table laughing, said he and Turk and little June were the three musketters, and all June could think of was the candy bar.

She remembered their hands, stacked six high, Armon's then Turk's then hers then Armon's again and Turk's again. and, finally, her's on top, on the white oilcloth. She remembered how black, curly hairs grew on her daddy's fingers, and she remembered how, even then, Turk had grease-stained hands, dirty broken fingernails.

Her own hands had been small and soft, then as now. Now her fingernails were longer and polished shiny as satin. She moved them through the silky hair, wet between her legs. Her finger went into her like a key, and turned, and she squeezed her eyes shut to see the rooms inside.

She slid her finger out of her and moved it back and forth over her skin, moved it like the tiny black brush she moved back and forth on her nails, the soft wet hair beneath her finger curved and bent like soft brush bristles. Her finger slid over the top of soft skin, warm and slick with the wetness she felt, and she lay there in the dim pink glow of the tree. She rolled the edge of the mink coat between her legs, the fur soft and cool.

227

Thinking she heard Cage's voice, she sat up, listening, but all she could hear was the far away voice of the television. The wet tips of the fur on the front of her coat stuck together like eyelashes and glistened in the Christmas tree light. She stood, passed close to the tree, going out the seldom-used front door, her heavy coat hitting a limb, dry needles sprinkling down the fur to the floor, hard and brown as wild rice.

Outside, the February air was cold. Cage's yellow Buick sat next to her Thunderbird. It reminded her of the fat, yellow suppository the doctor wanted her to give herself the night before she came in for some tests. She had been having more pains, cramps when her period was not due. She had not told Cage, but he knew she hadn't been feeling quite right and had insisted she see a doctor. She picked one out of the phone book and went, gave him a made-up name and address, paid cash for the visit. When the doctor suggested the tests, she said she didn't feel up to that yet but that she would call back in a few days. When she got home she ran the suppository he had given her through the garbage disposal. She didn't want to know anything bad that was happening inside her, didn't want anyone looking up into her rooms. They weren't going to get her into a hospital and do things to her with tubes and needles.

She walked around Cage's car, her face yellow on the hood, and she thought, *Cage will die in a car like this.* She got in his car, the light on when she opened the door. There was blood on her fur coat, blood on her fingers. She stared at the red smears on her fingers, pulled the door closed to make the light go out. She breathed the smell of after-shave, the smell of spice cake and rum sauce. We all die in heavy metal cars or airplanes or in metal beds with iron bars up on both sides. The smells of metal and rubber and fabric and after-shave lotion are the smells of death.

Cage will be riding smoothly over the new expressway, the tar seams in the concrete pavement, soft, regular thumps

228

somewhere beneath his feet, which will be relaxed on the soft gold carpet. He will speed around curves, gracefully passing smoking old Fords, passing red pickups, passing station wagons full of boys in blue baseball uniforms. He will slip around foreign sports cars, change lanes quickly and easily, pump the accelerator gently, nudging the big yellow Buick up inclines, over crowded streets, racing along at rooftop level. Out in front of the traffic he will suddenly twist the steering wheel too far, too quick.

The automobile responds. The gleaming grill, lips curled back, nervously twitching, exposing perfect rows of steel teeth, meets the guardrail, splinters of steel and concrete shooting into space like metal filings after a magnet. The automobile leaps, the wheels spin against air, the brown belly of the Buick exposed above the traffic below, the heavy engine roaring, out of pavement, smelling new surfaces beneath, gravity and traction, noses slowly down, arching its yellow back. Light, almost empty, the trunk rises, a box of pink and yellow real estate contracts floating, weightless, inside the trunk. Cage is leaning forward, the steering wheel broken off in his hands, the steering column pushing into his chest, fat bulging like rubber, seeing the gray sky of Ohio, the cornfield rising up to meet him, the hard, dry cornstalk entering his chest, ribs snapping like corncobs, skin rasping like husk. The Buick kisses earth, Cage kisses glass. Engine cutting into Texas dirt, brain spilling through broken skull and glass into dark Ohio night.

They will say it was a miracle no one else was killed. June will say, *yes, a miracle.* She will wish he had gone ahead and bought himself a Cadillac. The Buick will still smell like after-shave.

She got out of Cage's car, went around to her Thunderbird, got in. It started first time. She pulled on the parking lights, the dashboard glowed green, the driveway around her partially lit by the soft, low light of the parking lights.

A light that was like expectancy, like a suppressed laugh, like a hand covering a mouth, holding a secret. Like something warming up.

Or, June thought, he will die some other way, but it will be the same. It is always the same, like the Christmas tree balls and the old photographs.

He will be up early, the first time, before the sun, the stars still shining like new dimes in the dark sky. Jogging for his heart. A new sweat suit, new tennis shoes. Going around the block. One mile clocked the night before in the Buick. Will the last thing he hears be a Cadillac passing on the empty street? A dog barking at him? The roar of his blood in his ears? His knees, elbows, nose scraping into the damp sidewalk?

He is coming over a hill, his new rubber-soled shoes slapping the sidewalk, his chest hot, throat burning, arms light, out of control, jerking along, bouncing at the shoulders. He grins at the long downhill stretch of empty sidewalk, thinking of the quiet house waiting for him, the electric clock quiet on the dresser, June's breath regular in her sleep, the smell of the electric percolator in the kitchen, its red light on saying his coffee is waiting, the quiet turning and folding of his newspaper. Leaning forward into the air, his body quivers down to his thighs, the balls of his feet hitting the sidewalk, slap, slap, slap, slap, his legs don't seem to exist from his thighs down, but he knows they are moving because he hears his feet, slap, slap, slap. His chest crimps, a flower instantly blooming in reverse. Someone is pouring a sack of charcoal briquettes, white-hot off the backyard grill, down his throat. A giant windup key is rammed into his chest and tightened until he feels the spring explode into hard corkscrews of metal shooting up into his head. His knees return, he feels them hit, then they disappear again. He sees his hands trying to get the sweatshirt open, but nothing happens. He can't feel anything happening. The sun is not coming up. He cannot see his hands any longer. He is seeing scenes from a picture book. History. A sword sunk to the hilt into a Roman soldier's chest, Alexander trying to untie a huge knot, a cannonball opening a hole in a stone wall in France, a battering ram hitting castle doors in England, a giant cloud over Japan.

What is the last thing he sees? A plastic water pistol on the sidewalk? The thumb and first finger of his left hand? The antler blur of his eyelashes? The initials he cut on his school desk in Ohio? Those same initials on a gold money clip? June's face? The wide grin of the man who bought a lakefront lot from him yesterday?

June pulled the gearshift back to reverse, let the Thunderbird idle backwards, down the drive. Slowly it dipped and floated out onto the street until the incline slowed her to a stop, and she slid the gearshift forward into drive.

She moved slowly across the front of her house, looking straight ahead. She passed the Texaco, a streetlight bright on her left cheek.

Or will they be together? June and Cage eating supper in a very expensive restaurant. In San Antonio, in Dallas, perhaps, finally in Las Vegas. They will walk through the purple noon twilight of the Golden Nugget, Cage will win a nickel jackpot on an old slot machine, beginner's luck, three identical bananas, three sacks of gold with JACKPOT written across them, eight dollars in nickels spilling, spewing out of the little cash-register shaped machine.

They are celebrating. The table is small and the candlelight makes the room seem to shake. Cage can't see his steak and makes repeated jokes about seeing what he's eating. The yellow light flickers, is caught on his suit buttons, his gold tooth, his eyes. He has his fork in one hand, his glass of wine in the other. He is laughing, gesturing, joking, indicating the people around them, the red velvet wallpaper. June sees herself, small, in his glass of wine. He is talking fast, chewing the biggest cut of steak on the menu, another

231

hunk of meat on the end of his fork, using it as a pointer, moving it around like a sword swallower, a flame eater, before sticking it in his mouth. He sucks the second forkful in, swallows, throws his head back, laughing. He stops, silent. He leans forward over the table, his palms move, fish air, come down hard on the table, pink, almost red against the white tablecloth. The silverware jumps, the glass of wine falls over spilling red wine in his plate. His eyes open wide, wider. He can't believe it. His hands come up, he grabs his throat, he looks like he is strangling himself, his fingers wrapped around his neck, squeezing.

A crowd gathers, trying to reach him. Two or three men in suits, one with a napkin still stuck on his lap, hanging from his belt like a loincloth, they are all slapping him on the back. A woman is yelling for an ambulance, a man is shrieking. Cage opens his mouth, moves his jaws like a fish seen through glass in an aquarium, his tongue twists and flutters like a fish out of water. He has still not made noise, he is silent film. The men are trying to get him out of his chair, trying to hold him up by his legs. His head hits the table, his left cheek splats against the steak and spilled wine in his plate, his eyelids blink, there is not enough skin to cover his huge, bulged eyes. His face is the color of the tablecloth, the splattered wine an ugly birthmark on his cheek. Another man, the waiter, has the other leg, they pull him up, back. His head slides off the tabletop, his plate flips over, steak and potato hit the red carpet, his head swings into his chair, hitting the chair leg and tipping it over. The waiter reaches into Cage's mouth, pulls out steak and potato. The waiter grabs a spoon and pokes it into Cage's mouth. There is blood. Cage's mouth jerks, he bites the waiter, bites his tongue. They stretch him out, hold him down, push on his chest, his body bucking. The waiter has pulled all the meat out and now he puts his mouth over Cage's mouth, his lips on Cage's greasy lips. They try for half an hour. Once Cage makes a noise like

232

a burp, but that is all. The dinner music is still coming softly out of the speakers in the ceiling. June knows this will happen. She will go to Blanco and put Cage in one of the three new plots, not far from Turk, near enough to Armon, one of the family now. She will stay in the orange brick house. She will have insurance money. She will have the Thunderbird serviced at the new Texaco, like nothing happened.

She came to the stop sign and in one motion put on the power brakes and pulled on the headlights. A silent explosion. The bright lights hit the silver letters on the green sign of the new expressway like an electric charge, the white arrow sparkled. A direction to go. She goes, feeling the road climb, then open out into the wide lanes of the open road, the fast stream of pavement that would take her away, take her somewhere, set her loose with motion and speed.

She did not glance out the window at her house, did not look back. She looked straight ahead. She drove after the distant taillights ahead of her. She leaned forward without moving her eyes and turned the radio up all the way, the rear speaker loud. She didn't recognize the song, it was only sound. She rode.

She came to the newest section of the loop, just opened to traffic. She had not been over this ground before. The stripes that would separate the lanes had not been painted yet. The pavement was whiter than the rest of the expressway, like new skin after a wound has healed and the bandage is removed. She felt a soft bump where old pavement gave way to new, and she shot forward, speeding over congested streets, above traffic, rooftops, she kept going, around the city.

The new stretch of road was dark, the streetlights not yet functioning. She sped on, cutting into the darkness, her lights blazing a trail that continued to open before her.

She had left all the other traffic behind. She had been all around the city, almost one complete revolution. Ahead was the tall sign of the new Texaco station. She cut into the outside lane and looked for her house.

There. The pink lights in the window. The pink lights, the orange house, the dark and pink-lighted room.

She pressed down on the accelerator, surged ahead. Again. She pushed a silver button and all the windows opened, the glass sliding down into the silver body of the Thunderbird like the clear eyelids of some futuristic reptile. The Thunderbird filled with cold, with the loud breath of the wind. June felt suddenly alive, the cold air moving against her body, rushing up under her dress, filling the car, dress rising off her skin, a button snapping loose, her arms and legs moving freely beneath the dress that seemed ready to tear loose and go flying out the windows. And like a bright moving snake finally working free of its old dead skin and darting onto new spring grass, its senses awake to new life, June stared ahead and raced on into new territory.